'To say this is a terrific debut novel is really too mild . . . [it is] a relentlessly creepy family saga. I found myself dreading the last thirty pages or so, but was helpless to stop turning them. Then, after the lights were out, the story just stayed there in my head, coiled and hissing, like a snake in a cave'
Stephen King

'This is a stylish thriller about housewives who don't recognise their own desperations, while the reader recognises with fascinated clarity the nastiness and vacuity of life in an updated Stepford' *Literary Review*

'It is a stunningly accomplished evocation of the oppressiveness of small-town life and is just as assured in depicting the gradually revealed psychological disorder that links Camille to both killer and victims' *Sunday Times*

'Compulsively disturbing and . . . exciting' *Time Out*

'[A] striking first novel . . . a relentlessly dark tale, with some very disturbed characters, Camille among them, and it makes a powerful impact' *Sunday Telegraph*

'A stylish and compelling debut. A real winner' Harlan Coben

'If you love Martha O'Connor look out for Gillian Flynn's debut, *Sharp Objects* . . . a gothic fairytale-gone-bad' *Company*

'The horror creeps up slowly, with Flynn misdirecting the reader until the shocking, dreadful and memorable double ending' *Publisher's Weekly*

Gillian Flynn is the chief TV critic for *Entertainment Weekly*. This is her first novel.

SHARP OBJECTS

GILLIAN FLYNN

PHOENIX

A PHOENIX PAPERBACK

First published in Great Britain in 2006
by Weidenfeld & Nicolson
This paperback edition published in 2007
by Phoenix,
an imprint of Orion Books Ltd,
Orion House, 5 Upper St Martin's Lane,
London WC2H 9EA

A CIP catalogue record for this book
is available from the British Library.

Printed and bound in Great Britain by
Clays Ltd, St Ives plc

The Orion Publishing Group's policy is to use papers that
are natural, renewable and recyclable products and
made from wood grown in sustainable forests. The logging
and manufacturing processes are expected to conform to
the environmental regulations of the country of origin.

www.orionbooks.co.uk

For my parents,
Matt and Judith Flynn

SHARP OBJECTS

Chapter One

My sweater was new, stinging red and ugly. It was May 12 but the temperature had dipped to the forties, and after four days shivering in my shirtsleeves, I grabbed cover at a tag sale rather than dig through my boxed-up winter clothes. Spring in Chicago.

In my gunny-covered cubicle I sat staring at the computer screen. My story for the day was a limp sort of evil. Four kids, ages two through six, were found locked in a room on the South Side with a couple of tuna sandwiches and a quart of milk. They'd been left three days, flurrying like chickens over the food and feces on the carpet. Their mother had wandered off for a suck on the pipe and just forgotten. Sometimes that's what happens. No cigarette burns, no bone snaps. Just an irretrievable slipping. I'd seen the mother after the arrest: twenty-two-year-old Tammy Davis, blonde and fat, with pink rouge on her cheeks in two perfect circles the size of shot glasses. I could imagine her sitting on a shambled-down sofa, her lips on that metal, a sharp burst of smoke. Then all was fast floating, her kids way behind, as she shot back to junior high, when the boys still cared and she was the prettiest, a glossy-lipped thirteen-year-old who mouthed cinnamon sticks before she kissed.

A belly. A smell. Cigarettes and old coffee. My editor, esteemed, weary Frank Curry, rocking back in his cracked Hush Puppies. His teeth soaked in brown tobacco saliva.

"Where are you on the story, kiddo?" There was a silver tack on my desk, point up. He pushed it lightly under a yellow thumbnail.

"Near done." I had three inches of copy. I needed ten.

"Good. Fuck her, file it, and come to my office."

"I can come now."

"Fuck her, file it, then come to my office."

"Fine. Ten minutes." I wanted my thumbtack back.

He started out of my cubicle. His tie swayed down near his crotch.

"Preaker?"

"Yes, Curry?"

"Fuck her."

Frank Curry thinks I'm a soft touch. Might be because I'm a woman. Might be because I'm a soft touch.

Curry's office is on the third floor. I'm sure he gets panicky-pissed every time he looks out the window and sees the trunk of a tree. Good editors don't see bark; they see leaves – if they can even make out trees from up on the twentieth, thirtieth floor. But for the *Daily Post*, fourth-largest paper in Chicago, relegated to the suburbs, there's room to sprawl. Three floors will do, spreading relentlessly outward, like a spill, unnoticed among the carpet retailers and lamp shops. A corporate developer produced our township over three well-organized years – 1961–64 – then named it after his daughter, who'd suffered a serious equestrian accident a month before the job was finished. Aurora Springs, he ordered, pausing for a photo by a brand-new city sign. Then he took his family and left. The daughter, now in her fifties and fine except for an occasional tingling in her arms, lives in Florida and returns every few years to take a photo by her namesake sign, just like Pop.

I wrote the story on her last visit. Curry hated it, hates most slice-of-life pieces. He got smashed off old Chambord while he read it, left his office smelling like raspberries. Curry gets drunk fairly quietly, but often. It's not the reason, though, that he has such a cozy view of the ground. That's just yawing bad luck.

I walked in and shut the door to his office, which isn't how I'd ever imagined my editor's office would look. I craved big oak panels, a window pane in the door – marked Chief – so the cub reporters could watch us rage over First Amendment rights. Curry's office is bland and institutional, like the rest of the building. You could debate journalism or get a Pap smear. No one cared.

"Tell me about Wind Gap." Curry held the tip of a ballpoint pen at his grizzled chin. I could picture the tiny prick of blue it would leave among the stubble.

"It's at the very bottom of Missouri, in the boot heel. Spitting distance from Tennessee and Arkansas," I said, hustling for my facts. Curry loved to drill reporters on any topics he deemed pertinent – the number of murders in Chicago last year, the demographics for Cook County, or, for some reason, the story of my hometown, a topic I preferred to avoid. "It's been around since before the Civil War," I continued. "It's near the Mississippi, so it was a port city at one point. Now its biggest business is hog butchering. About two thousand people live there. Old money and trash."

"Which are you?"

"I'm trash. From old money." I smiled. He frowned.

"And what the hell is going on?"

I sat silent, cataloguing various disasters that might have befallen Wind Gap. It's one of those crummy towns prone to misery: A bus collision or a twister. An explosion at the silo or a toddler down a well. I was also sulking a bit. I'd hoped – as I always do when Curry calls me into his office – that he was going to compliment me on a recent piece, promote me to a better beat, hell, slide over a slip of paper with a 1 percent raise scrawled on it – but I was unprepared to chat about current events in Wind Gap.

"Your mom's still there, right, Preaker?"

"Mom. Stepdad." A half sister born when I was in college, her existence so unreal to me I often forgot her name. Amma. And then Marian, always long-gone Marian.

"Well dammit, you ever talk to them?" Not since Christmas: a chilly, polite call after administering three bourbons. I'd worried my mother could smell it through the phone lines.

4

"Not lately."

"Jesus Christ, Preaker, read the wires sometime. I guess there was a murder last August? Little girl strangled?"

I nodded like I knew. I was lying. My mother was the only person in Wind Gap with whom I had even a limited connection, and she'd said nothing. Curious.

"Now another one's missing. Sounds like it might be a serial to me. Drive down there and get me the story. Go quick. Be there tomorrow morning."

No way. "We got horror stories here, Curry."

"Yeah, and we also got three competing papers with twice the staff and cash." He ran a hand through his hair, which fell into frazzled spikes. "I'm sick of getting slammed out of news. This is our chance to break something. Big."

Curry believes with just the right story, we'd become the overnight paper of choice in Chicago, gain national credibility. Last year another paper, not us, sent a writer to his hometown somewhere in Texas after a group of teens drowned in the spring floods. He wrote an elegiac but well-reported piece on the nature of water and regret, covered everything from the boys' basketball team, which lost its three best players, to the local funeral home, which was desperately unskilled in cleaning up drowned corpses. The story won a Pulitzer.

I still didn't want to go. So much so, apparently, that I'd wrapped my hands around the arms of my chair, as if Curry might try to pry me out. He sat and stared at me a few beats with his watery hazel eyes. He cleared his throat, looked at his photo of his wife, and smiled like he was a doctor about to break bad news. Curry loved to bark – it fit his old-school image of an editor – but he was also one of the most decent people I knew.

"Look, kiddo, if you can't do this, you can't do it. But I think it might be good for you. Flush some stuff out. Get you back on your feet. It's a damn good story – we need it. You need it."

Curry had always backed me. He thought I'd be his best reporter, said I had a surprising mind. In my two years on the job I'd consistently fallen short of expectations. Sometimes strikingly. Now I could feel him across the desk, urging me to give him a little faith. I nodded in what I hoped was a confident fashion.

"I'll go pack." My hands left sweatprints on the chair.

I had no pets to worry about, no plants to leave with a neighbor. Into a duffel bag, I tucked away enough clothes to last me five days, my own reassurance I'd be out of Wind Gap before week's end. As I took a final glance around my place, it revealed itself to me in a rush. The apartment looked like a college kid's: cheap, transitory, and mostly uninspired. I promised myself I'd invest in a decent sofa when I returned as a reward for the stunning story I was sure to dig up.

On the table by the door sat a photo of a preteen me holding Marian at about age seven. We're both laughing. She has her eyes wide open in surprise, I have mine scrunched shut. I'm squeezing her into me, her short skinny legs dangling over my knees. I can't remember the occasion or what we were laughing about. Over the years it's become a pleasant mystery. I think I like not knowing.

I take baths. Not showers. I can't handle the spray, it gets my skin buzzing, like someone's turned on a switch. So I wadded a flimsy motel towel over the grate in the shower floor, aimed the nozzle at the wall, and sat in the three inches of water that pooled in the stall. Someone else's pubic hair floated by.

I got out. No second towel, so I ran to my bed and blotted myself with the cheap spongy blanket. Then I drank warm bourbon and cursed the ice machine.

Wind Gap is about eleven hours south of Chicago. Curry had graciously allowed me a budget for one night's motel stay and breakfast in the morning, if I ate at a gas station. But once I got in town, I was staying at my mother's. That he decided for me. I already knew the reaction I'd get when I showed up at her door. A quick, shocked flustering, her hand to her hair, a mismatched hug that would leave me aimed slightly to one side. Talk of the messy house, which wouldn't be. A query about length of stay packaged in niceties.

"How long do we get to have you for, sweetness?" she'd say. Which meant: "When do you leave?"

It's the politeness that I find most upsetting.

I knew I should prepare my notes, jot down questions. Instead I drank more bourbon, then popped some aspirin, turned off the light. Lulled by the wet purr of the air conditioner and the electric plinking of some video game next door, I fell asleep. I was only thirty miles outside my hometown, but I needed one last night away.

In the morning I inhaled an old jelly doughnut and headed south, the temperature shooting up, the lush forest imposing on both sides. This part of Missouri is ominously flat – miles of unmajestic trees broken only by the thin strip of highway I was on. The same scene repeating itself every two minutes.

You can't spot Wind Gap from a distance; its tallest building is only three stories. But after twenty minutes of driving, I knew it was coming: First a gas station popped up. A group of scraggly teenage boys sat out front, barechested and bored. Near an old pickup, a diapered toddler threw fistfuls of gravel in the air as his mother filled up the tank. Her hair was dyed gold, but her brown roots reached almost to her ears. She yelled something to the boys I couldn't make out as I passed. Soon after, the forest began to thin. I passed a scribble of a strip mall with tanning beds, a gun shop, a drapery store. Then came a lonely cul-de-sac of old houses, meant to be part of a development that never happened. And finally, town proper.

For no good reason, I held my breath as I passed the sign welcoming me to Wind Gap, the way kids do when they drive by cemeteries. It had been eight years since I'd been back, but the scenery was visceral. Head down that road, and I'd find the home of my grade-school piano teacher, a former nun whose breath smelled of eggs. That path led to a tiny park where I smoked my first cigarette on a sweaty summer day. Take that boulevard, and I'd be on my way to Woodberry, and the hospital.

I decided to head directly to the police station. It squatted at one end of Main Street, which is, true to its word, Wind Gap's main street. On Main Street you will find a beauty parlor and a hardware store, a five-and-dime called Five-and-Dime, and a library twelve shelves deep. You'll find a clothing store called Candy's Casuals, in which you may buy jumpers, turtlenecks, and sweaters that have ducks and schoolhouses on them. Most nice women in Wind Gap are teachers or mothers or work at places like Candy's Casuals. In a few years you may find a Starbucks, which will bring the town what it yearns for: prepackaged, preapproved mainstream hipness. For now, though, there's just a greasy spoon, which is run by a family whose name I can't remember.

Main Street was empty. No cars, no people. A dog loped down the sidewalk, with no owner calling after it. All the lampposts were papered with yellow ribbons and grainy photocopies of a little girl. I parked and peeled off one of the notices, taped crookedly to a stop sign at a child's height. The sign was homemade, "Missing," written at the top in bold letters that may have been filled in by Magic Marker. The photo showed a dark-eyed girl with a feral grin and too much hair for her head. The kind of girl who'd be described by teachers as a "handful." I liked her.

Natalie Jane Keene
Age: 10
Missing since 5/11
Last seen at Jacob J. Garrett Park, wearing
blue-jean shorts, red striped T-shirt
Tips: 555-7377

I hoped I'd walk into the police station and be informed
that Natalie Jane was already found. No harm done.
Seems she'd gotten lost or twisted an ankle in the woods
or ran away and then thought better of it. I would get in
my car and drive back to Chicago and speak to no one.

Turns out the streets were deserted because half the
town was out searching the forest to the north. The station's receptionist told me I could wait – Chief Bill
Vickery would be returning for lunch soon. The waiting
room had the false homey feel of a dentist's office; I sat
in an orange endchair and flipped through a *Redbook*. An
air freshener plugged into a nearby outlet hissed out a
plastic smell meant to remind me of country breezes.
Thirty minutes later I'd gone through three magazines
and was starting to feel ill from the scent. When Vickery
finally walked in, the receptionist nodded at me and
whispered with eager disdain, "Media."

Vickery, a slim fellow in his early fifties, had already
sweated through his uniform. His shirt clung to his
chest, and his pants puckered out in back where an ass
should have been.

"Media?" He stared at me over looming bifocals.
"What media?"

"Chief Vickery, I'm Camille Preaker, with the *Daily Post* in Chicago."

"Chicago? Why are you here from Chicago?"

"I'd like to speak with you about the little girls – Natalie Keene and the girl who was murdered last year."

"Jesus H. Christ. How'd you hear about this up there? Jesus Christ."

He looked at the receptionist, then back to me, as if we'd collaborated. Then he motioned to me to follow. "Hold my calls, Ruth."

The receptionist rolled her eyes.

Bill Vickery walked ahead of me down a wood-paneled hallway checked with cheap framed photos of trout and horses, then into his office, which had no window, which was in fact a tiny square lined with metal files. He sat down, lit a cigarette. Didn't offer me one.

"I don't want this to get out, Miss. I have no intention of letting this get out."

"I'm afraid, Chief Vickery, that there's not too much choice in the matter. Children are being targeted. The public should be aware." It's the line I'd been mouthing on the drive down. It directs fault to the gods.

"What do you care? They're not your kids, they're Wind Gap kids." He stood up, sat back down, rearranged some papers. "I bet I'm pretty safe to say Chicago never cared about Wind Gap kids before." His voice cracked at the end. Vickery sucked on his cigarette, twisted a chunky gold pinky ring, blinked in quick succession. I wondered suddenly if he was going to cry.

"You're right. Probably not. Look, this isn't going to be some sort of exploitive story. It's important. If it makes you feel any better, I'm from Wind Gap." *There you go, Curry. I'm trying.*

He looked back at me. Stared at my face.

"What's your name?"

"Camille Preaker."

"How do I not know you?"

"Never got in trouble, sir." I offered a slight smile.

"Your family's Preaker?"

"My mother married out of her maiden name about twenty-five years ago. Adora and Alan Crellin."

"Oh. Them I know." Them everybody knew. Money was none too common in Wind Gap, not real money. "But I still don't want you here, Miss Preaker. You do this story and from now on, people will only know us for . . . this."

"Maybe some publicity would help," I offered. "It's helped in other cases."

Vickery sat quiet for a second, pondering his paper-bag lunch crumpled at the corner of his desk. Smelled like bologna. He murmured something about JonBenet and shit.

"No thanks, Miss Preaker. And no comment. I have no comment on any ongoing investigations. You can quote me."

"Look, I have the right to be here. Let's make this easy. You give me some information. Something. Then I'll stay out of your way for a while. I don't want to make your job any harder. But I need to do mine." It was another little exchange I'd thought up somewhere near St. Louis.

I left the police station with a photocopied map of Wind Gap, on which Chief Vickery had drawn a tiny X to mark where the murdered girl's body was discovered last year.

Ann Nash, age nine, was found on August 27 in Falls Creek, a bumpy, noisy waterway that ran through the middle of the North Woods. Since nightfall on the twenty-sixth, when she went missing, a search party had combed the forest. But it was hunters who came across her just after 5 a.m. She'd been strangled close to midnight with a basic clothesline, looped twice around her neck. Then dumped in the creek, which was low from the long summer drought. The clothesline had snagged on a massive rock, and she'd spent the night drifting along in the lazy stream. The burial was closed coffin. This was all Vickery would give me. It took an hour of questions to get that much.

From the pay phone at the library I dialed the number on the Missing poster. An elderly female voice identified it as the Natalie Keene Hotline, but in the background I could hear a dishwasher churning. The woman informed me that so far as she knew, the search was still going in the North Woods. Those who wanted to help should report to the main access road and bring their own water. Record temperatures were expected.

At the search site, four blonde girls sat stiffly on a picnic towel spread in the sun. They pointed toward one of the trails and told me to walk until I found the group.

"What are you doing here?" asked the prettiest. Her flushed face had the roundness of a girl barely in her teens and her hair was parted in ribbons, but her breasts, which she aimed proudly outward, were those of a grown woman. A lucky grown woman. She smiled as if she knew me, impossible since she'd have been a pre-schooler the last time I was in Wind Gap. She looked familiar, though. Maybe the daughter of one of my old schoolmates. The age would be right if someone got knocked up straight out of high school. Not unlikely.

"Just here to help," I said.

"Right," she smirked, and dismissed me by turning all her interest to picking the polish off a toenail.

I walked off the crunch of the hot gravel and into the forest, which only felt warmer. The air was jungle wet. Goldenrod and wild sumac bushes brushed my ankles, and fuzzy white cottonwood seeds floated everywhere, slipping into my mouth, sticking to my arms. When I was a kid we called them fairy dresses, I remembered suddenly.

In the distance people were calling for Natalie, the three syllables rising and falling like song. Another ten minutes of hard hiking and I spotted them: about four dozen people walking in long rows, sifting the brush in front of them with sticks.

"Hello! Any news?" called out a beer-bellied man closest to me. I left the trail and threaded my way through the trees until I reached him.

"Can I help out at all?" I wasn't quite ready to whip out my notebook.

"You can walk beside me here," he said. "We can always use another person. Less ground to cover." We walked silently for a few minutes, my partner occasionally pausing to clear his throat with a wet, rocky cough.

"Sometimes I think we should just burn these woods," he said abruptly. "Seems like nothing good ever happens in them. You a friend of the Keenes?"

"I'm a reporter actually. *Chicago Daily Post.*"

"Mmmm. . . . Well how 'bout that. You writing about all this?"

A sudden wail shot through the trees, a girl's scream: "Natalie!" My hands began sweating as we ran toward the cry. I saw figures tumbling toward us. A teenager with white-blonde hair pushed past us onto the trail, her face red and bundled. She was stumbling like a frantic drunk, yelling Natalie's name at the sky. An older man, maybe her father, caught up with her, wrapped her in his arms, and began walking her out of the forest.

"They found her?" my friend called.

A collective head shaking. "She just got spooked, I think," another man called back. "Too much for her. Girls shouldn't be out here anyway, not as things stand." The man looked pointedly at me, took off his baseball cap to wipe his brow, then began sifting the grass again.

"Sad work," my partner said. "Sad time." We moved forward slowly. I kicked a rusted beer can out of my way. Then another. A single bird flew by at eye level, then shot straight up to the treetops. A grasshopper landed suddenly on my wrist. Creepy magic.

"Would you mind if I asked your thoughts on all this?" I pulled out my notebook, wagged it.

"Don't know I could tell you much."

"Just what you think. Two girls in a small town . . ."

"Well, no one knows these are related, right? Unless you know something I don't. For all we know, Natalie will turn up safe and sound. Hasn't even been two days."

"Are there any theories about Ann?" I asked.

"Some loony, some crazy man musta done it. Some guy rides through town, forgot to take his pills, voices are talking to him. Something like 'at."

"Why do you say that?"

He stopped, pulled a package of chaw from his back pocket, buried a fat pinch in his gumline and worked it until he got the first tiny cut to let the tobacco in. The lining of my mouth began tingling in sympathy.

"Why else would you pull out a dead little girl's teeth?"

"He took her teeth?"

"All but the back part of a baby molar."

After another hour with no results and not much more information, I left my partner, Ronald Kamens ("write my middle initial too, if you will: *J*"), and hiked south toward the spot where Ann's body was found last year. Took fifteen minutes before the sound of Natalie's name drifted away. Ten more minutes and I could hear Falls Creek, the bright cry of water.

It would be hard to carry a child through these

woods. Branches and leaves strangle the pathway, roots bump up from the ground. If Ann was a true girl of Wind Gap, a town that demands utmost femininity in its fairer sex, she'd have worn her hair long down her back. It would have tangled itself in the passing brush. I kept mistaking spiderwebs for glimmering strands of hair.

The grass was still flattened along the point where the body was discovered, raked through for clues. There were a few recent cigarette butts that the idle curious had left behind. Bored kids scaring each other with sightings of a madman trailing bloody teeth.

In the creek, there'd been a row of stones that had snagged the clothesline around Ann's neck, leaving her tethered and floating in the stream like the condemned for half a night. Now, just smooth water rolling over sand. Mr. Ronald J. Kamens had been proud when he told me: The townsfolk had pried out the rocks, loaded them in the back of a pickup, and smashed them just outside town. It was a poignant gesture of faith, as if such destruction would ward off future evil. Seems it didn't work.

I sat down at the edge of the creek, running my palms over the rocky soil. Picked up a smooth, hot stone and pressed it against my cheek. I wondered if Ann had ever come here when she was alive. Maybe the new generation of Wind Gap kids had found more interesting ways to kill summers. When I was a girl, we swam at a spot just downstream where huge table rocks made shallow pools. Crawdads would skitter around our feet and we'd jump for them, scream if we actually touched one.

No one wore swimsuits, it took too much planning. Instead you just rode your bike home in soaked shorts and halters, shaking your head like a wet dog.

Occasionally older boys, equipped with shotguns and stolen beer, would tromp through on their way to shoot flying squirrels or hare. Bloody pieces of meat swung from their belts. Those kids, cocky and pissed and smelling of sweat, aggressively oblivious of our existence, always compelled me. There are different kinds of hunting, I know now. The gentleman hunter with visions of Teddy Roosevelt and big game, who retires from a day in the field with a crisp gin and tonic, is not the hunter I grew up with. The boys I knew, who began young, were blood hunters. They sought that fatal jerk of a shot-spun animal, fleeing silky as water one second, then cracked to one side by their bullet.

When I was still in grammar school, maybe twelve, I wandered into a neighbor boy's hunting shed, a wood-planked shack where the animals were stripped and split. Ribbons of moist, pink flesh dangled from strings, waiting to be dried for jerky. The dirt floor was rusted with blood. The walls were covered with photographs of naked women. Some of the girls were spreading themselves wide, others were being held down and penetrated. One woman was tied up, her eyes glazed, breasts stretched and veined like grapes, as a man took her from behind. I could smell them all in the thick, gory air.

At home that night, I slipped a finger under my panties and masturbated for the first time, panting and sick.

Chapter Two

Happy Hour. I gave up on the search and stopped off at
Footh's, the town's low-key country bar, before dropping by 1665 Grove Street, home of Betsy and Robert
Nash, parents of Ashleigh, twelve; Tiffanie, eleven; the
deceased Ann, forever nine; and six-year-old Bobby Jr.

Three girls until, at last, their baby boy. As I sipped
my bourbon and cracked peanuts, I pondered the growing desperation the Nashes must have felt each time a
child popped out without a penis. There was the first,
Ashleigh, not a boy, but sweet and healthy. They'd
always wanted two anyway. Ashleigh got a fancy name
with extravagant spelling and a closet full of frosting-
cake dresses. They crossed their fingers and tried again
but still got Tiffanie. Now they were nervous, the welcome home less triumphant. When Mrs. Nash got
knocked up once again, her husband bought a tiny baseball glove to give the lump in her belly a nudge in the
right direction. Imagine the righteous dismay when Ann
arrived. She got slapped with some family name – didn't
even get the extra *e* to ornament it a bit.

Thank goodness for Bobby. Three years after the disappointing Ann – was he an accident or one last shot of brio? – Bobby was given his dad's name, was doted on, and the little girls suddenly realized how extraneous they were. Especially Ann. No one needs a third girl. But now she's getting some attention.

I took my second bourbon in one smooth shot, unclenched my shoulders, gave my cheeks a quick slap, got in my big blue Buick, and wished for a third drink. I'm not one of those reporters who relishes picking through people's privacy. It's probably the reason I'm a second-rate journalist. One of them, at least.

I still remembered the way to Grove Street. It was two blocks behind my high school, which served every kid within a seventy-mile radius. Millard Calhoon H.S. was founded in 1930, Wind Gap's last cough of effort before sinking into the Depression. It was named for the first mayor of Wind Gap, a Civil War hero. A Confederate Civil War hero, but that made no never mind, a hero nonetheless. Mr. Calhoon shot it out with a whole troop of Yankees in the first year of the Civil War over in Lexington, and single-handedly saved that little Missouri town. (Or so implies the plaque inside the school entrance.) He darted across farmyards and zipped through picket-fenced homes, politely shooing the cooing ladies aside so they wouldn't be damaged by the Yanks. Go to Lexington today and ask to see Calhoon House, a fine bit of period architecture, and you can still spot northern bullets in its planks. Mr. Calhoon's southern bullets, one assumes, were buried with the men they killed.

Calhoon himself died in 1929 as he closed in on his centennial birthday. He was sitting at a gazebo, which is now gone, in the town square, which has been paved over, being feted by a big brass band, when suddenly he leaned into his fifty-two-year-old wife and said, "It's all too loud." Then he had a massive coronary and pitched forward in his chair, smudging his Civil War finery in the tea cakes that had been decorated with the Stars and Bars just for him.

I have a special fondness for Calhoon. Sometimes it *is* all too loud.

The Nashs' house was much as I'd expected, a late-'70s piece of generica like all the houses on the west side of town. One of those homely ranch houses featuring the garage as its central point. As I drove up, a messy blond boy was sitting in the driveway in a Big Wheel several sizes too small for him, grunting with the effort to pedal the plastic bike. The wheels just spun in place under his weight.

"Want a push?" I said as I got out of the car. I'm not good with children as a rule, but it seemed an attempt wouldn't hurt. He looked at me silently for a second, stuck a finger in his mouth. His tank top slipped up as his round belly popped out to greet me. Bobby Jr. looked stupid and cowed. A boy for the Nashes, but a disappointing one.

I stepped toward him. He jumped off the Big Wheel, which remained clamped to him for a few steps, jammed on his body as it was, then clattered off sideways.

"Daddy!" He ran wailing toward the house as if I'd pinched him.

By the time I reached the front door, a man appeared. My eyes focused behind him, at a miniature fountain gurgling in the hallway. It had three tiers shaped like shells, with a statue of a little boy perched on top. Even from the other side of the screen door, the water smelled old.

"Can I help you?"

"Are you Robert Nash?"

He looked suddenly wary. It was probably the first question the police had asked him when they told him his daughter was dead.

"I'm Bob Nash."

"I'm so sorry to bother you at home. I'm Camille Preaker. I'm from Wind Gap."

"Mmhmmm."

"But now I'm with the *Daily Post* in Chicago. We're covering the story. . . . We're here because of Natalie Keene, and your daughter's murder."

I braced for yelling, door slams, curses, a punch. Bob Nash stuffed both hands deep into his front pockets and leaned back on his heels.

"We can talk in the bedroom."

He held the door open for me, and I began picking my way through the clutter of the living room, laundry baskets spurting over with rumpled sheets and tiny T-shirts. Then past a bathroom whose centerpiece was an empty roll of toilet paper on the floor, and down a hallway spackled with fading photos beneath grimy laminate: little blonde girls crowded dotingly around a baby boy; a young Nash with his arm stiffly circled around his new bride, each of them holding the edge of a cake knife. When I got to the bedroom – matching curtains and bedclothes, a tidy dresser – I realized why Nash had chosen the spot for our interview. It was the one area of the house that held a degree of civilization, like an outpost on the edge of a despairing jungle.

Nash sat on one edge of the bed, I on the other. There were no chairs. We could have been day players in an amateur porn flick. Except we each had a glass of cherry Kool-Aid he'd fetched for us. Nash was a well-kept man: clipped mustache, receding blond hair held down with gel, a glaring green polo tucked into jeans. I assumed he was the one who maintained the order of this room; it had the unadorned neatness of a bachelor trying very hard.

He needed no foreplay for the interview, and I was grateful. It's like sweet-talking your date when you both know you're about to get laid.

"Ann'd been riding her bike all last summer," he started without prompting. "All summer just around and around the block. My wife and me wouldn't let her go no further. She was only nine. We are very protective parents. But then at the end, right before she started school, my wife said fine. Ann had been whining, so my wife said fine, Ann could ride to her friend Emily's house. She never got there. It was eight o'clock before we realized."

"What time had she left?"

"About seven. So somewhere along the way, in those ten blocks, they got her. My wife will never forgive herself. Never."

"What do you mean, *they* got her?"

"Them, him, whatever. The bastard. The sick baby killer. While my family and I sleep, while you drive around doing your reporting, there is a person out there looking for babies to kill. Because you and I both know the little Keene girl isn't just lost."

He finished the rest of his Kool-Aid in one belt, wiped his mouth. The quotes were good, if overpolished. I find this common, and in direct proportion to the amount of TV a subject watches. Not long ago, I interviewed a woman whose twenty-two-year-old daughter had just been murdered by her boyfriend, and she gave me a line straight from a legal drama I happened to catch the night before: *I'd like to say that I pity him, but now I fear I'll never be able to pity again.*

"So Mr. Nash, you have no thoughts of anyone who might have wanted to harm you or your family by hurting Ann?"

"Miss, I sell *chairs*, ergonomic *chairs* for a living – over the *phone*. I work out of an office over in Hayti, with two other fellas. I don't meet anyone. My wife does part-time office work at the grade school. There's no drama here. Someone just decided to kill our little girl." He said the last part beleaguredly, as if he'd given in to the idea.

Bob Nash walked to the sliding glass door off the side

of the bedroom. It led onto a tiny deck. He opened the door but stayed inside. "Might be a homo did it," he said. The word choice was actually a euphemism in these parts.

"Why do you say that?"

"He didn't rape her. Everyone says that's unusual in a killing like this. I say it's the only blessing we got. I'd rather him kill her than rape her."

"There were no signs of molestation at all?" I asked in a murmur I hoped sounded gentle.

"None. And no bruises, no cuts, no sign of any kind of . . . torture. Just strangled her. Pried her teeth out. And I didn't mean what I said before, about her being better killed than raped. That was a stupid thing to say. But you know what I mean."

I said nothing, let my tape recorder whir on, capturing my breathing, Nash's ice clinking, the thunks of a volleyball game being played next door in the last of the daylight.

"Daddy?" A pretty blonde girl, hair in a ponytail down to her waist, peeked through the crack of the bedroom door.

"Not now, honey."

"I'm hungry."

"You can fix something," Nash said. "There's waffles in the freezer. Make sure Bobby eats, too."

The girl lingered a few seconds longer looking at the carpet in front of her, then quietly shut the door. I wondered where their mother was.

"Were you home when Ann left the house that last time?"

He cocked his head sideways at me, sucked his teeth. "No. I was on my way home from Hayti. It's an hour drive. I didn't hurt my daughter."

"I didn't mean that," I lied. "I was just wondering if you got to see her that night."

"Saw her that morning," he said. "Don't remember if we talked or not. Probably not. Four kids in the morning can be a little much, you know?"

Nash twirled his ice, now melted into one solid mass. He ran his fingers underneath his bristly mustache. "No one's been any help so far," he said. "Vickery's in over his head. There's some big-shot detective assigned here from Kansas City. He's a kid, smug too. Marking days till he can get out. You want a picture of Ann?" He said *picture* like *pitcher*. So do I if I don't watch it. He took from his wallet a school photo of a girl with a wide, crooked smile, her pale brown hair cut jaggedly above her chin.

"My wife wanted to put her hair in rollers the night before school photos. Ann chopped it off instead. She was a willful thing. A tomboy. I'm actually surprised she's the one they took. Ashleigh's always been the pretty one, you know. The one people look at." He stared at the photo one more time. "Ann must've given hell."

As I was leaving, Nash gave me the address of the friend Ann was going to visit the night she was grabbed. I drove there slowly over a perfectly squared few blocks. This west side was the newer section of town. You could tell because the grass was a brighter green, rolled out in prepaid patches just thirty summers ago. It wasn't like the dark, stiff, prickly stuff that grew in front of my mother's house. That grass made better whistles. You could split a blade in the middle, blow, and get a tweezy sound until your lips began to itch.

It would have taken Ann Nash only five minutes to pedal to her friend's house. Add an extra ten in case she decided to take a longer route, stretch her legs at the first chance to really ride that summer. Nine is too old to be stuck pedaling in circles around the same block. What happened to the bike?

I rolled slowly past the home of Emily Stone. As the night bloomed blue, I could see a girl run past a bright window. I bet Emily's parents tell their friends things like, "We hug her a little harder every night now." I bet Emily wonders where Ann was taken to die.

I did. Yanking out twenty-some teeth, no matter how small, no matter how lifeless the subject, is a tough task. It'd have to be done in a special place, somewhere safe so a person could take a few minutes to breathe now and then.

I looked at Ann's photo, the edges curling in as if to protect her. The defiant haircut and that grin reminded me of Natalie. I liked this girl, too. I tucked her picture away in my glove compartment. Then I lifted up the sleeve of my shirt and wrote her full name – Ann Marie Nash – in lush blue ballpoint on the inside of my arm.

I didn't pull into anyone's driveway to turn around as I needed to. I figured people here were jittery enough without unknown cars trolling around. Instead I turned left at the end of the block and took the long way to my mother's house. I debated whether to phone her first and decided against it three blocks from home. It was too late to call, too much misguided courtesy. Once you've crossed state lines, you don't phone to ask if you can drop in.

My mother's massive house is at the southernmost point of Wind Gap, the wealthy section, if you can count approximately three square blocks of town as a section. She lives in – and I once did too – an elaborate Victorian replete with a widow's walk, a wraparound veranda, a summer porch jutting toward the back, and a cupola arrowing out of the top. It's full of cubbyholes and nooks, curiously circuitous. The Victorians, especially southern Victorians, needed a lot of room to stray away from each other, to duck tuberculosis and flu, to avoid rapacious lust, to wall themselves away from sticky emotions. Extra space is always good.

The house is at the very top of a very steep hill. In first gear, you can drive up the cracked old driveway to the top, where a carriage porch keeps cars from getting wet. Or you can park at the bottom of the hill and walk the sixty-three stairs to the top, clutching the cigar-thin rail to the left. When I was a child, I always walked the stairs up, ran the driveway down. I assumed the rail was on the left side going up because I'm left-handed, and someone thought I might like that. Odd to think I ever indulged in such presumptions.

I parked at the bottom, so as to seem less intrusive.

Wet with sweat by the time I hit the top, I lifted up my hair, waved a hand at the back of my neck, flapped my shirt a few times. Vulgar pit stains on my French blue blouse. I smelled, as my mother would say, *ripe*.

I rang the doorbell, which had been a cat-calling screech when I was very young, now subdued and truncated, like the *bing!* you hear on children's records when it's time to turn the page. It was 9:15, just late enough that they might have gone to bed.

"Who is it, please?" My mother's reedy voice behind the door.

"Hi, Momma. It's Camille." I tried to keep my voice even.

"Camille." She opened the door and stood in the doorway, didn't seem surprised, and didn't offer a hug at all, not even the limp one I'd expected. "Is something the matter?"

"No, Momma, not at all. I'm in town on business."

"Business. Business? Well, goodness, I'm sorry, sweetheart, come in, come in. The house is not up to par for a visitor, I'm afraid."

The house was perfect, down to the dozens of cut tulips in vases at the entry hall. The air was so teasy with pollen, my eyes watered. Of course my mother didn't ask me what kind of business could possibly land me here. She rarely asked questions of any potency. It was either an exaggerated concern for others' privacy or she simply didn't care much about much. I'll let you guess which option I favored.

"Can I get you something to drink, Camille? Alan

and I were just having amaretto sours." She motioned to the glass in her hand. "I put just a little bit of Sprite in it, sharpens the sweet. But I also have mango juice, wine, and sweet tea, or ice water. Or soda water. Where are you staying?"

"Funny you ask that. I was hoping I could stay here. Just for a few days."

A quick pause, her long fingernails, a transparent pink, clicked on her glass. "Well, I'm sure that's fine. I wish you'd phoned. Just so I'd have known. I would have had dinner for you or something. Come say hello to Alan. We're on the back porch."

She began walking away from me, down the hallway – luminous white living rooms and sitting rooms and reading rooms blooming out on all sides – and I studied her. It was the first time we'd seen each other in almost a year. My hair was a different color – brown from red – but she didn't seem to notice. She looked exactly the same, though, not much older than I am now, although she's in her late forties. Glowing pale skin, with long blonde hair and pale blue eyes. She was like a girl's very best doll, the kind you don't play with. She was wearing a long, pink cotton dress with little white slippers. She was twirling her amaretto sour without spilling a drop.

"Alan, Camille's here." She disappeared into the back kitchen (the smaller of two) and I heard her crack a metal ice tray.

"Who?"

I peeked around the corner, offered up a smile. "Camille. I'm so sorry to drop in like this."

You'd think a lovely thing like my mother was born to be with a big ex-football star. She would have looked just right with a burly, mustached giant. Alan was, if anything, thinner than my mother, with cheekbones that jutted out of his face so high and sharp his eyes turned to almond slivers. I wanted to administer an IV when I saw him. He overdressed always, even for an evening of sweet drinks with my mother. Now he sat, needly legs jutting out of white safari shorts, with a baby blue sweater draped over a crisp oxford. He sweated not at all. Alan is the opposite of moist.

"Camille. It's a pleasure. A real pleasure," he murmured in his monotone drawl. "All the way down in Wind Gap. Thought you had a moratorium on anything south of Illinois."

"Just working, actually."

"Work." He smiled. It was the closest to a question as I would get. My mother reappeared, her hair now pulled up in a pale blue bow, Wendy Darling all grown up. She pressed a chilled glass of fizzing amaretto into my hand, patted my shoulder twice, and sat away from me, next to Alan.

"Those little girls, Ann Nash and Natalie Keene," I prompted. "I'm covering it for my paper."

"Oh, Camille." My mother hushed me, looking away. When my mother is piqued, she has a peculiar tell: She pulls at her eyelashes. Sometimes they come out. During some particularly difficult years when I was a child, she had no lashes at all, and her eyes were a constant gluey pink, vulnerable as a lab rabbit's. In winter time, they leaked streaks of tears whenever she went outdoors. Which wasn't often.

"It's my assignment."

"Goodness, what an assignment," she said, her fingers hovering near her eyes. She scratched the skin just below and put her hand in her lap. "Aren't those parents having a difficult enough time without you coming here to copy it all down and spread it to the world? 'Wind Gap Murders Its Children'! – is that what you want people to think?"

"A little girl has been killed, and another is missing. It's my job to let people know, yes."

"I knew those children, Camille. I'm having a very hard time, as you can imagine. Dead little girls. Who would do that?"

I took a slug of my drink. Granules of sugar stuck to my tongue. I was not ready to speak with my mother. My skin hummed.

"I won't stay long. Truly."

Alan refolded the cuffs of his sweater, smoothed his hand down the crease of his shorts. His contribution to our conversations generally came in the form of adjustments: a collar tucked in, a leg recrossed.

"I just can't have that kind of talk around me," my mother said. "About hurt children. Just don't tell me what you're doing, don't talk about anything you know. I'll pretend you're here for summer break." She traced the braided wicker of Alan's chair with her fingertip.

"How's Amma?" I asked to change the subject.

"Amma?" My mother looked alarmed, as if she suddenly remembered she'd left her child somewhere. "She's fine, she's upstairs asleep. Why do you ask?"

I knew from the footsteps I heard scampering up and down the second floor – from the playroom to the sewing room to the hall window that gave the best spying vantage of the back porch – that Amma was certainly not asleep, but I didn't begrudge her avoiding me.

"Just being polite, Momma. We do that up north, too." I smiled to show I was teasing her, but she buried her face into her drink. Came back up pink and resolute.

"Stay as long as you want, Camille, really," she said. "But you will have to be kind to your sister. Those girls were her schoolmates."

"I look forward to getting to know her," I mumbled. "I'm very sorry for her loss." The last words I couldn't resist, but my mother didn't notice their bitter spin.

"I'll give you the bedroom next to the sitting room. Your old bedroom. It has a tub. I'll buy fresh fruit and some toothpaste. And steaks. Do you eat steak?"

Four hours of threadbare sleep, like lying in a bathtub with your ears half submerged. Shooting up in bed every twenty minutes, my heart pounding so hard I wondered if it was the beating that woke me. I dreamt I was packing for a trip, then realized I'd laid out all the wrong clothes, sweaters for a summer vacation. I dreamt I'd filed the wrong story for Curry before I left: Instead of the item on miserable Tammy Davis and her four locked-up children, we'd run a puff piece about skin care.

I dreamt my mother was slicing an apple onto thick

cuts of meat and feeding it to me, slowly and sweetly, because I was dying.

Just after 5 a.m. I finally threw off the covers. I washed Ann's name off my arm, but somehow, between dressing, brushing my hair, and dabbing on some lipstick, I'd written Natalie Keene in its place. I decided to leave it for luck. Outside, the sun was just rising but my car handle was already hot. My face felt numb from lack of sleep and I stretched my eyes and mouth wide, like a B-movie scream queen. The search party was set to reconvene at 6 a.m. for continued work in the woods; I wanted to catch a quote from Vickery before the day began. Staking out the police station seemed a good bet.

Main Street looked vacant at first, but as I got out of my car I could see two people a few blocks down. It was a scene that made no sense. An older woman was sitting in the middle of the sidewalk, legs splayed, staring at the side of a building, while a man was stooped over her. The woman was shaking her head manically, like a child refusing to feed. Her legs shot out at angles that had to hurt her. A bad fall? Heart attack, maybe. I walked briskly toward them and could hear their staccato murmuring.

The man, white hair and ruined face, looked up at me with milky eyes. "Get the police," he said. His voice came out crumpled. "And call an ambulance."

"What's wrong?" I started, but then I saw it.

Wedged in the foot-wide space between the hardware store and the beauty parlor was a tiny body, aimed out at the sidewalk. As if she were just sitting and waiting for us, brown eyes wide open. I recognized the wild curls. But the grin was gone. Natalie Keene's lips caved in around her gums in a small circle. She looked like a plastic baby doll, the kind with a built-in hole for bottle feedings. Natalie had no teeth now.

The blood hit my face fast, and a shimmer of sweat quickly covered my skin. My legs and arms went slack, and for a second I thought I might smack the ground right next to the woman, who was now quietly praying. I backed up, leaned against a parked car, and put my fingers to my neck, willing my thumping pulse to slow. My eyes picked up images in meaningless flashes: The grimy rubber tip of the old man's cane. A pink mole on the back of the woman's neck. The Band-Aid on Natalie Keene's knee. I could feel her name glowing hotly under my shirtsleeve.

Then more voices, and Chief Vickery was running toward us with a man.

"Goddammit," Vickery grunted when he saw her. "Goddammit. Jesus." He put his face against the brick of the beauty parlor, and breathed hard. The second man, about my age, stooped next to Natalie. A loop of bruised purple circled her neck, and he pressed his fingers just above it to check for a pulse. A stalling tactic while he gathered his composure – the child was clearly dead. Big-shot detective from Kansas City, I guessed, the smug kid.

He was good, though, coaxing the woman out of her prayers and into a calm story of the discovery. The two were husband and wife, the owners of the diner whose

35

name I couldn't remember the day before. Broussard. They were on their way to open for breakfast when they found her. They'd been there maybe five minutes before I came along.

A uniformed officer arrived, pulled his hands over his face when he saw what he'd been called for.

"Folks, we're going to need you to head to the station with the officer here so we can get some statements," Kansas City said. "Bill." His voice had a parental sternness to it. Vickery was kneeling by the body, motionless. His lips moved as if he might be praying, too. His name had to be repeated twice before he snapped back.

"I hear you, Richard. Be human for a second." Bill Vickery put his arms around Mrs. Broussard and murmured to her until she patted his hand.

I sat in a room the color of egg yolk for two hours while the officer got my story down. The whole time I was thinking about Natalie going to autopsy, and how I would like to sneak in and put a fresh Band-Aid on her knee.

Chapter Three

My mother was wearing blue to the funeral. Black was hopeless and any other color was indecent. She also wore blue to Marian's funeral, and so did Marian. She was astonished I didn't remember this. I remembered Marian being buried in a pale pink dress. This was no surprise. My mother and I generally differ on all things concerning my dead sister.

The morning of the service Adora clicked in and out of rooms on her heels, here spraying perfume, there fastening an earring. I watched and drank hot black coffee with a burnt tongue.

"I don't know them well," she was saying. "They really kept to themselves. But I feel all the community should support them. Natalie was such a darling. People were so kind to me when . . ." Wistful downward glance. It may have been genuine.

I had been in Wind Gap five days and Amma was still an unseen presence. My mother didn't mention her. I'd also failed so far to get a quote from the Keenes. Nor had I gotten permission from the family to attend the funeral, but Curry wanted that coverage more than I'd ever heard him want anything, and I wanted to prove I could handle this. I figured the Keenes would never find out. No one reads our paper.

Murmured greetings and perfumed hugs at Our Lady of Sorrows, a few women nodding politely at me after they cooed over my mother (so *brave* of Adora to come) and shoved down to make room for her. Our Lady of Sorrows is a shiny '70s Catholic church: bronzy-gold and bejeweled, like a dime-store ring. Wind Gap is a tiny holdout of Catholicism in a region of booming Southern Baptists, the town having been founded by a pack of Irish. All the McMahons and Malones landed in New York during the Potato Famine, got generously abused, and (if they were smart) headed west. The French already reigned in St. Louis, so they turned south and started their own towns. But they were unceremoniously pushed out years later during Reconstruction. Missouri, always a conflicted place, was trying to shed its southern roots, reinvent itself as a proper nonslave state, and the embarrassing Irish were swept out with other undesirables. They left their religion behind.

Ten minutes till the service, and a line was forming to gain entry to the church. I surveyed the crowded seat holders inside. Something was wrong. There was not one child in the church. No boys in dark trousers, rolling trucks over their mothers' legs, no girls cradling rag dolls. Not a face younger than fifteen. I didn't know if it was out of respect for the parents, or fear-driven

38

defense. An instinct to prevent one's children from being picked as future prey. I pictured hundreds of Wind Gap sons and daughters tucked away in dark den rooms, sucking the backs of their hands while they watched TV and remained unmarked.

Without kids to tend to, the churchgoers seemed static, like paperboard cutouts holding the places of real people. In the back, I could see Bob Nash in a dark suit. Still no wife. He nodded at me, then frowned.

The organ pipes exhaled the muffled tones of "Be Not Afraid," and Natalie Keene's family, until then crying, and hugging, and fussing near the door like one massive failing heart, filed tightly together. Only two men were needed to carry the shiny white coffin. Any more and they would have been bumping into each other.

Natalie's mother and father led the procession. She was three inches taller than he, a large, warm-looking woman with sandy hair held back with a headband. She had an open face, the kind that would prompt strangers to ask for directions or the time. Mr. Keene was small and thin, with a round child's face made rounder by wire spectacles that looked like two gold bike wheels. Behind them walked a beautiful boy of eighteen or nineteen, his brunette head bowed into his chest, sobbing. Natalie's brother, a woman whispered behind me.

Tears ran down my mother's cheeks and dripped loudly onto the leather purse she held in her lap. The woman next to her patted her hand. I slipped my notepad from my jacket pocket and began scribbling notes to one side until my mother slapped her hand on mine and hissed, "You are being disrespectful and embarrassing. Stop or I will make you leave."

I quit writing but kept the pad out, feeling stabbingly defiant. But still blushing.

The procession moved past us. The coffin seemed ludicrously small. I pictured Natalie inside and could see her legs again – downy hair, knobby knees, the Band-Aid. I ached once, hard, like a period typed at the end of a sentence.

As the priest murmured the opening prayers in his best vestments, and we stood and sat, and stood again, prayer cards were distributed. On the front, the Virgin Mary beamed her bright red heart down on baby Jesus. On the back was printed:

> Natalie Jane Keene
> Darling daughter, sister and friend
> Heaven has a new angel

A large photo of Natalie perched near the coffin, a more formal photo than the one I'd seen before. She was a sweet, homely little thing, with a pointy chin and slightly bulbous eyes, the kind of girl who might have grown up to be strangely striking. She could have delighted men with ugly-duckling stories that were actually true. Or she might have remained a sweet, homely little thing. At ten, a girl's looks are fickle.

Natalie's mother made her way to the podium, clutching a piece of paper. Her face was wet, but her voice was solid when she began speaking.

"This is a letter to Natalie, my only daughter." She took a shaky breath and the words streamed out. "Natalie, you were my dearest girl. I can't believe you have been taken from us. Never again will I sing you to sleep or tickle your back with my fingers. Never again will your brother get to twirl your pigtails, or your father hold you on his lap. Your father will not walk you down the aisle. Your brother will never be an uncle. We will miss you at our Sunday dinners and our summer vacations. We will miss your laughter. We will miss your tears. Mostly, my dear daughter, we will miss you. We love you, Natalie."

As Mrs. Keene walked back to her seat, her husband rushed up to her, but she seemed to need no steadying. As soon as she sat down, the boy was back in her arms, crying in the crook of her neck. Mr. Keene blinked angrily at the church pews behind him, as if looking for someone to hit.

"It is a terrible tragedy to lose a child," intoned the priest. "It is doubly terrible to lose her to such evil doings. For evil is what they are. The Bible says, 'An eye for an eye and a tooth for a tooth.' But let us not dwell on revenge. Let us think instead of what Jesus urged: Love thy neighbor. Let us be good to our neighbors in this difficult time. Lift up your hearts to God."

"I liked the eye for an eye stuff better," grumbled a man behind me.

I wondered if the tooth for a tooth part disturbed anyone else.

When we emerged from the church into the day's glare, I could make out four girls sitting in a row along a stumpy wall across the street. Long colt legs dangling down. Breasts rounded out by pushup bras. The same girls I'd run into at the edge of the forest. They were huddled together laughing until one of them, again the prettiest, motioned over at me, and they all pretended to hang their heads. Their stomachs were still jiggling, though.

Natalie was buried in the family plot, next to a gravestone that already bore her parents' names. I know the wisdom, that no parents should see their child die, that such an event is like nature spun backward. But it's the only way to truly keep your child. Kids grow up, they forge more potent allegiances. They find a spouse or a lover. They will not be buried with you. The Keenes, however, will remain the purest form of family. Underground.

After the funeral, people gathered at the Keene home, a massive stone farmhouse, a moneyed vision of pastoral America. It was like nothing else in Wind Gap. Missouri money distances itself from bucolicry, from such country quaintness. Consider: In colonial America, wealthy women wore subtle shades of blues and grays to counter their crass New World image, while their wealthy counterparts in England tarted up like exotic birds. In short, the Keene home looked too Missouri to be owned by Missourians.

The buffet table held mainly meats: turkey and ham, beef and venison. There were pickles and olives and deviled eggs; shiny, hard rolls; and crusted casseroles. The guests segregated themselves into two groups, the tearful and the dry. The stoics stood in the kitchen, drinking coffee and liquor and talking about upcoming city-council elections and the future of the schools, occasionally pausing to whisper angrily about the lack of progress in the murder cases.

"I swear I see someone I don't know coming near my girls, I'll shoot the sumbitch before 'Hello' comes out his mouth," said one spade-faced man, flapping a roast beef sandwich. His friends nodded in agreement.

"I don't know why the hell Vickery hasn't emptied out the forest – hell, raze the whole goddam thing. You know he's in there," said a younger man with orange hair.

"Donnie, I'll go out there tomorrow with you," said the spade-faced man. "We can just take it acre by acre. We'll find the son of a bitch. Ya'll wanna come?" The men muttered assents and drank more liquor from their plastic cups. I made a note to cruise past the roads near the forest in the morning, to see if hangovers had given way to action or not. But I could already picture the sheepish phone calls in the morning:

You going?

Well, I don't know, I guess, you?

Well, I promised Maggie I'd take down the storm windows. . . .

Agreements to meet for beers later, and the receivers compressed very slowly to muffle the guilty click.

Those who wept, mostly women, did so in the front

room, on plush sofas and leather ottomans. Natalie's brother was there shaking in the arms of his mother, as she rocked him and cried silently, patting down his dark hair. Sweet kid, to cry so openly. I'd never seen such a thing. Ladies came by with paper-plate offerings of food, but mother and son just shook their heads no. My mother fluttered around them like a manic bluejay, but they took no notice, and soon she was off to her circle of friends. Mr. Keene stood in a corner with Mr. Nash, both of them smoking silently.

Recent evidence of Natalie was still scattered around the room. A small gray sweater folded over the back of a chair, a pair of tennis shoes with bright blue laces by the door. On one of the bookshelves sat a spiral note-book with a unicorn on the front, in a magazine rack was a dog-eared copy of *A Wrinkle in Time*.

I was rotten. I didn't approach the family, didn't announce myself. I walked through their home and I spied, my head down in my beer like a shamed ghost. I saw Katie Lacey, my old best friend from Calhoon High, in her own well-coiffed circle, the exact mirror of my mother's group, minus twenty years. She kissed me on the cheek when I approached.

"Heard you were in town, was hoping you'd phone," she said, wrinkling her thinly plucked eyebrows at me, then passing me off to the three other women, all of whom crowded in to give me limp hugs. All of whom had been my friends at one point, I suppose. We exchanged condolences and murmured about how sad this was. Angie Papermaker (née Knightley) looked like she was still battling the bulimia that'd whittled her down in high school – her neck was as thin and ropy as an old woman's. Mimi, a spoiled rich girl (Daddy owned acres of chicken lots down in Arkansas) who'd never liked me much, asked about Chicago and then immediately turned to talk to tiny little Tish, who had decided to hold my hand in a comforting but peculiar gesture.

Angie announced to me that she had a five-year-old daughter – her husband was at home with his gun, watching over her.

"It's going to be a long summer for the little ones," Tish murmured. "I think everyone's keeping their babies under lock and key." I thought about the girls I'd seen outside the funeral, not much older than Natalie, and wondered why their parents weren't worried.

"You have kids, Camille?" Angie asked in a voice as thin as her body. "I don't even know if you're married."

"No and no," I said, and took a slurp of my beer, flashing an image of Angie vomiting at my house after school, emerging from the bathroom pink and triumphant. Curry was wrong: Being an insider here was more distracting than useful.

"Ladies, you can't hog the out-of-towner all night!" I turned to see one of my mother's friends, Jackie O'Neele (née O'Keefe), who'd clearly just had a facelift. Her eyes were still puffy and her face was moist and red and stretched, as if she was an angry baby squeezing out of the womb. Diamonds flashed on her tanned fingers, and she smelled of Juicy Fruit and talc when she hugged me. The evening was feeling too much like a reunion.

And I was feeling too much like a kid again – I hadn't even dared to pull out my notebook with my mother still here, shooting me warning glances.

"Baby girl, you look so pretty," Jackie purred. She had a melon of a head, covered with overbleached hair, and a leering smile. Jackie was catty and shallow, but she was always completely herself. She also was more at ease with me than my own mother. It was Jackie, not Adora, who slipped me my first box of tampons, winking that I should phone her if I needed instructions, and Jackie who'd always teased me merrily about boys. Small huge gestures. "How are you, darling? Your momma didn't tell me you were in town. But your momma isn't talking to me right now – I disappointed her again somehow. You know how that goes. I *know* you know!" She let out a rocky smoker's laugh and squeezed my arm. I assumed she was drunk.

"I probably forgot to send her a card for something," she babbled on, overgesturing with the hand that held a glass of wine. "Or maybe that gardener I recommended didn't please her. I heard you're doing a story about *the girls*; that's just rough." Her conversation was so bumpy and abrupt it took me a minute to process everything. By the time I started to speak, she was caressing my arm and staring at me with wet eyes. "Camille, baby, it's been so damn long since I've seen you. And now – I look at you and I see you when you were the same age as those girls. And I just feel so sad. So much has gone wrong. I can't make sense of it." A tear trailed down her cheek. "Look me up, okay? We can talk."

I left the Keene house with no quotes. I was already tired of talking, and I'd said very little.

I called the Keenes later, after I'd had more to drink – a to-go cup of vodka from their stash – and was safely segregated by phone lines. Then I explained myself and what I would write. It didn't go well.

Here's what I filed that night:

> In tiny Wind Gap, Missouri, posters pleading for the return of 10-year-old Natalie Jane Keene were still hanging as they buried the little girl on Tuesday. A vibrant funeral service, at which the priest spoke of forgiveness and redemption, did little to calm nerves or heal wounds. That's because the healthy, sweet-faced young girl was the second victim of what police presume to be a serial killer. A serial killer who's targeting children.
>
> "All the little ones here are sweethearts," said local farmer Ronald J. Kamens, who assisted in the search for Keene. "I can't imagine why this is happening to us."
>
> Keene's strangled body was discovered May 14, crammed into a space between two buildings on Wind Gap's Main Street. "We will miss her laughter," said Jeannie Keene, 52, mother of Natalie. "We will miss her tears. Mostly, we will miss Natalie."
>
> This, however, is not the first tragedy Wind Gap, located in the boot heel of the state, has with-

stood. Last August 27, nine-year-old Ann Nash was found in an area creek, also strangled. She had been bicycling just a few blocks to visit a friend when she was abducted the night before. Both victims reportedly had their teeth removed by the killer.

The murders have left the five-person Wind Gap police force baffled. Lacking experience in such brutal crimes, they have elicited help from the Kansas City homicide division, which has sent an officer trained in the psychological profiling of murderers. Residents of the town (pop. 2,120) are, however, sure of one thing: The person responsible for the slayings is killing with no particular motive.

"There is a man out there looking for babies to kill," says Ann's father, Bob Nash, 41, a chair salesman. "There's no hidden drama here, no secrets. Someone just killed our little girl."

The removal of the teeth has remained a point of mystery, and clues thus far have been minimal. Local police have declined to comment. Until these murders are resolved, Wind Gap protects its own – a curfew is in effect, and neighborhood watches have sprung up over this once-quiet town.

The residents also try to heal themselves. "I don't want to talk to anyone," says Jeannie Keene. "I just want to be left alone. We all want to be left alone."

Hack work – you don't need to tell me that. Even as I e-mailed Curry the file, I was already regretting nearly everything about it. Stating that police presumed the murders were committed by a serial killer was a stretch. Vickery never said anything of the sort. The first Jeannie Keene quote I stole from her eulogy. The second yanked from the vitriol she spewed at me when she realized my phone condolences were a front. She knew I planned to dissect her girl's murder, lay it out on butcher paper for strangers to chew on. "We all want to be left alone!" she yelped. "We buried our baby today. Shame on you." A quote nonetheless, a quote I needed, since Vickery was shutting me out.

Curry thought the piece was solid – not great, mind you, but a solid start. He even left in my overfried line: "A serial killer who's targeting children." That should have been cut, I knew it myself, but I craved the dramatic padding. He must have been drunk when he read it.

He ordered a larger feature on the families, soon as I could scrape it together. Another chance to redeem myself. I was lucky – it looked like the *Chicago Daily Post* might have Wind Gap to ourselves for a bit longer. A congressional sex scandal was unraveling delightfully, destroying not just one austere House member, but three. Two of them women. Lurid, juicy stuff. More importantly, there was a serial killer stalking a more glamorous city, Seattle. Amid the fog and coffeehouses, someone was carving up pregnant women, opening their bellies, and arranging the contents in shocking tableaux for his own amusement. Thus it was our good fortune that reporters for this type of thing were out of commission. There was just me, left wretched in my childhood bed.

I slept late into Wednesday, sweaty sheets and blankets pulled over my head. Woke several times to phones ringing, the maid vacuuming outside my door, a lawn mower. I was desperate to remain asleep, but the day kept bobbing through. I kept my eyes closed and imagined myself back in Chicago, on my rickety slice of a bed in my studio apartment facing the brick back of a supermarket. I had a cardboard dresser purchased at that supermarket when I moved in four years ago, and a plastic table on which I ate from a set of weightless yellow plates and bent, tinny flatware. I worried that I hadn't watered my lone plant, a slightly yellow fern I'd found by my neighbors' trash. Then I remembered I'd tossed the dead thing out two months ago. I tried to imagine other images from my life in Chicago: my cubicle at work, my superintendent who still didn't know my name, the dull green Christmas lights the supermarket had yet to take down. A scattering of friendly acquaintances who probably hadn't noticed I'd been gone.

I hated being in Wind Gap, but home held no comfort either.

I pulled a flask of warm vodka from my duffel bag and got back in bed. Then, sipping, I assessed my surroundings. I'd expected my mother to pave over my bedroom as soon as I'd left the house, but it looked exactly as it was more than a decade before. I regretted what a serious teenager I'd been: There were no posters of pop stars or favorite movies, no girlish collections of photos or corsages. Instead there were paintings of sailboats, proper pastel pastorals, a portrait of Eleanor Roosevelt. The latter was particularly strange, since I'd known little about Mrs. Roosevelt, except that she was good, which at the time I suppose was enough. Given my druthers now, I'd prefer a snapshot of Warren Harding's wife, "the Duchess," who recorded the smallest offenses in a little red notebook and avenged herself accordingly. Today I like my first ladies with a little bite.

I drank more vodka. There was nothing I wanted to do more than be unconscious again, wrapped in black, gone away. I was raw. I felt swollen with potential tears, like a water balloon filled to burst. Begging for a pin prick. Wind Gap was unhealthy for me. This home was unhealthy for me.

A quiet knock at the door, little more than a rattling gust.

"Yes?" I tucked my glass of vodka to the side of the bed.

"Camille? It's your mother."

"Yes?"

"I brought you some lotion."

I walked to the door a bit blurrily, the vodka giving me that first necessary layer to deal with this particular place on this particular day. I'd been good about booze for six months, but nothing counted here. Outside my door my mother hovered, peering in warily as if it were the trophy room of a dead child. Close. She held out a large pale green tube.

"It has vitamin E. I picked it up this morning."

My mother believes in the palliative effects of vitamin E, as if slathering enough on will make me smooth and flawless again. It hasn't worked yet.

"Thank you."

Her eyes scanned across my neck, my arms, my legs, all bared by the lone T-shirt I'd worn to bed. Then back with a frown to my face. She sighed and shook her head slightly. Then she just stood there.

"Was the funeral very hard on you, Momma?" Even now, I couldn't resist making a small conversational offering.

"It was. So much was similar. That little casket."

"It was hard for me, too," I nudged. "I was actually surprised how hard. I miss her. Still. Isn't that weird?"

"It would be *weird* if you didn't. She's your sister. It's almost as painful as losing a child. Even though you were so young." Downstairs, Alan was whistling elaborately, but my mother seemed not to hear. "I didn't care much for that open letter Jeannie Keene read," she continued. "It's a funeral, not a political rally. And why were they all dressed so informally?"

"I thought the letter was nice. It was heartfelt," I said. "Didn't you read anything at Marian's funeral?"

"No, no. I could barely stand, much less give speeches. I can't believe you can't remember these things, Camille. I'd think you'd be embarrassed to have forgotten so much."

"I was only thirteen when she died, Momma.

Remember, I was young." Nearly twenty years ago, can that be right?

"Yes, well. Enough. Is there anything you'd like to do today? The roses are in bloom at Daly Park, if you'd like a walk."

"I should go over to the police station."

"Don't say that while you're staying here," she snapped. "Say you have errands to run, or friends to see."

"I have errands to run."

"Fine. Enjoy."

She padded away down the plush corridor, and I heard the stairs creak quickly downward.

I washed up in a cool, shallow bath, lights off, another glass of vodka balanced on the side of the tub, then dressed and entered the hallway. The house was silent, as silent as its century-old structure would allow. I heard a fan whirring in the kitchen as I stood outside to make sure no one was there. Then I slipped in, grabbed a bright green apple, and bit into it as I walked out of the house. The sky was cloudless.

Outside on the porch I saw a changeling. A little girl with her face aimed intently at a huge, four-foot doll-house, fashioned to look exactly like my mother's home. Long blonde hair drifted in disciplined rivulets down her back, which was to me. As she turned, I realized it was the girl I'd spoken to at the edge of the woods, the girl who'd been laughing with her friends outside Natalie's funeral. The prettiest one.

"Amma?" I asked, and she laughed.

"Naturally. Who else would be playing on Adora's front porch with a little Adora house?"

The girl was in a childish checked sundress, matching straw hat by her side. She looked entirely her age – thirteen – for the first time since I'd seen her. Actually, no. She looked younger now. Those clothes were more appropriate for a ten-year-old. She scowled when she saw me assessing her.

"I wear this for Adora. When I'm home, I'm her little doll."

"And when you're not?"

"I'm other things. You're Camille. You're my half sister. Adora's first daughter, before *Marian.* You're Pre and I'm Post. You didn't recognize me."

"I've been away too long. And Adora stopped sending out Christmas photos five years ago."

"Stopped sending them to you, maybe. We still take the dang pictures. Every year Adora buys me a red-and-green checked dress just for the occasion. And as soon as we're done I throw it in the fire."

She plucked a footstool the size of a tangerine from the dollhouse's front room and held it up to me. "Needs repolstering now. Adora changed her color scheme from peach to yellow. She promised me she'd take me to the fabric store so I can make new coverings to match. This dollhouse is my fancy." She almost made it sound natural, *my fancy*. The words floated out of her mouth sweet and round like butterscotch, murmured with just a tilt of her head, but the phrase was definitely my mother's. Her little doll, learning to speak just like Adora.

"Looks like you do a very good job with it," I said, and motioned a weak wave good-bye.

"Thank you," she said. Her eyes focused on my room in the dollhouse. A small finger poked the bed. "I hope you enjoy your stay here," she murmured into the room, as if she were addressing a tiny Camille no one could see.

I found Chief Vickery banging the dent out of a stop sign at the corner of Second and Ely, a quiet street of small houses a few blocks from the police station. He used a hammer, and with each tinny bang he winced. The back of his shirt was already wet, and his bifocals were slung down to the end of his nose.

"I have nothing to say, Miss Preaker." *Bang.*

"I know this is an easy thing to resent, Chief Vickery. I didn't really even want this assignment. I was forced into it because I'm from here."

"Haven't been back in years, from what I hear." *Bang.*

I didn't say anything. I looked at the crabgrass splurting up through a crack in the sidewalk. The *Miss* stung me a bit. I couldn't tell if it was politeness I wasn't accustomed to or a jab at my unmarried state. A single woman even a hair over thirty was a queer thing in these parts.

"A decent person would have quit before writing about dead children." *Bang.* "Opportunism, Miss Preaker."

Across the street, an elderly man clutching a carton

of milk was shuffling half-steps toward a white clapboard house.

"I'm not feeling so decent right now, you're right." I didn't mind gingering Vickery along a little bit. I wanted him to like me, not just because it would make my job easier, but because his bluster reminded me of Curry, who I missed. "But a little publicity might bring some attention to this case, help get it solved. It's happened before."

"Goddam." He threw the hammer with a thud on the ground and faced me. "We already asked for help. Got some special detective from Kansas City down here, off and on for months. And he hasn't been able to figure out one goddam thing. Says it might be some crazed hitchhiker dropped off the road here, liked the looks of the place, and stayed for near on a year. Well this town ain't that big, and I sure as hell haven't seen anyone looks like they don't belong." He glanced pointedly at me.

"We've got some pretty big woods around here, pretty dense," I suggested.

"This isn't some stranger, and I would guess you know it."

"I would have thought you'd prefer it to be a stranger."

Vickery sighed, lit a cigarette, put his hand around the sign post protectively. "Hell, of course I would," he said. "But I'm not too dumb myself. Ain't worked no homicide before, but I ain't a goddam idiot."

I wished then that I hadn't sucked down so much vodka. My thoughts were vaporizing, I couldn't hold on to what he was saying, couldn't ask the right questions.

"You think someone from Wind Gap is doing this?"

"No comment."

"Off record, why would someone from Wind Gap kill kids?"

"Got called out one time because Ann had killed a neighbor's pet bird with a stick. She'd sharpened it herself with one of her daddy's hunting knifes. Natalie, hell, her family moved here two years ago because she stabbed one of her classmates in the eye with a pair of scissors back in Philadelphia. Her daddy quit his job at some big business, just so they could start over. In the state where his granddad grew up. In a small town. Like a small town don't come with its own set of problems."

"Not the least of which is everyone knows who the bad seeds are."

"Damn straight."

"So you think this could be someone who didn't like the children? These girls specifically? Maybe they had done something to him? And this was revenge?"

Vickery pulled at the end of his nose, scratched his mustache. He looked back at the hammer on the ground, and I could tell he was debating whether to pick it up and dismiss me or keep talking. Just then a black sedan whooshed up next to us, the passenger-side window zipping down before the car even stopped. The driver's face, blocked by sunglasses, peered out to look at us.

"Hey, Bill. Thought we were supposed to meet at your office right about now."

"Had some work to do."

It was Kansas City. He looked at me, lowering his glasses in a practiced way. He had a flip of light brown hair that kept dropping over his left eye. Blue. He smiled at me, teeth like perfect Chiclets.

"Hi there." He glanced at Vickery, who pointedly bent down to pick up the hammer, then back at me.

"Hi," I said. I pulled my sleeves down over my hands, balled the ends up in my palms, leaned on one leg.

"Well, Bill, want a ride? Or are you a walking man – I could pick us up some coffee and meet you there."

"Don't drink coffee. Something you should've noticed by now. I'll be there in fifteen minutes."

"See if you can make it ten, huh? We're already running late." Kansas City looked at me one more time. "Sure you don't want a lift, Bill?"

Vickery said nothing, just shook his head.

"Who's your friend, Bill? I thought I'd met all the pertinent Wind Gappers already. Or is it ... Wind Gapians?" He grinned. I stood silent as a schoolgirl, hoping Vickery would introduce me.

Bang! Vickery was choosing not to hear. In Chicago I would have jabbed my hand out, announced myself with a smile, and enjoyed the reaction. Here I stared at Vickery and stayed mute.

"All right then, see you at the station."

The window zipped back up, the car pulled away.

"Is that the detective from Kansas City?" I asked.

In answer, Vickery lit another cigarette, walked off. Across the street, the old man had just reached his top step.

Chapter Four

Someone had spray-painted blue curlicues on the legs of the water tower at Jacob J. Garrett Memorial Park, and it was left looking oddly dainty, as if it were wearing crochet booties. The park itself – the last place Natalie Keene was seen alive – was vacant. The dirt from the baseball field hovered a few feet above the ground. I could taste it in the back of my throat like tea left brewing too long. The grasses grew tall at the edge of the woods. I was surprised no one had ordered them cut, eradicated like the stones that snagged Ann Nash.

When I was in high school, Garrett Park was the place everyone met on weekends to drink beer or smoke pot or get jerked off three feet into the woods. It was where I was first kissed, at age thirteen, by a football player with a pack of chaw tucked down in his gums. The rush of the tobacco hit me more than the kiss; behind his car I vomited wine cooler with tiny, glowing slices of fruit.

"James Capisi was here."

I turned around to face a blond, buzz-cut boy of about ten, holding a fuzzy tennis ball.

"James Capisi?" I asked.

"My friend, he was here when she got Natalie," the kid said. "James saw her. She was wearing her nightgown. They were playing Frisbee, over by the woods, and she took Natalie. It would've been James, but he decided to stay here on the field. So Natalie was the one right by the trees. James was out here because of the sun. He's not supposed to be in the sun, because his mom's got skin cancer, but he does anyway. Or he did." The boy bounced the tennis ball, and a puff of dirt floated up around him.

"He doesn't like the sun anymore?"

"He doesn't like nothing no more."

"Because of Natalie?"

He shrugged belligerently.

"Because James is a pussy."

The kid looked me up and down, then suddenly threw the ball at me, hard. It hit my hip and bounced off.

He blurted out a little laugh. "Sorry." He scrambled after the ball, dove on top of it dramatically, then leapt up and hurled it against the ground. It bounced about ten feet in the air, then dribbled to a stop.

"I'm not sure I understood what you said. Who was wearing a nightgown?" I kept my eye on the bouncing ball.

"The woman who took Natalie."

"Wait, what do you mean?" The story I'd heard was that Natalie had been playing here with friends who left to go home one by one, and that she was assumed to have been abducted somewhere along her short walk home.

"James saw the woman take Natalie. It was just the two of them, and they were playing Frisbee, and Natalie missed and it went into the grasses by the woods, and the woman just reached out and grabbed her. Then they were gone. And James ran home. And he don't come out since."

"Then how do you know what happened?"

"I visited him once. He told me. I'm his buddy."

"Does James live around here?"

"Fuck him. I might go to my grandma's for the summer anyway. In Arkansas. Better'n here."

The boy threw the ball at the chain-link fence outlining the baseball diamond, and it lodged there, rattling the metal.

"You from here?" He began kicking dirt in the air.

"Yeah. I used to be. I don't live here anymore. I'm visiting." I tried again: "Does James live around here?"

"You in high school?" His face was deeply tanned. He looked like a baby Marine.

"No."

"College?" His chin was wet with spit.

"Older."

"I got to go." He hopped away backward, yanked the ball out of the fence like a bad tooth, turned around and looked at me again, waggled his hips in a nervous dance. "I got to go." He threw the ball toward the street, where it bounced off my car with an impressive thunk. He ran after it and was gone.

I looked up *Capisi, Janel,* in a magazine-thin phone book at Wind Gap's lone FaStop. Then I filled a Big Mouth with strawberry pop and drove to 3617 Holmes.

The Capisi home sat on the edge of the low-rent section to the far east of town, a cluster of broken-down, two-bedroom houses, most of whose inhabitants work at the nearby pig factory-farm, a private operation that delivers almost 2 percent of the country's pork. Find a poor person in Wind Gap, and they'll almost always tell you they work at the farm, and so did their old man. On the breeding side, there are piglets to be clipped and crated, sows to be impregnated and penned, manure pits to be managed. The killing side's worse. Some employees load the pigs, forcing them down the gangway, where stunners await. Others grab the back legs, fasten the catch around them, release the animal to be lifted, squealing and kicking, upside down. They cut the throats with pointy slaughter knives, the blood spattering thick as paint onto the tile floors. Then on to the scalding tank. The constant screams – frantic, metallic squeals – drive most of the workers to wear earplugs, and they spend their days in a soundless rage. At night they drink and play music, loud. The local bar, Heelah's, serves nothing pork related, only chicken tenders, which are, presumably, processed by equally furious factory workers in some other crappy town.

For the sake of full disclosure, I should add that my mother owns the whole operation and receives approximately $1.2 million in profits from it annually. She lets other people run it.

A tomcat was yowling on the Capisis' front porch, and as I walked toward the house, I could hear the din of a daytime talk show. I banged on the screen door and waited. The cat rubbed up against my legs; I could feel its ribs through my pants. I banged again, and the TV switched off. The cat stalked under the porch swing and cried. I traced the word *yelp* on my right palm with a fingernail and knocked again.

"Mom?" A child's voice at the open window.

I walked over, and through the dust of the screen could see a thin boy with dark curls and gaping eyes.

"Hi there, I'm sorry to bug you. Are you James?"

"What do you want?"

"Hi James, I'm sorry to bother you. Were you watching something good?"

"Are you the police?"

"I'm trying to help figure out who hurt your friend. Can I talk to you?"

He didn't leave, just traced a finger along the window ledge. I sat down on the swing at the far end away from him.

"My name's Camille. A friend of yours told me what you'd seen. A boy with real short blonde hair?"

"Dee."

"Is that his name? I saw him at the park, the same park where you were playing with Natalie."

"She took her. No one believes me. I'm not scared. I just need to stay in the house is all. My mom has cancer. She's sick."

"That's what Dee said. I don't blame you. I hope I

didn't scare you, coming by like this." He began scraping an overlong fingernail down the screen. The clicking sound made my ears itch.

"You don't look like her. If you looked like her, I'd call the police. Or I'd shoot you."

"What did she look like?"

He shrugged his shoulders. "I've said it already. A hundred times."

"One more time."

"She was old."

"Old like me?"

"Old like a mother."

"What else?"

"She was wearing a white bed dress with white hair. She was just all white, but not like a ghost. That's what I keep saying."

"White like how?"

"Just like she'd never been outside before."

"And the woman grabbed Natalie when she went toward the woods?" I asked it in the same coaxing voice my mother used on favored waitstaff.

"I'm not lying."

"Of course not. The woman grabbed Natalie while y'all were playing?"

"Real fast," he nodded. "Natalie was walking in the grass to find the Frisbee. And I saw the woman moving from inside the woods, watching her. I saw her before Natalie did. But I wasn't scared."

"Probably not."

"Even when she grabbed Natalie, at first I wasn't scared."

"But then you were?"

"No." His voice trailed off. "I wasn't."

"James, could you tell me what happened when she grabbed Natalie?"

"She pulled Natalie against her, like she was hugging her. And then she looked up at me. She stared at me."

"The woman did?"

"Yeah. She smiled at me. For a second I thought it might be all right. But she didn't say anything. And then she stopped smiling. She put her finger to her lips to be quiet. And then she was gone into the woods. With Natalie." He shrugged again. "I've already told all this before."

"To the police?"

"First to my mom, then the police. My mom made me. But the police didn't care."

"Why not?"

"They thought I was lying. But I wouldn't make that up. It's stupid."

"Did Natalie do anything while this was happening?"

"No. She just stood there. I don't think she knew what to do."

"Did the woman look like anyone you'd seen before?"

"No. I told you." He stepped away from the screen then, began looking over his shoulder into the living room.

"Well, I'm sorry to bother you. Maybe you should have a friend come by. Keep you company." He shrugged again, chewed on a fingernail. "You might feel better if you get outside."

"I don't want to. Anyway, we have a gun." He pointed back over his shoulder at a pistol balanced on the arm of a couch, next to a half-eaten ham sandwich. Jesus.

"You sure you should have that out, James? You don't want to use that. Guns are very dangerous."

"Not so dangerous. My mom doesn't care." He looked at me straight on for the first time. "You're pretty. You have pretty hair."

"Thank you."

"I've got to go."

"Okay. Be careful, James."

"That's what I'm doing." He sighed purposefully and walked away from the window. A second later I heard the TV squabble on again.

There are eleven bars in Wind Gap. I went to one I didn't know, Sensors, which must have blossomed during some flash of '80s idiocy, judging by the neon zigzags on the wall and the mini dance floor in its center. I was drinking a bourbon and scribbling down my notes from the day when KC Law plopped down in the cushioned seat opposite me. He rattled his beer on the table between us.

"I thought reporters weren't supposed to talk to minors without permission." He smiled, took a gulp. James's mother must have made a phone call.

"Reporters have to be more aggressive when the police completely shut them out of an investigation," I said, not looking up.

"Police can't really do their work if reporters are detailing their investigations in Chicago papers."

This game was old. I went back to my notes, soggy from glass sweat.

"Let's try a new approach. I'm Richard Willis." He took another gulp, smacked his lips. "You can make your dick joke now. It works on several levels."

"Tempting."

"Dick as in asshole. Dick as in cop."

"Yes, I got it."

"And you are Camille Preaker, Wind Gap girl made good in the big city."

"Oh, that's me all right."

He smiled his alarming Chiclet smile and ran a hand through his hair. No wedding ring. I wondered when I began to notice such things.

"Okay, Camille, what do you say you and I call a détente? At least for now. See how it goes. I assume I don't need to lecture you about the Capisi boy."

"I assume you realize there's nothing to lecture about. Why have the police dismissed the account of the one eyewitness to the kidnapping of Natalie Keene?" I picked up my pen to show him we were on record.

"Who says we dismissed it?"

"James Capisi."

"Ah, well, there's a good source." He laughed. "I'll let you in on a little something here, *Miss* Preaker." He was doing a fairly good Vickery imitation, right down to twisting an imaginary pinky ring. "We don't let nine-year-old boys be particularly privy to an ongoing investigation one way or another. Including whether or not we believe his story."

"Do you?"

"I can't comment."

"It seems that if you had a fairly detailed description of a murder suspect, you might want to let people around here know, so they can be on the lookout. But you haven't, so I'd have to guess you'd dismissed his story."

"Again, I can't comment."

"I understand Ann Nash was not sexually molested," I continued. "Is that also the case with Natalie Keene?"

"*Ms.* Preaker. I just can't comment right now."

"Then why are you sitting here talking to me?"

"Well, first of all, I know you spent a lot of your time, probably work time, with our officer the other day, giving him your version of the discovery of Natalie's body. I wanted to thank you."

"My *version*?"

"Everyone has their own version of a memory," he said. "For instance, you said Natalie's eyes were open. The Broussards said they were closed."

"I can't comment." I was feeling spiteful.

"I'm inclined to believe a woman who makes her living as a reporter over two elderly diner owners," Willis said. "But I'd like to hear how positive you are."

"Was Natalie sexually molested? Off the record." I set down my pen.

He sat silent for a second, twirling his beer bottle. "No."

"I'm positive her eyes were open. But you were there."

"I was," he said.

"So you don't need me for that. What's the second thing?"

"What?"

"You said, 'first of all . . .' "

"Oh, right. Well, the second reason I wanted to speak with you, to be frank — a quality it seems you'd appreciate — is that I'm desperate to talk to a nontownie." The teeth flashed at me. "I mean, I know you're from here. And I don't know how you did it. I've been here off and on since last August and I'm going crazy. Not that Kansas City is a seething metropolis, but there's a night life. A cultural . . . some culture. There's people."

"I'm sure you're doing fine."

"I'd better. I may be here for a while now."

"Yes." I pointed my notebook at him. "So what's your theory, Mr. Willis?"

"That's Detective Willis, actually." He grinned again. I finished my drink in another swallow, began chewing on the stunted cocktail straw. "So, Camille, can I buy you a round?"

I jiggled my glass and nodded. "Bourbon straight up."

"Nice."

While he was at the bar, I took my ballpoint and wrote the word *dick* on my wrist in looping cursive. He came back with two Wild Turkeys.

"So." He wiggled his eyebrows at me. "My proposal is that maybe we can just talk for a little bit. Like civilians? I'm really craving it. Bill Vickery isn't exactly dying to get to know me."

"That makes two of us."

"Right. So, you're from Wind Gap, and now you work for a paper in Chicago. *Tribune?*"

"Daily Post."

"Don't know that one."

"You wouldn't."

"That high on it, huh?"

"It's fine. It's just fine." I wasn't in the mood to be charming, not even sure I'd remember the drill. Adora is the schmoozer in the family – even the guy who sprays for termites once a year sends doting Christmas cards.

"You're not giving me a lot to work with here, Camille. If you want me to leave, I will."

I didn't, in truth. He was nice to look at, and his voice made me feel less ragged. It didn't hurt that he didn't belong here either.

"I'm sorry, I'm being curt. Been a rocky reentry. Writing about all this doesn't help."

"How long since you've been back?"

"Years. Eight to be precise."

"But you still have family here."

"Oh, yes. Fervent Wind Gapians. I think that's the preferred term, in answer to your question earlier today."

"Ah, thanks. I'd hate to insult the nice people around

here. More than I already have. So your folks like it here?"

"Mm-hmm. They'd never dream of leaving here. Too many friends. Too perfect a house. Etcetera."

"Both your parents were born here then?"

A table of familiar guys about my age plopped down at a nearby booth, each sloshing a pitcher of beer. I hoped they wouldn't see me.

"My mom was. My stepdad's from Tennessee. He moved here when they got married."

"When was that?"

"Almost thirty years ago, I'd guess." I tried to slow my drinking down so I didn't outpace him.

"And your father?"

I smiled pointedly. "You raised in Kansas City?"

"Yep. Never dream of leaving. Too many friends. Too perfect a house. Etcetera."

"And being a cop there is . . . good?"

"You see some action. Enough so I won't turn into Vickery. Last year I did some high-profile stuff. Murders mostly. And we got a guy who was serially assaulting women around town."

"Rape?"

"No. He straddled them and then reached inside their mouths, scratched their throats to pieces."

"Jesus."

"We caught him. He was a middle-aged liquor sales-man who lived with his mother, and still had tissue from the last woman's throat under his fingernails. Ten *days* after the attack."

I wasn't clear if he was bemoaning the guy's stupidity or his poor hygiene.

"Good."

"And now I'm here. Smaller town, but bigger proving grounds. When Vickery first phoned us, the case wasn't that big yet, so they sent someone mid-range on the totem pole. Me." He smiled, almost self-effacingly. "Then it turned into a serial. They're letting me keep the case for now – with the understanding that I'd better not screw up."

His situation sounded familiar.

"It's strange to get your big break based on something so horrible," he continued. "But you must know about that – what kind of stories do you cover in Chicago?"

"I'm on the police beat, so probably the same kind of junk you see: abuse, rape, murder." I wanted him to know I had horror stories, too. Foolish, but I indulged. "Last month it was an eighty-two-year-old man. Son killed him, then left him in a bathtub of Drano to dissolve. Guy confessed, but, of course, couldn't come up with a reason for doing it."

I was regretting using the word *junk* to describe abuse, rape, and murder. Disrespectful.

"Sounds like we've both seen some ugly things," Richard said.

"Yes." I twirled my drink, had nothing to say.

"I'm sorry."

"Me too."

He studied me. The bartender switched the house

lights to low, an official signal of nighttime hours.

"We could catch a movie sometime." He said it in a conciliatory tone, as if an evening at the local cineplex might make everything work out for me.

"Maybe." I swallowed the rest of my drink. "Maybe."

He peeled the label off the empty beer bottle next to him and smoothed it out onto the table. Messy. A sure sign he'd never worked in a bar.

"Well, Richard, thank you for the drink. I've got to get home."

"It was nice talking with you, Camille. Can I walk you to your car?"

"No, I'm fine."

"You okay to drive? I promise, I'm not being a cop."

"I'm fine."

"Okay. Have good dreams."

"You too. Next time, I want something on record."

Alan, Adora, and Amma were all gathered in the living room when I returned. The scene was startling, it was so much like the old days with Marian. Amma and my mother sat on the couch, my mother cradling Amma – in a woolen nightgown despite the heat – as she held an ice cube to her lips. My half sister stared up at me with blank contentment, then went back to playing with a glowing mahogany dinner table, exactly like the one in the next room, except that it was about four inches high.

"Nothing to worry about," Alan said, looking up from a newspaper. "Amma's just got the summer chills."

I felt a shot of alarm, then annoyance: I was sinking back into old routines, about to run to the kitchen to heat some tea, just like I always did for Marian when she was sick. I was about to linger near my mother, waiting for her to put an arm around me, too. My mother and Amma said nothing. My mother didn't even look up at me, just nuzzled Amma in closer to her, and cooed into her ear.

"We Crellins run a bit delicate," Alan said somewhat guiltily. The doctors in Woodberry, in fact, probably saw a Crellin a week – both my mother and Alan were sincere overreactors when it came to their health. When I was a child, I remember my mother trying to prod me with ointments and oils, homemade remedies and homeopathic nonsense. I sometimes took the foul solutions, more often refused. Then Marian got sick, really sick, and Adora had more important things to do than coaxing me into swallowing wheat-germ extract. Now I had a pang: all those syrups and tablets she proffered, and I rejected. That was the last time I had her full attention as a mother. I suddenly wished I'd been easier.

The Crellins. Everyone here was a Crellin but me, I thought childishly.

"I'm sorry you're sick, Amma," I said.

"The pattern on the legs is wrong," Amma whined abruptly. She held the table up to my mother, indignant.

"You've got such eyes, Amma," Adora said, squinting at the miniature. "But it's barely noticeable, baby. Only you will ever know." She smoothed back Amma's damp hairline.

"I can't have it wrong," Amma said, glaring at it. "We have to send it back. What's the point of getting it special-made if it's not right?"

"Darling, I promise you, you can't even tell." My mother patted Amma's cheek, but she was already standing up.

"You said it would all be perfect. You promised!" Her voice wavered and tears started dripping down her face. "Now it's ruined. The whole thing is ruined. It's the dining room – it can't have a table that doesn't match. I hate it!"

"Amma . . ." Alan folded his paper and went to put his arms around her, but she wrenched away.

"This is all I want, it's all I asked for, and you don't even care that it's wrong!" she was screaming through her tears now, a full-blown tantrum, her face mottled in anger.

"Amma, calm yourself," Alan said coolly, trying to get a hold of her again.

"It's all I want!" Amma yelped, and smashed the table on the floor, where it cracked into five shards. She hit it until it was in pieces, then buried her face in the sofa cushion and wailed.

"Well," my mother said. "Looks like we'll have to get a new one now."

I retreated to my room, away from that horrible little girl, who was not like Marian at all. My body was heading into a flare. I paced a bit, tried to remember how to breathe right, how to calm my skin. But it blared at me. Sometimes my scars have a mind of their own.

I am a cutter, you see. Also a snipper, a slicer, a carver, a jabber. I am a very special case. I have a purpose. My skin, you see, screams. It's covered with words – *cook, cupcake, kitty, curls* – as if a knife-wielding first-grader learned to write on my flesh. I sometimes, but only sometimes, laugh. Getting out of the bath and seeing, out of the corner of my eye, down the side of a leg: *baby-doll*. Pulling on a sweater and, in a flash of my wrist: *harmful*. Why these words? Thousands of hours of therapy have yielded a few ideas from the good doctors. They are often feminine, in a Dick and Jane, pink vs. puppy dog tails sort of way. Or they're flat-out negative. Number of synonyms for anxious carved in my skin: eleven. The one thing I know for sure is that at the time, it was crucial to see these letters on me, and not just see them, but feel them. Burning on my left hip: *petticoat*.

And near it, my first word, slashed on an anxious summer day at age thirteen: *wicked*. I woke up that morning, hot and bored, worried about the hours ahead. How do you keep safe when your whole day is as wide and empty as the sky? Anything could happen. I remember feeling that word, heavy and slightly sticky across my pubic bone. My mother's steak knife. Cutting like a child along red imaginary lines. Cleaning myself. Digging in deeper. Cleaning myself. Pouring bleach over the knife and sneaking through the kitchen to return it. *Wicked*. Relief. The rest of the day, I spent ministering to my wound. Dig into the curves of *W* with an alcohol-soaked Q-tip. Pet my cheek until the sting went away. Lotion. Bandage. Repeat.

The problem started long before that, of course. Problems always start long before you really, really see them. I was nine and copying, with a thick polka-dotted pencil, the entire *Little House on the Prairie* series word by word into spiral notebooks with glowing green covers.

I was ten and writing every other word my teacher said on my jeans in blue ballpoint. I washed them, guiltily, secretly, in my bathroom sink with baby shampoo. The words smudged and blurred, left indigo hieroglyphics up and down the pant legs, as if a tiny ink-stained bird had hopped across them.

By eleven, I was compulsively writing down everything anyone said to me in a tiny blue notepad, a mini reporter already. Every phrase had to be captured on paper or it wasn't real, it slipped away. I'd see the words hanging in midair – Camille, pass the milk – and anxiety coiled up in me as they began to fade, like jet exhaust. Writing them down, though, I had them. No worries that they'd become extinct. I was a lingual conservationist. I was the class freak, a tight, nervous eighth-grader frenziedly copying down phrases ("Mr. Feeney is totally gay," "Jamie Dobson is ugly," "They never have chocolate milk") with a keenness bordering on the religious.

Marian died on my thirteenth birthday. I woke up, padded down the hall to say hello – always the first thing I did – and found her, eyes open, blanket pulled up to her chin. I remember not being that surprised. She'd been dying for as long as I could remember.

That summer, other things happened. I became quite

suddenly, unmistakably beautiful. It could have fallen either way. Marian was the confirmed beauty: big blue eyes, tiny nose, perfect pointy chin. My features changed by the day, as if clouds floated above me casting flattering or sickly shadows on my face. But once it was settled – and we all seemed to realize it that summer, the same summer I first found blood speckling my thighs, the same summer I began compulsively, furiously masturbating – I was hooked. I was taken with myself, an incredible flirt in any mirror I could find. Unabashed as a colt. And people loved me. I was no longer the pity case (with, how weird, the dead sister). I was the pretty girl (with, how sad, the dead sister). And so I was popular.

It was that summer, too, that I began the cutting, and was almost as devoted to it as to my newfound loveliness. I adored tending to myself, wiping a shallow red pool of my blood away with a damp washcloth to magically reveal, just above my naval: *queasy*. Applying alcohol with dabs of a cottonball, wispy shreds sticking to the bloody lines of: *perky*. I had a dirty streak my senior year, which I later rectified. A few quick cuts and *cunt* becomes *can't*, *cock* turns into *back*, *clit* transforms to a very unlikely *cat*, the *l* and *i* turned into a teetering capital *A*.

The last word I ever carved into myself, sixteen years after I started: *vanish*.

Sometimes I can hear the words squabbling at each other across my body. Up on my shoulder, *panty* calling down to *cherry* on the inside of my right ankle. On the underside of a big toe, *sew* uttering muffled threats to *baby,* just under my left breast. I can quiet them down by thinking of *vanish*, always hushed and regal, lording over the other words from the safety of the nape of my neck.

Also: At the center of my back, which was too difficult to reach, is a circle of perfect skin the size of a fist.

Over the years I've made my own private jokes. *You can really read me. Do you want me to spell it out for you? I've certainly given myself a life sentence.* Funny, right? I can't stand to look at myself without being completely covered. Someday I may visit a surgeon, see what can be done to smooth me, but now I couldn't bear the reaction. Instead I drink so I don't think too much about what I've done to my body and so I don't do any more. Yet most of the time that I'm awake, I want to cut. Not small words either. *Equivocate. Inarticulate. Duplicitous.* At my hospital back in Illinois they would not approve of this craving.

For those who need a name, there's a gift basket of medical terms. All I know is that the cutting made me feel safe. It was proof. Thoughts and words, captured where I could see them and track them. The truth, stinging, on my skin, in a freakish shorthand. Tell me you're going to the doctor, and I'll want to cut *worrisome* on my arm. Say you've fallen in love and I buzz the outlines of *tragic* over my breast. I hadn't necessarily wanted to be cured. But I was out of places to write, slicing myself between my toes – *bad, cry* – like a junkie looking for one last vein. *Vanish* did it for me. I'd saved the neck, such a nice prime spot, for one final good cutting. Then I turned myself in. I stayed at the hospital twelve weeks. It's a special place for people who cut, almost all of them women, most under twenty-five. I went when I was thirty. Just six months out. Delicate times.

Curry came to visit once, brought yellow roses. They chiseled off all the thorns before he was allowed into the reception room, deposited the shards in plastic containers – Curry said they looked like prescription bottles – which they locked away until the trash pickup came. We sat in the dayroom, all rounded edges and plush couches, and as we talked about the paper and his wife and the latest news in Chicago, I scanned his body for anything sharp. A belt buckle, a safety pin, a watch fob.

"I'm so sorry, my girl," he said at the end of his visit, and I could tell he meant it because his voice sounded wet.

When he left I was so sick with myself I vomited in the bathroom, and as I was vomiting, I noticed the rubber-covered screws at the back of the toilet. I pried the cap off one and sanded the palm of my hand – *I* – until orderlies hauled me out, blood splurting from the wound like stigmata.

My roommate killed herself later that week. Not by cutting, which was, of course, the irony. She swallowed a bottle of Windex a janitor left out. She was sixteen, a former cheerleader who cut herself above the thigh so no one would notice. Her parents glared at me when they came to pick up her things.

They always call depression the blues, but I would have been happy to waken to a periwinkle outlook. Depression to me is urine yellow. Washed out, exhausted miles of weak piss.

The nurses gave us meds to alleviate our tingling skins. And more meds to soothe our burning brains. We were body searched twice weekly for any sharp objects, and sat in groups together purging ourselves, theoretically, of anger and self-hatred. We learned not to turn on ourselves. We learned to blame. After a month of good behavior, we earned silky baths and massages. We were taught the goodness of touch.

My only other visitor was my mother, who I hadn't seen in half a decade. She smelled of purple flowers and wore a jangling charm bracelet I coveted as a child. When we were alone, she talked about the foliage and some new town rule that required Christmas lights be taken down by January 15. When my doctors joined us, she cried and petted and fretted at me. She stroked my hair and wondered why I had done this to myself.

Then, inevitably, came the stories of Marian. She'd already lost one child, you see. It had nearly killed her. Why would the older (though necessarily less beloved) deliberately harm herself? I was so different from her lost girl, who – *think of it* – would be almost thirty had she lived. Marian embraced life, what she had been spared. Lord, she had soaked up the world – *remember, Camille, how she laughed even in the hospital?*

I hated to point out to my mother that such was the nature of a bewildered, expiring ten-year-old. Why bother? It's impossible to compete with the dead. I wished I could stop trying.

Chapter Five

Alan was wearing white pants, the creases like folded paper, and a pale green oxford when I came down to breakfast. He sat alone at the massive mahogany dining-room set, his light shadow glowing in the polished wood. I peeked pointedly at the table legs to see what all the fuss of last night was about. Alan chose not to notice. He was eating milky eggs from a bowl with a teaspoon. When he looked up at me, a rubbery string of yolk swung like spit past his chin.

"Camille. Sit down. What can I have Gayla bring you?" He tinkled the silver bell next to him, and through the swinging kitchen door came Gayla, a former farm girl who ten years ago traded in pigs for daily work cleaning and cooking in my mother's home. She was my height – tall – but couldn't have weighed much more than a hundred pounds. The white starched nursing dress she wore as her uniform swayed loosely on her, like a bell.

My mother walked in past her, kissed Alan on the cheek, sat a pear in front of her place on a white cotton napkin.

"Gayla, you remember Camille."

"Of course I do, Mrs. Crellin," she said, pointing her vulpine face at me. Smiled with mismatched teeth and cracked, flaky lips. "Hi Camille. I have eggs, toast, fruit?"

"Just coffee please. Cream and sugar."

"Camille, we picked up food just for you," my mother said, nibbling on the plump end of the pear. "Have a banana at least."

"And a banana." Gayla headed back into the kitchen with a smirk.

"Camille, I must apologize to you for last night," Alan started. "Amma is going through one of those stages."

"She's very clingy," my mother said. "Mostly in a sweet way, but sometimes she gets a bit out of hand."

"Or more than a bit," I said. "That was a serious tantrum for a thirteen-year-old. It was a little scary." That was the Chicago me coming back – more assured and definitely more mouthy. I was relieved.

"Yes, well, you weren't exactly placid yourself at that age." I didn't know what my mother meant – my cutting, my crying jags over my lost sister, or the overactive sex life I'd embarked on. I decided just to nod.

"Well, I hope she's okay," I said with finality, and stood up to leave.

"Please, Camille, sit back down," said Alan thinly, wiping the corners of his mouth. "Tell us about the Windy City. Spare us a minute."

"Windy City's fine. Job's still good, been getting good feedback."

"What comprises good feedback?" Alan leaned toward me, hands folded, as if he thought his question quite charming.

"Well, I've been doing some more high-profile stories. I've covered three murders just since the beginning of the year."

"And that's a good thing, Camille?" My mother stopped nibbling. "I will never understand where your penchant for ugliness comes from. Seems like you have enough of that in your life without deliberately seeking it out." She laughed: a shrill lilt, like a balloon lifted in a gust.

Gayla returned with my coffee and a banana wedged awkwardly in a bowl. As she exited, Amma entered, like two players in a drawing-room farce. She kissed my mother on the cheek, greeted Alan, and sat across from me. Kicked me once under the table and laughed. *Oh, was that you?*

"I'm sorry you had to see me that way, Camille," Amma said. "Especially since we don't really know each other. I'm just going through a stage." She flashed an overdone smile. "But now we're reunited. You're like poor Cinderella, and I'm the evil stepsister. Half sister."

"There's not a speck of evil in you, sweetheart," Alan said.

"But Camille was the first. First is usually best. Now that she's back, will you love Camille more than me?" asked Amma. She started the question teasingly, but her cheeks were flushed as she waited for my mother to respond.

"No," Adora said quietly. Gayla set a plate of ham in front of Amma, who poured honey on it in lacy circles.

"Because you love *me*," Amma said, between mouthfuls of ham. The sick smell of meat and sweetness wafted over. "I wish I'd be murdered."

"Amma, don't say such a thing," my mother said, blanching. Her fingers fluttered to her eyelashes, then back determinedly down on the table.

"Then I'd never have to worry again. When you die, you become perfect. I'd be like Princess Diana. Everyone loves her now."

"You are the most popular girl in your whole school, and at home you are adored, Amma. Don't be greedy."

Amma kicked me again under the table and smiled emphatically, as if some important matter had been settled. She swung a corner of the garment she was wearing over her shoulder, and I realized what I'd thought was a housedress was a cleverly wrapped blue sheet. My mother noticed, too.

"What in the world are you wearing, Amma?"

"It's my maiden cloak. I'm going to the forest to play Joan of Arc. The girls will burn me."

"You'll do no such thing, darling," my mother snapped, grabbing the honey from Amma, who was about to soak her ham further. "Two girls your age are dead, and you think you're going to the forest to play?"

The children in the woods play wild, secret games. The

beginning of a poem I once knew by heart.

"Don't worry, we'll be fine." Amma smiled in a cloying exaggeration.

"You'll stay here."

Amma stabbed at her ham and muttered something nasty. My mother turned to me with her head cocked, the diamond on her wedding finger flashing in my eyes like an SOS.

"Now, Camille, can we at least do something pleasant while you're here?" she asked. "We could have a picnic in the backyard. Or we could take out the convertible, go for a drive, maybe play some golf over in Woodberry. Gayla, bring me some iced tea, please."

"That all sounds nice. I just need to figure out how much longer I'm here for."

"Yes, that'd be nice for us to know also. Not that you're not welcome to stay as long as you want," she said. "But it would be nice for us to know, so we could make our own plans."

"Sure." I took a bite of the banana, which tasted like pale green nothing.

"Or maybe Alan and I can come up there sometime this year. We've never really seen Chicago." My hospital was ninety minutes south of the city. My mother flew into O'Hare and had a taxi drive her. It cost $128, $140 with tip.

"That'd be good, too. We have some great museums. You'd love the lake."

"I don't know that I can enjoy any kind of water anymore."

"Why not?" I already knew.

"After that little girl, little Ann Nash, was left in the creek to drown." She paused to take a sip of her iced tea. "I knew her, you know."

Amma whined and began fidgeting in her seat.

"She wasn't drowned though," I said, knowing my correction would annoy her. "She was strangled. She just ended up in the creek."

"And then the Keene girl. I was fond of both of them. Very fond." She stared away wistfully, and Alan put his hand over hers. Amma stood up, released a little scream the way an excited puppy might suddenly bark, and ran upstairs.

"Poor thing," my mother said. "She's having nearly as hard a time as I am."

"She actually saw the girls every day, so I'm sure she is," I said peevishly in spite of myself. "How did you know them?"

"Wind Gap, I need not remind you, is a small town. They were sweet, beautiful little girls. Just beautiful."

"But you didn't really know them."

"I did know them. I knew them well."

"How?"

"Camille, please try not to do this. I've just told you that I am upset and unnerved, and instead of being comforting, you attack me."

"So. You've sworn off all bodies of water in the future, then?"

My mother emitted a quick, creaky sound. "You need to shut up now, Camille." She folded the napkin around the remains of her pear like a swaddling and left the room. Alan followed her with his manic whistling, like an old-time piano player lending drama to a silent movie.

Every tragedy that happens in the world happens to my mother, and this more than anything about her turns my stomach. She worries over people she's never met who have a spell of bad chance. She cries over news from across the globe. It's all too much for her, the cruelty of human beings.

She didn't come out of her room for a year after Marian died. A gorgeous room: canopy bed the size of a ship, vanity table studded with frosted perfume bottles. A floor so glorious it had been photographed by several decorating magazines: Made from pure ivory, cut into squares, it lit up the room from below. That room and its decadent floor had me awestruck, all the more so because it was forbidden to me. Notables like Truman Winslow, the mayor of Wind Gap, paid weekly visits, brought fresh flowers and classic novels. I could glimpse my mother on occasion when the door opened to admit these people. She'd be in bed always, propped up on a snowdrift of pillows, dressed in a series of thin, flowered robes. I never got to go in.

Curry's deadline for the feature was only two days away, and I had little to report. Sitting in my room, spread formally on my bed with my hands clasped like a corpse, I summed up what I knew, forced it into structure. No one had witnessed the abduction of Ann Nash last

August. She'd simply vanished, her body turning up a few miles away in Falls Creek ten hours later. She'd been strangled about four hours after she was taken. Her bike was never found. If forced to guess, I'd say she knew the person. Grabbing a child and her bike against her will would be a noisy business on those still streets. Was it someone from church, or even the neighborhood? Someone who looked safe.

But with the first murder committed cautiously, why take Natalie in the day, in front of a friend? It didn't make sense. If James Capisi had been standing at the edge of those woods, instead of guiltily sucking up sun-rays, would he be dead now? Or had Natalie Keene been a deliberate target? She was held longer, too: She was more than two days missing before her body appeared, wedged in the twelve inches between the hardware store and a beauty parlor on the very public Main Street.

What did James Capisi see? The boy left me uneasy. I didn't think he was lying. But children digest terror differently. The boy saw a horror, and that horror became the wicked witch of fairy tales, the cruel snow queen. But what if this person simply looked feminine? A lanky man with long hair, a transvestite, an androgynous boy? Women didn't kill this way, they just didn't. You could count the list of female serial killers on one hand, and their victims were almost always male – generally sex business gone bad. But then the girls hadn't been sexually assaulted, and that also didn't fit the pattern.

The choice of the two girls also seemed senseless. If

not for Natalie Keene, I'd believe they were victims of sheer dumb luck. But if James Capisi wasn't lying, effort had been made to get that girl at the park, and if it was indeed that particular girl the killer wanted, then Ann was not sheer caprice, either. Neither girl was beautiful in a way that would nurture obsession. Like Bob Nash had said, *Ashleigh's the prettiest*. Natalie came from a moneyed family, still fairly new to Wind Gap. Ann was on the low end of middle class, and the Nashes had been in Wind Gap for generations. The girls weren't friends. Their only connection was a shared viciousness, if Vickery's stories were to be believed. And then there was the hitchhiker theory. Could that really be what Richard Willis was thinking? We were near a major trucking route to and from Memphis. But nine months is a long time for a stranger to go unnoticed, and the surrounding woods of Wind Gap had yielded nothing so far, not even many animals. They were hunted out years ago.

I could feel my thoughts blowing back on themselves, dirtied with old prejudices and too much insider knowledge. I suddenly felt a desperate need to talk to Richard Willis, a person not from Wind Gap, who saw what was happening as a job, a project to assemble and complete, the last nail in place, tidy and contained. I needed to think like that.

I took a cool bath with the lights off. Then I sat on the edge of the tub and rubbed my mother's lotion all over my skin, once, quickly. Its bumps and ridges made me cringe.

On went a pair of light cotton pants and a long-sleeved crew neck. I brushed my hair and looked at myself in the mirror. Despite what I'd done to the rest of my body, my face was still beautiful. Not in the way that a person could pick out a single outstanding feature, but in the way that it was all in perfect balance. It made a stunning sort of sense. Big blue eyes, high cheekbones framing a small triangle of a nose. Full lips that turned slightly downward at the corners. I was lovely to look at, as long as I was fully clothed. Had things turned out differently, I might have amused myself with a series of heart-wretched lovers. I might have dallied with brilliant men. I might have married.

Outside, our section of Missouri sky was, as ever, electric blue. It made my eyes water to even think of it.

I found Richard at the Broussards' diner, eating waffles without syrup, a stack of folders nearly as high as his shoulder on the table. I plopped down across from him and felt strangely happy – conspiratorial and comfortable.

He looked up and smiled. "Ms. Preaker. Have some toast. Every time I come here I tell them no toast. Doesn't seem to work. Like they're trying to meet a quota."

I took a slice, spread a flower of butter over it. The bread was cold and hard, and my bite sprayed flecks onto the table. I brushed them under the plate and got to the point.

"Look, Richard. Talk to me. On record or off. I can't make anything out of this. I can't get objective enough."

He patted the stack of files next to him, waved his yellow legal pad at me. "I've got all the objectivity you want – from 1927 on at least. No one knows what happened to any records before 1927. Probably some receptionist tossed them out, my guess, keep the poh-lice station uncluttered."

"What kind of records?"

"I'm compiling a criminal profile of Wind Gap, a history of the town's violence," he said, flapping a folder at me. "Did you know that in 1975, two teenage girls were found dead at the edge of Falls Creek, very near where Ann Nash turned up, wrists cut? Police ruled it was self-inflicted. Girls were 'overly close, unhealthily intimate for their age. A homosexual attachment is suspected.' But they never found the knife. Weird."

"One of them was named Murray."

"Ah, you do know."

"She'd just had a baby."

"Yes, a little girl."

"That would be Faye Murray. She went to my high school. They called her Fag Murray. The boys would take her out after school into the woods and take turns having sex with her. Her mother kills herself, and sixteen years later, Faye has to fuck every boy in school."

"I don't follow."

"To prove she isn't a lesbian. Like mother, like daughter, right? If she didn't fuck those boys, no one would have had anything to do with her. But she did. So she proved she wasn't a lesbian, but that she *was* a slut. So no one had anything to do with her. That's

Wind Gap. We all know each other's secrets. And we all use them."

"Lovely place."

"Yes. Give me a comment."

"I just did."

It made me laugh, and I was surprised. I could picture turning in my copy to Curry: *Police have no leads, but believe that Wind Gap is a "lovely place."*

"Look, Camille, I'll make a deal. I'll give you a comment you can use on the record, and you help me fill in these back stories. I need someone who'll tell me what this town is really like, and Vickery won't. He's very . . . protective."

"Give me a comment on record. But work with me off record. I won't use anything you give me unless you say it's okay. You can use anything I give you." It wasn't the straightest of deals, but it would have to do.

"What should my comment be?" Richard smiled.

"Do you really believe these killings were committed by an outsider?"

"For print?"

"Yeah."

"We have not ruled anyone out." He took a last bite of waffle and sat thinking, his eyes to the ceiling. "We are looking very closely at potential suspects within the community, but are also carefully considering the possibility that these killings may be the work of an outsider."

"So you have no clue."

He grinned, shrugged his shoulders. "I gave you my comment."

"Okay, off record, you have no clue?"

He clicked the cap of the sticky syrup bottle up and down a few times, placed his silverware crossways on his plate.

"Off record, Camille, do you really think this seems like an outsider crime? You're a police reporter."

"I don't." Saying it out loud agitated me. I tried to keep my eyes off the prongs of the fork in front of me.

"Smart girl."

"Vickery said you thought it was a hitchhiker or something like that."

"Oh, damn it, I mentioned that as a possibility when I first got here – nine months ago. He holds on to it like it's proof of my incompetence. Vickery and I have communication issues."

"Do you have any real suspects?"

"Let me take you for drinks this week. I want you to spill everything you know about everyone in Wind Gap."

He grabbed the check, pushed the syrup bottle back against the wall. It left a sugary ring on the table, and without thinking, I dipped a finger into it, put it to my mouth. Scars peeked out of a shirtsleeve. Richard looked up just as I was putting my hands back beneath the table.

I didn't mind the idea of spilling Wind Gap's stories to Richard. I felt no particular allegiance to the town. This was the place my sister died, the place I started cutting myself. A town so suffocating and small, you tripped over people you hated every day. People who knew things about you. It's the kind of place that leaves a mark.

Although it's true that on the surface, I couldn't have been treated better when I lived here. My mother saw to that. The town loved her, she was like a cake topping: the most beautiful, sweet girl Wind Gap had ever raised. Her parents, my grandparents, had owned the pig farm and half the houses around it, and kept my mother under the same strict rules they applied to their workers: no drinking, no smoking, no cursing, church service mandatory. I can only imagine how they must have taken the news when my mother became pregnant at seventeen. Some boy from Kentucky who she met at church camp came for a Christmas visit and left me in her belly. My grandparents grew angry twin tumors to match my mother's expanding tummy, and were dead of cancer within a year of my birth.

My mother's parents had friends in Tennessee, and their son began wooing Adora before I was on solids, making visits nearly every weekend. I cannot picture this courtship as anything but awkward. Alan, pleated and pressed, elaborating on the weather. My mother, alone and untended for the first time in her life, in need of a good match, laughing at . . . jokes? I'm not sure Alan has ever made a joke in his life, but I'm sure my mother found some reason to giggle girlishly for him. And where was I in this picture? Probably in some far corner room, kept quiet by the maid, Adora slipping her an extra five bucks for the trouble. I can imagine Alan, proposing to my mother while pretending to look over her shoulder, or fiddling with a plant, anything to avoid eye contact. My mother accepting graciously and then pouring him more tea. A dry kiss was exchanged, perhaps.

No matter. By the time I could talk, they were married. I know almost nothing about my real father. The name on the birth certificate is fake: Newman Kennedy, for my mother's favorite actor and president, respectively. She refused to tell me his true name, lest I hunt him down. No, I was to be considered Alan's child. This was difficult, as she soon had Alan's child, eight months after he married her. She was twenty, he was thirty-five, with family money that my mother didn't need, having plenty of her own. Neither of them have ever worked. I've learned little else of Alan over the years. He's a ribbon-winning equestrian who doesn't ride anymore because it makes Adora nervous. He's often ill, and even when he's not, he's mostly immobile. He reads countless books on the Civil War and seems content to let my mother do most of the talking. He's as smooth and shallow as glass. Then again, Adora has never tried to forge a bond between us. I was considered Alan's child but never really fathered by him, never encouraged to call him anything but his proper name. Alan never gave me his last name and I never asked for it. I remember trying out *Dad* once when I was little, and the shock on his face was enough to scotch any further attempts. Frankly, I think Adora prefers us to feel like strangers. She wants all relationships in the house to run through her.

Ah, but back to the baby. Marian was a sweet series

of diseases. She had trouble breathing from the start, would wake in the night spluttering for air, splotchy and gray. I could hear her like a sick wind down the hall from me, in the bedroom next to my mother. Lights would click on and there would be cooing, or sometimes crying or shouting. Regular trips to the emergency room, twenty-five miles away in Woodberry. Later she had trouble digesting and sat murmuring to her dolls in a hospital bed set up in her room, while my mother poured sustenance into her through IVs and feeding tubes.

During those last years, my mother pulled out all her eyelashes. She couldn't keep her fingers off them. She left little piles of them on tabletops. I told myself they were fairy nests. I remember finding two long blonde lashes stuck to the side of my foot, and I kept them for weeks next to my pillow. At night I tickled my cheeks and lips with them, until one day I woke to find them blown away.

By the time my sister finally died, I was grateful in a way. It seemed to me that she'd been expelled into this world not quite formed. She was not ready for its weight. People whispered comfort about Marian being called back to heaven, but my mother would not be distracted from her grief. To this day it remains a hobby.

My car, faded blue, covered with bird crap, its leather seats sure to be steaming, didn't exactly beckon me, so I decided to take a turn around town. On Main Street, I passed the poultry shop, where chickens are dropped off fresh from the Arkansas killing fields. The smell flared my nostrils. A dozen or more stripped birds hung lasciviously in the window, a few white feathers papering the ledge beneath them.

Toward the end of the street, where a makeshift shrine to Natalie had sprung up, I could see Amma and her three friends. They were sifting through the balloons and drugstore gifts, three standing guard while my half sister snatched up two candles, a bouquet of flowers, and a teddy bear. All but the bear went into her oversized purse. The teddy she held as the girls locked arms and skipped mockingly toward me. Straight at me actually, not stopping until they were an inch from me, filling the air with the kind of heavy perfume dispensed on powdered strips in magazines.

"Did you see us do that? Are you going to put it in your newspaper story?" Amma shrieked. She'd definitely gotten over her dollhouse tantrum. Such childish things, clearly, were left at home. Now she'd traded in her sundress and was wearing a miniskirt, platform sandals, and a tube top. "If you are, get my name right: Amity Adora Crellin. Guys, this is . . . my sister. From Chicago. *The bastard of the family.*" Amma wiggled her eyebrows at me, and the girls giggled. "Camille, these are my loooovely friends, but you don't need to write about them. I'm the leader."

"She's just the leader because she's the loudest," said a small honey-haired girl with a husky voice.

"And she has the biggest tits," said a second girl, with hair the color of a brass bell.

The third girl, a strawberry blonde, grabbed Amma's left breast, gave it a squeeze: "Part real, part padding."

"Fuck off, Jodes," Amma said, and as if disciplining a cat, smacked her on the jaw. The girl flushed splotchy red and muttered a sorry.

"Anyway, what's your deal, sister?" Amma demanded, looking down at her teddy. "Why are you writing a story about two dead girls who no one noticed to begin with? Like getting killed makes you popular." Two of the girls forced loud laughs; the third was still staring at the ground. A tear splashed on the sidewalk.

I recognized this provocative girl talk. It was the verbal equivalent of farming my yard. And while part of me appreciated the show, I was feeling protective of Natalie and Ann, and my sister's aggressive disrespect raised my hackles. To be honest, I should add that I was also feeling jealous of Amma. (Her middle name was *Adora*?)

"I bet Adora wouldn't be happy to read that her daughter stole items from a tribute to one of her schoolmates," I said.

"Schoolmate isn't the same as friend," said the tall girl, glancing around for confirmation of my stupidity.

"Oh, Camille, we're just kidding," Amma said. "I feel horrible. They were nice girls. Just weird."

"Definitely weird," one of them echoed.

"Ohhh guys, what if he's killing all the freaks?" Amma giggled. "Wouldn't that be perfect?" The crying girl looked up at this and smiled. Amma pointedly ignored her.

"He?" I asked.

"Everyone knows who did it," the husky blonde said.

"Natalie's brother. Freaks run in families," Amma proclaimed.

"He's got a little-girl thing," the girl called Jodes said sulkily.

"He's always finding excuses to talk to me," Amma said. "At least now I know he won't kill me. Too cool." She blew an air kiss and handed the teddy to Jodes, looped her arms around the other girls, and, with a cheeky "'Scuse," bumped past me. Jodes trailed behind.

In Amma's snideness, I caught a whiff of desperation and righteousness. Like she'd whined at breakfast: *I wish I'd be murdered.* Amma didn't want anyone to get more attention than her. Certainly not girls who couldn't compete when they were alive.

I phoned Curry near midnight, at his home. Curry does a reverse commute, ninety minutes to our suburban office from the single-family his parents left him in Mt. Greenwood, a working-class Irish enclave on the South Side. He and his wife, Eileen, have no children. Never wanted any, Curry always barks, but I've seen the way he eyes his staffers' toddlers from afar, what close attention he pays when a baby makes a rare appearance in our office. Curry and his wife married late. I guessed they'd been unable to conceive.

Eileen is a curvy woman with red hair and freckles that he met at his neighborhood car wash when he was forty-two. It turned out, later on, that she was a second cousin of his childhood best friend. They married three months to the day they first spoke. Been together for twenty-two years. I like that Curry likes to tell the story.

Eileen was warm when she answered the phone, which was what I needed. Of course they weren't asleep, she laughed. Curry was, in fact, working on one of his puzzles, 4,500 pieces. It had all but taken over the living room, and she had given him one week to complete it.

I could hear Curry rumble to the phone, could almost smell his tobacco. "Preaker, my girl, what gives? You okay?"

"I'm okay. There's just not a lot of headway down here. It's taken this long just to get an official police statement."

"Which is?"

"They're looking at everyone."

"Fah. That's crap. There's got to be more. Find out. You talk to the parents again?"

"Not yet."

"Talk to the parents. If you can't break anything, I want that profile on the dead girls. This is human-interest stuff, not just straight police reporting. Talk to other parents, too, see if they have theories. Ask if they're taking extra precautions. Talk to locksmiths and gun dealers, see if they're getting extra business. Get a clergyman in there or some teachers. Maybe a dentist, see how hard it is to pull out that many teeth, what kind of tool you'd use, whether you have to have some sort of experience. Talk to some kids. I want voices, I want faces. Give me thirty inches for Sunday; let's work this while we still have it exclusive."

I took notes first on a legal pad, then in my head, as I began outlining the scars on my right arm with my felt-tip pen.

"You mean before there's another murder."

"Unless the police know a damn lot more than they're giving you, there's going to be another, yeah. This kind of guy doesn't stop after two, not when it's this ritualistic."

Curry doesn't know a thing firsthand about ritualistic killings, but he plows through a few low-grade true-crimers a week, yellowed paperbacks with glossy covers he picks up at his used bookstore. *Two for a buck, Preaker, that's what I call entertainment.*

"So, Cubby, any theories on whether it's a local?"

Curry seemed to like the nickname for me, his favorite cub reporter. His voice always tickled when he used it, as if the word itself was blushing. I could picture him in the living room, eyeing his puzzle, Eileen taking a quick drag on his cigarette while she stirred up tuna salad with sweet pickles for Curry's lunch. He ate it three days a week.

"Off record, they say yes."

"Well, dammit, get them to say it on record. We need that. That's good."

"Here's something strange, Curry. I talked to a boy who says he was with Natalie when she was taken. He said it was a woman."

"A woman? It's not a woman. What do the police say?"

"No comment."

"Who's the kid?"

"Son of a hog worker. Sweet boy. He seems really scared, Curry."

"The police don't believe him, or you'd've heard about it. Right?"

"I honestly don't know. They're tight here."

"Christ, Preaker, break those boys. Get something on record."

"Easier said. I kind of feel it's almost a detriment that I'm from here. They resent me carpetbagging back home for this."

"Make them like you. You're a likable person. Your mom will vouch for you."

"My mom's not so happy I'm here, either."

Silence, then a sigh from Curry's end of the line that buzzed my ears. My right arm was a road map of deep blue.

"You doing okay, Preaker? You taking care of yourself?"

I didn't say anything. I suddenly felt like I might cry.

"I'm okay. This place does bad things to me. I feel . . . wrong."

"You keep it together, girl. You're doing real good. You're going to be fine. And if you feel unfine, call me. I'll get you out."

"Okay, Curry."

"Eileen says be careful. Hell, I say be careful."

Chapter Six

Small towns usually cater to one kind of drinker. That kind may vary: There are the honky-tonk towns, which keep their bars on the outskirts, make their patrons feel a little bit outlaw. There are the upscale sipping-drink towns, with bars that overcharge for a gin ricky so the poor people have to drink at home. There are the middle-class strip-mall towns, where beers come with onion blossoms and cutely named sandwiches.

Luckily everyone drinks in Wind Gap, so we have all those bars and more. We may be small, but we can drink most towns under the table. The watering hole closest to my mother's home was an expensive, glassy box that specialized in salads and wine spritzers, Wind Gap's sole upscale eatery. It was brunch-time, and I couldn't stand the idea of Alan and his soupy eggs, so I walked myself over to La Mère. My French goes only to eleventh grade, but judging from the restaurant's aggressively nautical theme, I think the owners meant to name it La Mer, The Sea, and not La Mère, The Mother. Still, the name was appropriate, as The Mother, my mother, frequented this place, as did her friends. They all just love the chicken Caesar, which is neither French nor seafood, but I'm not going to be the one to press the point.

"Camille!" A blonde in a tennis outfit came trotting across the room, glowing with gold necklaces and chunky rings. It was Adora's best friend, Annabelle Gasser, née Anderson, nicknamed Annie-B. It was commonly known that Annabelle absolutely hated her husband's last name – she even crumpled up her nose when she said it. It never occurred to her that she didn't have to take it.

"Hi sweetheart, your momma told me you were in town." Unlike poor, Adora-ousted Jackie O'Neele, who I also spotted at the table, looking just as tipsy as she had at the funeral. Annabelle kissed both my cheeks and stepped back to assess me. "Still pretty-pretty. Come on, come sit with us. We're just having a few bottles of wine and gabbing. You can lower the age ratio for us."

Annabelle pulled me over to a table where Jackie sat chatting up two more blonde, tanned women. She didn't even stop talking while Annabelle made introductions, she just continued droning about her new bedroom set, then knocked over a glass of water as she jerked back to me.

"Camille? You're here! I'm so happy to see you again, sweetie." She seemed sincere. That Juicy Fruit smell wafted off her again.

"She's been here for five minutes," snapped another blonde, wiping the ice and water onto the floor with a swipe of her dark hand. Diamonds flashed from two fingers.

"Right, I remember. You're here covering the murders, bad girl," Jackie continued. "Adora must hate that. Sleeping in her house with your dirty little brain." She smiled a smile that must have been saucy twenty years ago. Now it seemed slightly mad.

"Jackie!" said a blonde, aiming bright saucer eyes at her.

"'Course before Adora took it over, we all slept over at Joya's house with our dirty little brains. Same house, different crazy lady running it," she said to me, fingering the flesh behind her ears. Stitches from that facelift?

"You never knew your grandma Joya, did you, Camille?" purred Annabelle.

"Woo! She was a piece of work, sweetie," said Jackie. "Scary, scary woman."

"How so?" I asked. I'd never heard such detail about my grandmother. Adora allowed that she was strict, but said little else.

"Oh, Jackie's exaggerating," Annabelle said. "No one likes their mother when they're in high school. And Joya was dead pretty soon after. They never really had time to establish an adult relationship."

For a second I had a pitiful dash of hope, that this was why my mother and I were so distant: She had no practice. The idea was dead before Annabelle finished refilling my glass.

"Right, Annabelle," Jackie said. "I'm sure if Joya were alive today, they'd have a grand old time. At least Joya would. She'd just love to tear at Camille. Remember those long, long nails of hers? Never painted them. I always thought that was weird."

"Change of subject," Annabelle smiled, each word like the tinkle of a silver dinner bell.

"I think Camille's job must be so fascinating," said one of the blondes dutifully.

"Especially this one," said another.

"Yeah Camille, tell us who did it," blurted Jackie. She smiled leeringly again and clicked her round brown eyes open and shut. She reminded me of a ventriloquist dummy come alive. With hard skin and broken capillaries.

I had a few calls to make, but decided this could be better. A quartet of drunk, bored, and bitchy housewives who knew all the gossip of Wind Gap? I could write it off as a business lunch.

"Actually I'd be interested to know what you all think." A sentence they couldn't hear very often.

Jackie dipped her bread into a side dish of ranch dressing, then dripped it down her front. "Well you all know what I think. Ann's daddy, Bob Nash. He's a pervert. He always stares at my chest when I see him at the store."

"What chest there is," said Annabelle, and nudged me jokingly.

"I'm serious, it's out of line. I've been meaning to tell Steven about it."

"I've got yummy news," said the fourth blonde. Dana or Diana? I forgot it as soon as Annabelle introduced us.

"Oh, DeeAnna always has good scoop, Camille," Annabelle said, squeezing my arm. DeeAnna paused for effect, licked her teeth, poured herself another glass of wine, and peeked over it at us.

"John Keene has moved out of his parents' house," she announced.

"What?" said a blonde.

"You are joooking," said another.

"My word," gushed a third.

"And . . ." said DeeAnna triumphantly, smiling like a game-show hostess about to bestow a prize. "Into Julie Wheeler's home. The carriage house out back."

"That is too good," said Melissa or Melinda.

"Oh, you *know* they're doing it now," laughed Annabelle. "No way Meredith can keep her Little Miss Perfect thing going. See, Camille," she turned to me, "John Keene is Natalie's big brother, and when that family moved here, the whole town went loony for him. I mean, he's gorgeous. He. Is. Gorgeous. Julie Wheeler, she's a friend of your momma's and ours. Didn't have babies till she was, like, thirty, and when she did, she became just insufferable. One of those people whose kids can do no wrong. So when Meredith – her daughter – snagged John, oh my God. We thought we'd never hear the end of it. Meredith, this A-student little virgin girl gets the Big Man on Campus. But no way a boy like that, his age, goes with a girl who isn't putting out. Just doesn't work that way. And now, it's so convenient for them. We should get Polaroids and stick them under Julie's windshield wipers."

"Well, you know how she's playing it," Jackie interrupted. "It's going to be all about how good they are to take John in and give him a little breathing room while he mourns."

"Why is he moving out, though?" asked Melissa/Melinda, who I was starting to think was the voice of reason. "I mean, shouldn't he be with his folks at a time like this? Why would he need breathing room?"

"Because *he's* the killer," DeeAnna blurted, and the table began laughing.

"Oh, that would be so delicious if Meredith Wheeler were giving it to some serial killer," Jackie said. Suddenly the table stopped laughing. Annabelle emitted a sneezy hiccup and looked at her watch. Jackie rested her chin on her hand, breathed out hard enough to bluster the bread crumbs on her plate.

"I can't believe this is really happening," said DeeAnna, looking down at her nails. "In our town, where we grew up. Those little girls. It makes me feel sick to my stomach. Just sick."

"I'm so glad my girls are grown up," Annabelle said. "I just don't think I'd be able to take it. Poor Adora must be worried sick about Amma."

I nabbed a piece of bread in the birdy, girlish way of my hostesses, and steered the conversation away from Adora. "Do people really think John Keene could have had anything to do with it? Or is that just mean gossip?" I could feel myself spitting out the last part. I'd forgotten how unlivable women like these could make Wind Gap for people they didn't like. "I ask only because a group of girls, probably junior-high-schoolers, said the same thing to me yesterday." I thought it best not to mention Amma was one of them.

"Let me guess, four little mouthy blonde things who think they're prettier than they are," Jackie said.

"Jackie, sweetheart, do you realize who you just said that to?" Melissa/Melinda said, slapping her hand on Jackie's shoulder.

"Oh shit. I always forget Amma and Camille are even related – different lifetimes, you know?" Jackie smiled. A hearty pop sounded behind her and she lifted her wineglass without even looking at the waiter. "Camille, you might as well hear it here: Your little Amma is truuuuble."

"I hear they come to all the high-school parties," DeeAnna said. "And take all the boys. And do things we didn't do till we were old married women – and then only after the transaction of a few nice pieces of jewelry." She twirled a diamond tennis bracelet.

They all laughed; Jackie actually pounded the table with both fists like a toddler in a fit.

"But do . . ."

"I don't know if people really think John did it. I know the police talked to him," Annabelle said. "They're definitely a strange family."

"Oh, I thought you were close," I said. "I saw you at their house after the funeral." *You fucking cunts*, I added in my head.

"Everybody important in the town of Wind Gap was in that house after the funeral," DeeAnna said. "Like we were going to miss a function like that." She tried to start the laughter going again, but Jackie and Annabelle were nodding solemnly. Melissa/Melinda looked around the restaurant as if she could wish herself to another table.

"Where's your momma?" Annabelle suddenly blurted. "She needs to come down here. Could do her good. She's been acting so strange since this all started."

"She was acting strange before this started, too," Jackie said, working her jaw. I wondered if she was going to vomit.

"Oh please, Jackie."

"I'm serious. Camille, let me say this: Right now, way things are with your mother, you're better in Chicago. You should go back soon." Her face had lost its manicness – she looked completely solemn. And genuinely concerned. I felt myself liking her again.

"Truly, Camille . . ."

"Jackie, shut up," Annabelle said, and threw a roll, hard, at Jackie's face. It bounced off her nose and thumped onto the table. A silly flash of violence, like when Dee threw his tennis ball at me – you're less shocked by the impact than the fact it happened at all. Jackie registered the hit with a wave of her hand and kept talking.

"I'll say what I please, and I'm saying, Adora can harm . . ."

Annabelle stood up and walked over to Jackie's side, pulled her up by her arm.

"Jackie, you need to make yourself throw up," she said. Her voice was a cross between a coo and a threat. "You've had too much to drink, and you're going to feel real sick otherwise. Let me take you to the lady's room and help make you feel better."

Jackie smacked her hand away at first, but Annabelle's grip tightened and the two soon tottered away. Silence at the table. My mouth hung open.

"That's nothing," DeeAnna said. "We old girls have little fights the same way you young girls do. So Camille, have you heard we might be getting a Gap?"

Jackie's words stuck with me: *Way things are with your mother, you're better in Chicago.* How much more of a sign did I need to leave Wind Gap? I wondered exactly why she and Adora had fallen out. Had to be more than a forgotten greeting card. I made a mental note to drop by Jackie's when she was less looped. If she ever was. Then again, I was hardly the one to frown on a drinker.

Sailing on a nice wine buzz, I called the Nashes from the convenience store, and a quivering girl's voice said hello and then went silent. I could hear breathing, but no answer to my requests to speak with Mom or Dad. Then a slow, sliding click before the line went dead. I decided to try my luck in person.

A boxy disco-era minivan sat in the Nash driveway next to a rusty yellow Trans Am, which I assumed meant both Bob and Betsy were home. The eldest daughter answered the bell, but simply stood inside the screen door staring at my stomach when I asked if her folks were home. The Nashes were built tiny. This one, Ashleigh, I knew was twelve, but like the pudgy boy I'd met on my first visit, she looked several years younger than her age. And acted it. She sucked on her hair and hardly blinked when little Bobby waddled next to her and began crying at the sight of me. Then howling. A good minute went by before Betsy Nash came to the door. She looked as dazed as both her children, and seemed confused when I introduced myself.

"Wind Gap don't have a local daily paper," she said.

"Right, I'm from the *Chicago Daily Post*," I said. "Up in Chicago. Illinois."

"Well, my husband deals with purchases like that," she said, and began running her fingers through her son's blond hair.

"I'm not selling a subscription or anything. . . . Is Mr. Nash home? Maybe I could just chat with him real quick?"

All three Nashes moved away from the door en masse, and after another few minutes, Bob Nash had me ushered inside and was throwing laundry off the couch to make room for me to sit.

"Goddammit, this place is a pit," he muttered loudly toward his wife. "I apologize for the state of our home, Miss Preaker. Things have kinda gone to hell ever since Ann."

"Oh, don't worry about it at all," I said, pulling a pair of tiny boys' undies from beneath me. "This is what my place looks like all the time." This was the opposite of true. One quality I did inherit from my mother was a compulsive neatness. I have to stop myself from ironing socks. When I got back from the hospital, I even went through a period of boiling things: tweezers and eyelash curlers, bobby pins and toothbrushes. It was an indulgence I allowed myself. I ended up trashing the tweezers, though. Too many late-night thoughts about their shiny, warm points. Dirty girl, indeed.

I was hoping Betsy Nash would disappear. Literally. She was so insubstantial, I could imagine her slowly evaporating, leaving only a sticky spot on the edge of the sofa. But she lingered, eyes darting between me and her husband before we even began speaking. Like she was winding up for the conversation. The children, too, hovered about, little blonde ghosts trapped in a limbo between indolence and stupidity. The pretty girl might do all right. But the piggy middle child, who now waddled dazedly into the room, was destined for needy sex and snack-cake bingeing. The boy was the type who'd end up drinking in gas-station parking lots. The kind of angry, bored kid I saw on my way into town.

"Mr. Nash, I need to speak some more with you about Ann. For a larger piece," I started. "You've been very kind with your time, and I was hoping to get a little bit more."

"Anything that might get this case a little attention, we don't mind," he said. "What do you need to know?"

"What kind of games did she like, what kind of foods did she like? What would be some words you'd use to describe her? Did she tend to be a ringleader or a follower? Did she have lots of friends or just a few close ones? How did she like school? What did she do on her Saturdays?" The Nashes stared at me in silence for a second. "Just for starters," I smiled.

"My wife would be the one to answer most of those questions," Bob Nash said. "She's the . . . caregiver." He turned to Betsy Nash, who was folding and refolding the same dress on her lap.

"She liked pizza and fishsticks," she said. "And she had lots of girls she was friendly with, but only a few close friends, if you know what I mean. She played by herself a lot."

"Look, Mommy, Barbie needs clothes," said Ashleigh, wielding a naked plastic doll in front of her mother's face. All three of us ignored her, and she tossed the toy to the floor and began twirling around the room in fake ballerina moves. Seeing a rare chance, Tiffanie pounced on the Barbie and began splaying the rubbery tan legs open and shut, open and shut.

"She was tough, she was my toughest," Bob Nash said. "She could have played football if she'd been a boy. She'd knock herself silly just running around, always had scrapes and bruises."

"Ann was my mouth," Betsy said quietly. Then she said no more.

"How is that, Mrs. Nash?"

"She was a real talker, said whatever come into her mind. In a good way. Mostly." She was silent again for a few beats, but I could see her thinking back behind her eyes so I said nothing. "You know, I thought maybe she'd be a lawyer or college debater or something someday, because she was just . . . she never stopped to measure her words. Like me. I think everything I say is stupid. Ann thought everyone should hear everything she had to say."

"You mentioned school, Miss Preaker," interrupted

Bob Nash. "That's where her talkativeness got her in trouble. She could be a little bossy, and we got a few calls from her teachers over the years about her not taking too well to class. She was a little wild."

"But sometimes I think it was because she was just so smart," added Betsy Nash.

"She was whip smart, yup," Bob Nash nodded. "Sometimes I thought she was smarter than her old man. Sometimes *she* thought she was smarter than her old man."

"Look at me, Mommy!" Piggy Tiffanie, who had been chewing mindlessly on Barbie's toes, ran to the center of the living room and began doing somersaults. Ashleigh, seized by some phantom anger, yelped at the sight of her mother's attention on the second daughter, and gave her a hard shove. Then yanked her hair emphatically once. Tiffanie's face split in a red wail, which started Bobby Jr. crying again.

"It's Tiffanie's *fault*," Ashleigh screamed, and began whimpering also.

I had shattered some delicate dynamic. A multichild household is a pit of petty jealousies, this I knew, and the Nash children were panicking at the idea of competing not just with one another, but with a dead sister. They had my sympathies.

"Betsy," muttered Bob Nash quietly, eyebrows slightly raised. Bobby Jr. was quickly scooped up and propped on a hip, Tiffanie pulled up from the floor with one hand, another arm around the now inconsolable Ashleigh, and soon the four were moving out of the room.

Bob Nash stared after them a beat.

"Been like that for almost a year now, those girls," he said. "Them acting like little babies. Thought they were supposed to be anxious to grow up. Ann being gone changes this home more than . . ." He shifted on the sofa. "It's just that she was a real *person*, you know? You think: Nine years old, what's that? What's there? But Ann had a *personality*. I could guess what she'd think about things. I knew, when we were watching TV, what stuff she'd think was funny and what stuff she'd think was dumb. I can't do that with my other kids. Hell, I can't do that with my wife. Ann, you just felt her *there*. I just . . ." Bob Nash's throat shut up on him. He stood and turned away from me, turned back once, then away, walked in a circle behind the couch, then stood in front of me. "Goddammit, I want her back. I mean, what now? Is this it?" He threw his hand around the room, toward the doorway where his wife and kids had exited. "Because if this is it, there ain't much point is there? And goddammit, someone needs to find that man, because he needs to tell me: Why Ann? I need to know that. She was the one I'd always thought would do ok."

I sat quiet for a second, could feel my pulse in my neck.

"Mr. Nash, it has been suggested to me that maybe Ann's personality, which you mention was very strong, might have rubbed some people the wrong way. Do you think that could have anything to do with this?"

I could feel him get wary on me, see it in the way he sat down and deliberately leaned back onto the couch, spread his arms and pretended to be casual.

"Rubbed who the wrong way?"

"Well, I understand there were troubles about Ann and a neighbor's bird? That she may have hurt a neighbor's bird?"

Bob Nash rubbed his eyes, looked at his feet.

"God, people gossip in this town. No one ever proved Ann did that. She and the neighbors already had bad blood. Joe Duke across the way. His girls, they're older, they messed with Ann a lot, teased her a lot. Then they have her over to play one day. I don't really know what happened, but by the time Ann got back here, they were all screaming that she'd killed their goddam bird." He laughed, shrugged his shoulders. "Be fine by me if she had, it was a noisy old thing."

"Do you think Ann would be likely to do something like that, if provoked?"

"Well, it was a fool who provoked Ann," he said. "She didn't take that kind of thing well. She wasn't exactly a little lady."

"Do you think she knew the person who killed her?"

Nash picked up a pink T-shirt from the sofa, folded it in squares like a kerchief. "Used to think no. Now, I think yes. I think she went with someone she knew."

"Would she be more likely to go with a man or a woman?" I asked.

"So you heard the James Capisi story?"

I nodded.

"Well, a little girl is more likely to trust a person who reminds her of her momma, right?"

Depends on what her momma's like, I thought.

"But I still think it's a man. Can't picture a woman doing all . . . that to a baby. I hear John Keene has no alibi. Maybe he wanted to kill a little girl, saw Natalie all day every day, and couldn't take it, the urge, so he went out and killed another little tomboy, girl kind of like Natalie. But then in the end he couldn't resist, took Natalie too."

"Is that the talk?" I asked.

"Some of it, I s'pose."

Betsy Nash appeared suddenly in the doorway. Looking down at her knees, she said, "Bob. Adora is here." My stomach clenched without my permission.

My mother breezed in, smelling like bright blue water. She looked more comfortable in the Nash house than Mrs. Nash did. It was a natural gift for Adora, making other women feel incidental. Betsy Nash retired from the room, like some maid from a 1930s movie. My mother refused to look at me, but went straight to Bob Nash.

"Bob, Betsy told me there was a reporter here, and I knew right then it was my daughter. I'm so sorry. I can't apologize enough for the intrusion."

Bob Nash stared at Adora, then at me. "This is your daughter? I had no idea."

"No, probably not. Camille's not the family type."

"Why didn't you say anything?" Nash asked me.

"I told you I was from Wind Gap. I had no idea you'd be interested in who my mother was."

"Oh, I'm not angry, don't get me wrong. It's just that your mother is a very good friend to us," he said, as if she were some big-hearted patron. "She tutored Ann in English and spelling. Your mother and Ann were very close. Ann was very proud she had an adult friend."

My mother sat with her hands folded in her lap, skirt spread out along the couch, and blinked at me. I felt as if I were being warned not to say something, but I didn't know what.

"I had no idea," I finally said. True. I'd thought my mother was overplaying her mourning, pretending to know those girls. Now I was surprised at how subtle she'd been. But why in the world was she tutoring Ann? She'd done the mother's-aide thing at my school when I was a kid – mainly to spend time with other Wind Gap housewives – but I couldn't picture her noblesse oblige extending to spending afternoons with an unkempt girl from the west side of town. Occasionally I underestimated Adora. I suppose.

"Camille, I think you should leave," Adora said. "I'm here on a social visit and it's difficult for me to relax around you these days."

"I'm not quite done talking with Mr. Nash."

"Yes, you are." Adora looked at Nash for confirmation, and he smiled awkwardly, like someone staring down the sun.

"Maybe we can pick this up later, Miss . . . Camille." A word suddenly flashed on my lower hip: *punish*. I could feel it getting hot.

"Thanks for your time, Mr. Nash," I said, and strode out of the room, not looking at my mother. I began crying before I'd even reached my car.

Chapter Seven

Once I was standing on a cold corner in Chicago waiting for the light to change when a blind man came clicking up. *What are the cross streets here*, he asked, and when I didn't reply he turned toward me and said, *Is anybody there?*

I'm here, I said, and it felt shockingly comforting, those words. When I'm panicked, I say them aloud to myself. *I'm here.* I don't usually feel that I am. I feel like a warm gust of wind could exhale my way and I'd be disappeared forever, not even a sliver of fingernail left behind. On some days, I find this thought calming; on others it chills me.

My sense of weightlessness, I think, comes from the fact that I know so little about my past – or at least that's what the shrinks at the clinic came up with. I've long since given up trying to discover anything about my dad; when I picture him, it's as a generic "father" image. I can't stand to think about him too specifically, to imagine him shopping for groceries or having a cup of morning coffee, coming home to kids. Will I someday run smack into a girl who looks like me? As a child, I struggled to find a solid resemblance between my mother and myself, some link that would prove I came from her. I'd study her when she wasn't looking, steal the framed portraits from her room and try to convince myself I had her eyes. Or maybe it was something not in the face. The turn of a calf or the hollow of my neck.

She never even told me how she'd met Alan. What I know of their story has come from other people. Questions are discouraged, considered prying. I remember the shock of hearing my college roommate talk to her mother on the phone: The detailed minutia, her lack of censorship seemed decadent. She would say silly things, like how she forgot she'd enrolled for a class – completely forgot she was supposed to be in Geography 101 three days a week – and she'd say it in the same boastful tone of a kindergartner with a gold-star crayon drawing.

I remember finally meeting her mom, how she zipped around our suite asking so many questions, knowing already so much about me. She gave Alison a big plastic bag of safety pins that she thought might come in handy, and when they left for lunch, I surprised myself by bursting into tears. The gesture – so random and kind – baffled me. Is this what mothers did, wonder if you might need safety pins? Mine phoned once a month and always asked the same practical questions (grades, classes, upcoming expenses).

As a child, I don't remember ever telling Adora my favorite color, or what I'd like to name my daughter when I grew up. I don't think she ever knew my favorite dish, and I certainly never padded down to her room in the early-morning hours, teary from nightmares. I always feel sad for the girl that I was, because it never occurred to me that my mother might comfort me. She has never told me she loved me, and I never assumed she did. She tended to me. She administrated me. Oh, yes, and one time she bought me lotion with vitamin E.

For a while I convinced myself that Adora's distance was a defense constructed after Marian. But in truth, I think she's always had more problems with children than she'd ever admit. I think, in fact, she hates them. There's a jealousy, a resentfulness that I can feel even now, in my memory. At one point, she probably liked the idea of a daughter. When she was a girl, I bet she daydreamed of being a mother, of coddling, of licking her child like a milk-swelled cat. She has that voraciousness about children. She swoops in on them. Even I, in public, was a beloved child. Once her period of mourning for Marian was over, she'd parade me into town, smiling and teasing me, tickling me as she spoke with people on the sidewalks. When we got home, she'd trail off to her room like an unfinished sentence, and I would sit outside with my face pressed against her door and replay the day in my head, searching for clues to what I'd done to displease her.

I have one memory that catches in me like a nasty clump of blood. Marian was dead about two years, and my mother had a cluster of friends come over for afternoon drinks. One of them brought a baby. For hours, the child was cooed over, smothered with red-lipstick kisses, tidied up with tissues, then lipstick smacked again. I was supposed to be reading in my room, but I sat at the top of the stairs watching.

My mother finally was handed the baby, and she cuddled it ferociously. *Oh, how wonderful it is to hold a baby again!* Adora jiggled it on her knee, walked it around the rooms, whispered to it, and I looked down from above like a spiteful little god, the back of my hand placed against my face, imagining how it felt to be cheek to cheek with my mother.

When the ladies went into the kitchen to help tidy up the dishes, something changed. I remember my mother, alone in the living room, staring at the child almost lasciviously. She pressed her lips hard against the baby's apple slice of a cheek. Then she opened her mouth just slightly, took a tiny bit of flesh between her teeth, and gave it a little bite.

The baby wailed. The blotch faded as Adora snuggled the child, and told the other women it was just being fussy. I ran to Marian's room and got under the covers.

Back at Footh's for a drink after my mother and the Nashes. I was boozing too much, but never to the point of drunkenness, I reasoned with myself. I needed just a nip. I've always been partial to the image of liquor as lubrication – a layer of protection from all the sharp thoughts in your head. The barkeep was a round-faced guy two classes behind me who I was pretty sure was named Barry but not sure enough to actually call him that. He muttered, "Welcome back," as he filled my Big Mouth cup two-thirds full of bourbon, splashed some coke on top. "On the house," he said to the napkin holder. "We don't take money from pretty women here." His neck shot red, and he suddenly pretended he had urgent business at the other end of the counter.

I took Neeho Drive on the way back to the house. It was a street several of my friends had lived on, slicing through town and growing increasingly more posh as it neared Adora's. I spotted Katie Lacey's old home, a flimsy mansion her parents built when we were ten – after they'd smashed their old Victorian into shards.

A block ahead of me, a little girl on a golf cart decorated with flower stickers putt-putted along. She wore her hair in elaborate braids like a little Swiss maid on a cocoa box. Amma. She'd taken advantage of Adora's visit to the Nashes to make an escape – girls traveling solo were an oddity in Wind Gap since Natalie's killing.

Rather than continue home, she turned and headed east, which meant dirtbox houses and the pig farm. I turned the corner and followed her so slowly I almost stalled out.

The route offered a nice downhill slope for Amma, and the cart glided so fast her braids flew out behind her. In ten minutes, we were in the country. Tall yellow grasses and bored cows. Barns leaning like old men. I let the car idle for a few minutes to give Amma a good head start, then drove just far enough to keep her in sight. I trailed her past farmhouses and a roadside walnut stand that was manned by a boy who held his cigarette jaunty as a movie star. Soon the air smelled like shit and stale saliva and I knew where we were heading. Another ten minutes and the metal pig holds came into sight, long and glinty like rows of staples. The squeals made my ears sweat. Like screams from a rusty well pump. My nose flared involuntarily and my eyes started watering. You ever been near an animal-processing plant, you know what I mean. The smell isn't like water or air; it's a solid. Like you should be able to cut a hole in the stink to get some relief. You can't.

Amma zipped through the gates of the plant. The guy at the booth just waved at her. I had a tougher time until I said the magic word: *Adora.*

"Right. Adora's got a grown-up daughter. I remember," said the old guy. His nametag said *Jose.* I tried to see if he was missing any fingers. Mexicans don't get cushy box jobs unless they're owed. That's the way plants down here work: The Mexicans get the shittiest, most dangerous jobs, and the whites still complain.

Amma parked her cart next to a pickup and dusted herself off. Then, with a businesslike beeline, she walked straight past the slaughtering house, past the lines of pig holds, those wet pink snouts squirming between the air slats, and to a big metal barn of a building where the nursing happens. Most sows are repeatedly inseminated, brood after brood, till their bodies give way and they go to slaughter. But while they're still useful, they're made to nurse – strapped to their sides in a farrowing crate, legs apart, nipples exposed. Pigs are extremely smart, sociable creatures, and this forced assembly-line intimacy makes the nursing sows want to die. Which, as soon as they dry up, they do.

Even the idea of this practice I find repulsive. But the sight of it actually does something to you, makes you less human. Like watching a rape and saying nothing. I saw Amma at the far end of the barn, standing at the edge of one metal farrowing crate. A few men were pulling one pack of squealing piglets out of the stall, throwing another pack in. I moved to the far side of the barn so I could stand behind Amma without her seeing me. The pig lay nearly comatose on its side, its belly exposed between metal bars, red, bloody nipples pointing out like fingers. One of the men rubbed oil on the goriest one, then flicked it and giggled. They paid no attention to Amma, as if it were quite normal that she was there. She winked at one as they snapped another sow in a crate and drove off to get the next pack.

The piglets in the stall were swarming over the sow like ants on a glob of jelly. The nipples were fought over, bouncing in and out of mouths, jiggling tautly like rubber. The sow's eyes rolled up into her head. Amma sat down cross-legged and gazed, fascinated. After five minutes she was in the same position, now smiling and squirming. I had to leave. I walked, first slowly, then broke into a scramble to my car. Door shut, radio blasting, warm bourbon stinging my throat, I drove away from the stink and sound. And that child.

Chapter Eight

Amma. All this time I'd had little real interest in her. Now I did. What I saw at the farm kept my throat clenched.

My mother said she was the most popular girl in school, and I believed it. Jackie said she was the meanest, and I believed that, too. Living in the swirl of Adora's bitterness had to make one a bit crooked. And what did Amma make of Marian, I wondered? How confusing to live in the shadow of a shadow. But Amma was a smart girl – she did her acting out away from home. Near Adora she was compliant, sweet, needy – just what she had to be, to get my mother's love.

But that violent streak – the tantrum, the smacking of her friend, and now this ugliness. A penchant for doing and seeing nasty things. It suddenly reminded me of the stories about Ann and Natalie. Amma wasn't like Marian, but maybe she was a little bit like them.

It was late afternoon, just before suppertime, and I decided to make a second pass at the Keenes. I needed a quote for my feature piece and if I couldn't get it, Curry was going to pull me out. Leaving Wind Gap would cause me no pain personally, but I needed to prove I could handle myself, especially with my credibility faltering. A girl who slices herself open isn't the first on the list for tough assignments.

I drove past the spot where Natalie's body was discovered. What Amma deemed unworthy of stealing sat in a sad clump: three stumpy candles, long since blown out, along with cheap flowers still in their supermarket wrappers. A limp helium balloon in the shape of a heart bobbing listlessly.

In the driveway outside the Keene home, Natalie's brother sat in the passenger seat of a red convertible talking with a blonde girl who almost matched his beauty. I parked behind them, saw them sneak quick looks, then pretend not to notice me. The girl began laughing animatedly, weaving her red-lacquered nails through the back of the boy's dark hair. I gave them a quick, awkward nod, which I'm sure they didn't see, and slipped past them to the front door.

Natalie's mother answered. Behind her the house was dark and quiet. Her face stayed open; she didn't recognize me.

"Mrs. Keene, I am so sorry to bother you at a time like this, but I really need to talk with you."

"About Natalie?"

"Yes, may I come in?" It was a nasty trick to sneak my way into her home without identifying myself. Reporters are like vampires, Curry likes to say. They can't come into your home without your invitation, but once they're there, you won't get them out till they've sucked you dry. She opened the door.

"Oh, it feels nice and cool in here, thanks," I said. "It was supposed to peak at ninety today, but I think we passed that."

"I heard ninety-five."

"I believe it. Could I trouble you for a glass of water?" Another time-honored ploy: A woman is less likely to throw you out if she's offered her hospitality. If you have allergies or a cold, asking for a tissue is even better. Women love vulnerability. Most women.

"Of course." She paused, looking at me, as if she felt she should know who I was and was too embarrassed to ask. Morticians, priests, police, medics, mourners – she'd probably met more people in the past few days than she had the previous year.

While Mrs. Keene disappeared into the kitchen, I peered around. The room looked completely different today, with furniture moved back into the proper places. On a table not far away sat a photo of the two Keene children. They were each leaning on a side of a big oak tree, dressed in jeans and red sweaters. He was smiling uncomfortably, like he was doing something best left undocumented. She was maybe half his height, and looked determinedly serious, like the subject of an old daguerreotype.

"What's your son's name?"

"That's John. He's a very kind, gentle boy. I've always been proudest of that. He just graduated from high school."

"They bumped it up a little – when I went to school here, they made us wait till June."

"Mmmm. Nice to have the longer summers."

I smiled. She smiled. I sat down and sipped my water. I couldn't remember what Curry advised once you tricked your way into someone's living room.

"We actually haven't properly met. I'm Camille Preaker. From the *Chicago Daily Post*? We spoke briefly on the phone the other night."

She stopped smiling. Her jaw started working.

"You should have said that before."

"I know what a horrible time this is for you, and if I could just ask you a few questions . . ."

"You may not."

"Mrs. Keene, we want to be fair to your family, that's why I'm here. The more information we can give people . . ."

"The more papers you can sell. I'm sick and tired of all this. Now I will tell you one last time: Do not come back here. Do not try to contact us. I have absolutely nothing to say to you." She stood over me, leaned down. She wore, as she had at the funeral, a beaded necklace made of wood, with a big red heart at its center. It bobbed back and forth off her bosom like a hypnotist's watch. "I think you are a parasite," she spat at me. "I think you are disgusting. I hope some-day you look back and see how ugly you are. Now please leave."

She trailed me to the door, as if she wouldn't believe I was truly gone until she saw me step outside her home.

She closed the door behind me with enough force to make her doorbell chime lightly.

I stood on the stoop blushing, thinking to myself what a nice detail that heart necklace would make in my story, and saw the girl in the red convertible staring at me. The boy was gone.

"You're Camille Preaker, right?" she called out.

"Yes."

"I remember you," the girl said. "I was just a little thing when you lived here, but we all knew you."

"What's your name?"

"Meredith Wheeler. You wouldn't remember me, I was just a little goofball when you were in high school."

John Keene's girlfriend. Her name was familiar, thanks to my mother's friends, but I wouldn't have remembered her personally. Hell, she'd have been all of six or seven last time I lived here. Still, I wasn't surprised she knew me. Girls growing up in Wind Gap studied the older girls obsessively: who dated the football stars, who was homecoming queen, who mattered. You traded favorites like baseball cards. I still remember CeeCee Wyatt, Calhoon High prom queen from when I was a girl. I once bought eleven drugstore lipsticks trying to find the exact shade of pink she wore when she said hello to me one morning.

"I remember you," I said. "I can't believe you're driving."

She laughed, seemed pleased by my lie.

"You're a reporter now, right?"

"Yes, in Chicago."

"I'll get John to talk to you. We'll be in touch."

Meredith zipped away. I'm sure she felt quite pleased with herself – *We'll be in touch* – reapplying her lip gloss and thinking not at all of the dead ten-year-old that was to be the subject of conversation.

I phoned the main hardware store in town – the one where Natalie's body had been found. Without identifying myself, I began chatting about maybe redoing a bathroom, maybe getting new tiles. Not too hard to steer the conversation to the killings. I suppose a lot of people have been rethinking their home security lately, I suggested.

"That's a fact, ma'am. We've had a run on chain locks and double bolts in the past few days," said the grumbly voice.

"Really? How many have you gone through?"

"About three dozen, I'd guess."

"Mostly families? People with children?"

"Oh, yeah. They're the ones got reason to worry, right? Horrible thing. We're hoping to make some sort of donation to little Natalie's family." He paused. "You want to come down, look at some tile samples?"

"I might just do that, thanks."

One more reporting chore off my list, and I didn't even have to subject myself to namecalling from a grieving mother.

For our dinner meeting, Richard picked Gritty's, a "family restaurant" with a salad bar that featured every kind of food but salad. The lettuce always sat in a small container at the end, a greasy, pale afterthought. Richard was chatting up the jolly-fat hostess when I flustered in twelve minutes late. The girl, whose face matched the pies revolving in the case behind her, didn't seem to notice me hovering. She was immersed in the possibilities of Richard: In her head, she was already writing her diary entry for the night.

"Preaker," he said, eyes still on the girl. "Your tardiness is a scandal. You're lucky JoAnn was here to keep me company." The girl giggled, then glared at me, leading us to a corner booth where she slapped a greasy menu in front of me. On the table, I could still see the outline of the previous customer's glassware.

The waitress appeared, slid me a glass of water the size of a shot, then handed Richard a styrofoam trough of soda pop. "Hey Richard – I remembered, see?"

"That's why you're my favorite waitress, Kathy." Cute.

"Hi, Camille; I heard you were in town." I didn't want to hear that phrase ever again. The waitress, upon second look, was a former classmate of mine. We'd been friends for a semester sophomore year because we'd dated best buddies – mine was Phil, hers was Jerry – jock guys who played football in the fall and wrestled in the winter, and threw parties year-round in Phil's basement rec room. I had a flash memory of us holding hands for balance while we peed in the snow just outside the sliding glass doors, too drunk to face his mom upstairs. I remember her telling me about having sex with Jerry on the pool table. Which explained why the felt was sticky.

"Hey, Kathy, it's good to see you. How's it going?"

She threw her arms out and cast a glance around the restaurant.

"Oh, you can probably guess. But hey, that's what you get for sticking around here, right? Bobby says hi. Kidder."

"Oh, right! God . . . " I'd forgotten they got married. "How is he?"

"Same old Bobby. You should drop by some time. If you have time. We're over on Fisher."

I could picture the clock ticking loudly as I sat in the living room of Bobby and Kathy Kidder, trying to come up with something to say. Kathy would do all the talking, she always had. She was the kind of person who'd read street signs aloud rather than suffer silence. If he was still the same old Bobby, he was quiet but affable, a guy with few interests and slate blue eyes that flicked into focus only when talk turned to hunting. Back in high school, he saved the hooves of all the deer he killed, always had the latest pair in his pocket, and would pull them out and tap drumbeats with them on whatever hard surface was available. I always felt like it was the dead deer's Morse code, a delayed mayday from tomorrow's venison.

"Anyway, you guys doing the buffet?"

I asked for a beer, which brought forth a mighty pause. Kathy glanced back over her shoulder at the clock on the wall. "Mmmm, we're not supposed to serve till eight. But I'll see if I can sneak you one – old times' sake, right?"

"Well, I don't want to get you in trouble." Just like Wind Gap to have arbitrary drinking rules. Five o'clock would make sense, at least. Eight o'clock was just someone's way of making you feel guilty.

"Lord, Camille, it'd be the most interesting thing that's happened to me in quite a while."

While Kathy went to purloin me a drink, Richard and I filled plates with chicken-fried steak, grits, mashed potatoes, and, in Richard's case, a jiggly slab of Jell-O that was melting into his food by the time we returned to our table. Kathy had left a bottle of beer discreetly on my seat cushion.

"Always drink this early?"

"I'm just having a beer."

"I could smell liquor on your breath when you came in, underneath a layer of Certs – wintergreen?" He smiled at me, as if he were simply curious, no judgments. I bet he glowed in the interrogation room.

"Certs, yes; liquor, no."

In truth, that's why I'd been late. Right before I pulled into the parking lot, I realized the quick nip I took after leaving the Keenes needed some quick covering up, and drove another few blocks to the convenience store to buy some mints. Wintergreen.

"Okay, Camille," he said gently. "No worries. It's none of my business." He took a bite of mashed potatoes, dyed red from the Jell-O, and stayed silent. Seemed slightly abashed.

"So, what do you want to know about Wind Gap?"

I felt I'd disappointed him keenly, like I was a careless parent reneging on a birthday promise to take him to the zoo. I was willing to tell him the truth then, to answer unfailingly the next question he asked in order to make it up to him – and I suddenly wondered if that was the reason he'd challenged my drinking to begin with. Smart cop.

He stared me down. "I want to know about its violence. Every place has its own particular strain. Is it in the open, is it hidden? Is it committed as a group – bar fights, gang rapes – or is it specific, personal? Who commits it? Who's the target?"

"Well, I don't know that I can just make a sweeping statement of the entire history of violence here."

"Name a truly violent incident you saw growing up."

My mother with the baby.

"I saw a woman hurt a child."

"Spanking? Hitting?"

"She bit it."

"Okay. Boy or girl?"

"Girl, I think."

"The child was hers?"

"No."

"Okay, okay, this is good. So a very personal act of violence on a female child. Who committed it, I'll check it out."

"I don't know the person's name. It was someone's relative from out of town."

"Well, who would know her name? I mean, if she has ties here, it'd be worth looking into."

I could feel my limbs disconnecting, floating nearby like driftwood on an oily lake. I pressed my fingertips against my fork tines. Just saying the story aloud panicked me. I hadn't even thought Richard might want specifics.

"Hey, I thought this was just supposed to be a profile of violence," I said, my voice hollow behind the blood in my ears. "I don't have any details. It was a woman I didn't recognize, and I don't know who she was with. I just assumed she was from out of town."

"I thought reporters didn't assume." He was smiling again.

"I wasn't a reporter at the time, I was only a girl. . . ."

"Camille, I'm giving you a hard time, I'm sorry." He plucked the fork from my fingers, placed it deliberately on his side of the table, picked my hand up and kissed it. I could see the word *lipstick* crawling out from my right shirtsleeve. "I'm sorry, I didn't mean to grill you. I was playing bad cop."

"I find it difficult to see you as bad cop."

He grinned. "True, it's a stretch. Curse these boyish good looks!"

We sipped our drinks for a second. He twirled the salt shaker and said, "Can I ask a few more questions?" I nodded. "What's the next incident you can think of?"

The overpowering smell of the tuna salad on my plate was making my stomach twist. I looked for Kathy to get another beer.

"Fifth grade. Two boys cornered a girl at recess and

had her put a stick inside herself."

"Against her will? They forced her?"

"Mmmm . . . a little bit I guess. They were bullies, they told her to, and she did."

"And you saw this or heard about it?"

"They told a few of us to watch. When the teacher found out, we had to apologize."

"To the girl?"

"No, the girl had to apologize too, to the class. 'Young ladies must be in control of their bodies because boys are not.'"

"Jesus. You forget sometimes how different things were, and not that many years ago. How just . . . uninformed." Richard jotted in his notebook, slid some Jell-O down his throat. "What else do you remember?"

"Once, an eighth-grade girl got drunk at a high-school party and four or five guys on the football team had sex with her, kind of passed her around. Does that count?"

"Camille. Of course it counts. You know that, right?"

"Well, I just didn't know if that counted as outright violence or . . ."

"Yeah, I'd count a bunch of punks raping a thirteen-year-old outright violence, yes I sure would."

"How is everything?" Kathy was suddenly smiling over us.

"You think you could sneak me one more beer?"

"Two." Richard said.

"All right, this one I do only as a favor to Richard,

since he's the best tipper in town."

"Thanks, Kathy." Richard smiled.

I leaned across the table. "I'm not arguing that it's wrong, Richard; I'm just trying to get your criteria for violence."

"Right, and I'm getting a good picture of exactly the kind of violence we're dealing with here, just by the fact that you're asking me if that counts. Were the police notified?"

"Of course not."

"I'm surprised she wasn't made to apologize for allowing them to rape her in the first place. Eighth grade. That makes me sick." He tried to take my hand again, but I tucked it away in my lap.

"So it's the age that makes it rape."

"It'd be rape at any age."

"If I got a little too drunk tonight, and was out of my head and had sex with four guys, that would be rape?"

"Legally, I don't know, it'd depend on a lot of things – like your attorney. But ethically, hell yes."

"You're sexist."

"What?"

"You're sexist. I'm so sick of liberal lefty men practicing sexual discrimination under the guise of protecting women against sexual discrimination."

"I can assure you I am doing nothing of the sort."

"I have a guy in my office – *sensitive*. When I got passed over for a promotion, he suggested I sue for discrimination. I wasn't discriminated against, I was a mediocre reporter. And sometimes drunk women aren't raped; they just make stupid choices – and to say we deserve special treatment when we're drunk because we're women, to say we need to be *looked after*, I find offensive."

Kathy came back with our beers and we sipped in silence until they were drained.

"Geez Preaker, okay, I give."

"Okay."

"You do see a pattern, though, right? In the attacks on females. In the attitude about the attacks."

"Except neither the Nash or Keene girl was sexually molested. Right?"

"I think in our guy's mind, the teeth pulling is equivalent to rape. That's all about power – it's invasive, it requires a goodly amount of force, and as each tooth comes out . . . release."

"Is this on record?"

"If I see this in your paper, if I see even a hint of this conversation under your byline, you and I will never speak again. And that would be really bad, because I like talking to you. Cheers." Richard clicked his empty against mine. I stayed silent.

"In fact, let me take you out," he said. "Just for fun. No shop talk. My brain desperately needs a night off from this stuff. We could do something appropriately small town."

I raised my eyebrows.

"Pull taffy? Catch a greased pig?" he began ticking activities on his fingers. "Make our own ice cream? Ride down Main Street in one of those little Shriners cars? Oh, is there a quaint county fair anywhere near here – I could perform a feat of strength for you."

"That attitude must really endear you to the locals."

"Kathy likes me."

"Because you tip her."

We ended up at Garrett Park, jammed on swings that were too small for us, wobbling back and forth in the hot evening dust. The place Natalie Keene was last seen alive, but neither of us mentioned it. Across the ballpark, an old stone drinking fountain spurted water endlessly, would never go off until Labor Day.

"I see a lot of high-school kids partying here at nighttime," Richard said. "Vickery's too busy these days to chase them off."

"It was like that even when I was in high school. Drinking's not that big a deal down here. Except, apparently at Gritty's."

"I'd like to have seen you at sixteen. Let me guess: You were like the wild preacher's daughter. Looks, money, and a brain. That's a recipe for trouble around here I'd guess. I can picture you right over there," he said, pointing to the cracked bleachers. "Outdrinking the boys."

The least of the outrages I'd committed in this park. Not only my first kiss, but my first blow job, at age thirteen. A senior on the baseball team took me under his wing, then took me into the woods. He wouldn't kiss me until I serviced him. Then he wouldn't kiss me because of where my mouth had been. Young love. Not long after was my wild night at the football party, the story that had gotten Richard so riled. Eighth grade, four guys. Got more action then than I've had in the past ten years. I felt the word *wicked* blaze up by my pelvis.

"I had my share of fun," I said. "Looks and money get you a long way in Wind Gap."

"And brains?"

"Brains you hide. I had a lot of friends, but no one I was close to, you know?"

"I can imagine. Were you close to your mom?"

"Not particularly." I'd had one too many drinks; my face felt closed and hot.

"Why?" Richard twisted his swing to face me.

"I just think some women aren't made to be mothers. And some women aren't made to be daughters."

"Did she ever hurt you?" The question unnerved me, particularly after our dinner conversation. Hadn't she hurt me? I felt sure someday I'd dream a memory of her, scratching or biting or pinching. I felt like that had happened. I pictured myself pulling off my blouse to show him my scars, screaming, *yes, look!* Indulgent.

"That's a bizarre question, Richard."

"I'm sorry, you just sounded so . . . sad. Mad. Something."

"That's the mark of someone who has a healthy relationship with his parents."

"Guilty." He laughed. "What about I change the subject?"

"Yes."

"Okay, let's see . . . light conversation. Swing-set conversation." Richard scrunched his face up to mime thinking. "Okay, so what's your favorite color, your favorite ice cream flavor, and your favorite season?

"Blue, coffee, and winter."

"Winter. No one likes winter."

"It gets dark early, I like that."

"Why?"

Because that means the day has ended. I like checking days off a calendar – 151 days crossed and nothing truly horrible has happened. 152 and the world isn't ruined. 153 and I haven't destroyed anyone. 154 and no one really hates me. Sometimes I think I won't ever feel safe until I can count my last days on one hand. Three more days to get through until I don't have to worry about life anymore.

"I just like the night." I was about to say more, not much more, but more, when a broken-down yellow IROC rumbled to a stop across the street and Amma and her blondes piled out the back. Amma leaned into the driver's window, cleavage teasing the boy, who had the long greasy dirt-blond hair you'd expect of someone who still drove a yellow IROC. The three girls stood behind her, hips jutted out, the tallest turning her ass to them and bending over, lean and long to pretend to tie her shoe. Nice moves.

The girls glided toward us, Amma waving her hands extravagantly in protest of the black exhaust cloud. They were hot little things, I had to admit. Long blonde hair, heart-shaped faces, and skinny legs. Miniskirts with tiny

Ts exposing flat baby tummies. And except for the girl Jodes, whose bosom was too high and stiff to be anything but padding, the rest had breasts, full and wobbly and way overripe. All those milk-fed, hog-fed, beef-fed early years. All those extra hormones we put in our livestock. We'll be seeing toddlers with tits before long.

"Hey, Dick," Amma called. She was sucking on a red oversized Blow Pop.

"Hi, ladies."

"Hi, Camille, make me a star yet?" Amma asked, rolling her tongue around the sucker. The Alps-inspired braids were gone, as were the clothes she'd worn to the plant, which had to reek with odors of all kinds and species. Now she wore a tank and a skirt that passed her crotch by an inch.

"Not yet." She had peach skin, so free of blotches or wrinkles, her face so perfect and character-free she could have just popped out of the womb. They all seemed unfinished. I wanted them to go away.

"Dick, when are you going to take us for a ride?" Amma asked, plopping down in the dirt in front of us, her legs pulled up to reveal a glimpse of her panties.

"To do that, I'd have to arrest you. I might have to arrest those boys you keep hanging around with. High-school boys are too old for you."

"They're not in high school," said the tall girl.

"Yeah," Amma giggled. "They dropped out."

"Amma, how old are you?" Richard asked.

"Just turned thirteen."

"Why do you always care so much about Amma?"

interrupted the brassy blonde. "We're here, too, you know. You probably don't even know our names."

"Camille, have you met Kylie, Kelsey, and Kelsey?" Richard said, pointing to the tall girl, the brassy girl, and the girl my sister called . . .

"That's Jodes," Amma said. "There are two Kelseys, so she goes by her last name. To avoid confusion. Right, Jodes?"

"They can call me Kelsey if they want," said the girl, whose low spot in the pecking order was likely punishment for being the least of the beauties. Weak chin.

"And Amma is your half sister, right?" Richard continued. "I'm not as out of the loop as all that."

"No, it looks like you're right in the loop," Amma said. She made the words sound sexual, even though I could think of no double entendre. "So, are you guys dating or what? I heard little Camille here is a real hot ticket. At least she was."

Richard let out a burp of a laugh, a shocked croak. *Unworthy* flared up my leg.

"It's true, Richard. I was something back in the day."

"*Some*thing," Amma mocked. The two girls laughed. Jodes drew frantic lines in the dirt with a stick. "You should hear the stories, Dick. They'd get you pretty hot. Or maybe you already have."

"Ladies, we've got to be going, but as always, it was definitely *something*," Richard said, and took my hand to help me out of the swing. Held on to it, squeezed it twice as we walked toward the car.

"Isn't he a gentleman," Amma called, and the four got to their feet and began following us. "Can't solve crime, but he can take the time to help Camille into his crappy-ass car." They were right on us, Amma and Kylie stepping on our heels, literally. I could feel *sickly* glowing where Amma's sandal had scuffed my Achilles tendon. Then she took her wet sucker and twirled it in my hair.

"Stop it," I muttered. I twirled around and grabbed her wrist so hard I could feel her pulse. Slower than mine. She didn't squirm, in fact, just pushed closer into me. I could feel her strawberry breath fill the hollow of my neck.

"Come on, do something." Amma smiled. "You could kill me right now and Dick still wouldn't be able to figure it out." I let go, pushed her away from me, and Richard and I shuffled to the car faster than I would have liked.

Chapter Nine

I fell asleep, accidentally and hard, at nine o'clock, woke to an angry sun at seven the next morning. A dried-out tree rustled its branches against my window screen as if it wanted to climb in next to me for comfort.

I donned my uniform – the long sleeves, the long skirt – and wandered downstairs. Gayla was glowing in the backyard, her white nurse's dress brilliant against the greenery. She held a silver tray on which my mother was placing imperfect roses. My mother wore a butter-colored sundress that matched her hair. She was stalking through the clumps of pink and yellow blooms with a pair of pliers. She examined each flower hungrily, pluck-ing off petals, pushing and prying.

"You need to water these more, Gayla. Look what you've done to them."

She separated a light pink rose from a bush, pulled it to the ground, secured it with a dainty foot, and clipped it off at its root. Gayla must have had two dozen roses on her tray. I could see little wrong with them.

"Camille, you and I are going shopping in

Woodberry today," my mother called without looking up. "Shall we?" My mother said nothing about the square-off at the Nashes the day before. That would be too direct.

"I have a few things to do," I said. "By the way, I didn't know you were friends with the Nashes. With Ann." I had a catch of guilt for my taunting her about the girl at breakfast the other morning. It wasn't that I truly felt bad that I'd upset my mother – it was more that I hated any debits in her column.

"Mmmm-hmm. Alan and I are having a party next Saturday. It was planned long before we knew you were coming. Although I suppose we didn't really know you were coming until you were here."

Another rose snapped off.

"I thought you barely knew the girls. I didn't real-ize . . ."

"Fine. It will be a nice summer party, a lot of really fine people, and you'll need a dress. I'm sure you didn't bring a dress?"

"No."

"Good then, it will be a nice chance for us to catch up. You've been here over a week, I think it's time." She placed a final stem on the tray. "Okay, Gayla, you can throw these away. We'll pick some decent ones for the house later."

"I'll take those for my room, Momma. They look fine to me."

"They're not."

"I don't mind."

"Camille, I was just looking at them, and they're not good blooms." She dropped the pliers to the ground, began tugging at a stem.

"But they're fine for me. For my room."

"Oh, now look what you've done. I'm bleeding." My mother held up thorn-pricked hands, and trails of deep red began to roll down her wrists. End of conversation. She walked toward the house, Gayla following her, me following Gayla. The back-door knob was sticky with blood.

Alan bandaged both my mother's hands extravagantly, and when we nearly tumbled over Amma, working again on her dollhouse on the porch, Adora plucked teasingly at her braid and told her to come with us. She followed obligingly, and I kept waiting for those knicks at my heels. Not with Mother around.

Adora wanted me to drive her baby blue convertible to Woodberry, which boasted two high-end boutiques, but she didn't want the top down. "We get cold," she said with a conspiratorial smile at Amma. The girl sat silently behind my mother, twisted her mouth into a smart-ass smile when I caught her staring at me in the rearview. Every few minutes, she'd brush her fingertips against my mother's hair, lightly so she wouldn't notice.

As I parked the Mercedes outside her favorite shop, Adora requested weakly that I open the car door for her. It was the first thing she'd said to me in twenty minutes. Nice to catch up. I opened the boutique's door for her too, and the feminine bell matched the saleswoman's delighted greeting.

"Adora!" And then a frown. "My goodness, darling, what's happened to your hands?"

"Just an accident, really. Doing some work around the house. I'll see my doctor this afternoon." Of course she would. She'd go for a paper cut.

"What happened?"

"Oh, I really don't want to talk about it. I *do* want to introduce you to my daughter, Camille. She's visiting."

The saleswoman looked at Amma, then gave me a wavering smile.

"Camille?" A quick recovery: "I think I'd forgotten that you have a third daughter." She lowered her voice on the word "daughter," as if it were an oath. "She must take after her father," the woman said, peering into my face as if I were a horse she might buy. "Amma looks so much like you, and Marian too, in your pictures. This one, though . . ."

"She doesn't take after me much," my mother said. "She has her father's coloring, and his cheekbones. And his temperament."

It was the most I'd ever heard my mother say about my father. I wondered how many other salesladies had received such casual tidbits about him. I had a quick vision of chatting up all the store clerks in southern Missouri, putting together a blurry profile of the man.

My mother petted my hair with gauzy hands. "We need to get my sweetheart a new dress. Something colorful. She's prone to blacks and grays. Size four."

The woman, so thin her hip bones poked from her

skirt like antlers, started weaving in and out of the circular racks, creating a bouquet of splashy green and blue and pink dresses.

"This would look beautiful on you," Amma said, holding a glittery gold top to my mother.

"Stop it, Amma," my mother said. "That's tacky."

"Do I really remind you of my father?" I couldn't help asking Adora. I could feel my cheeks get hot at my presumptuousness.

"I knew you wouldn't just let that go," she said, touching up her lipstick in a store mirror. The gauze on her hands remained impossibly unsmeared.

"I was just curious; I'd never heard you say my personality reminded you of . . ."

"Your personality reminds me of someone very unlike me. And you certainly don't take after Alan, so I assume it must be your father. Now, no more."

"But Momma, I just wanted to know . . ."

"Camille, you're making me bleed more." She held up her bandaged hands, now pocked with red. I wanted to scratch her.

The saleslady bumped up on us with a swatch of dresses. "This is the one you're absolutely going to have to have," she said, holding up a turquoise sundress. Strapless.

"And what about sweetie-pie here," the woman said, nodding at Amma. "She can probably already fit into our petites."

"Amma's only thirteen. She's not ready for these types of clothes," my mother said.

"Only thirteen, good god. I keep forgetting, she looks like such a big girl. You must be worried sick with all that's going on in Wind Gap now."

My mother put an arm around Amma, kissed the top of her head. "Some days I think I won't be able to take the worry. I want to lock her away somewhere."

"Like Bluebeard's dead wives," Amma mumbled.

"Like Rapunzel," my mother said. "Well, go on, Camille – show your sister how pretty you can be."

She trailed me into the dressing area, silent and righteous. In the little mirrored room, with my mother perched on a chair outside, I surveyed my options. Strapless, spaghetti straps, cap sleeves. My mother was punishing me. I found a pink dress with three-quarter sleeves and, quickly doffing my blouse and skirt, pulled it on. The neckline was lower than I'd thought: The words on my chest looked swollen in the fluorescent light, like worms tunneled beneath my skin. *Whine, milk, hurt, bleed.*

"Camille, let me see."

"Uh, this won't work."

"Let me see." *Belittle* burned on my right hip.

"Let me try another." I rifled through the other dresses. All just as revealing. I caught sight of myself again in the mirror. I was horrifying.

"Camille, open the door."

"What's wrong with Camille?" Amma chimed.

"This won't work." The side zipper was sticking. My bared arms flashed scars in deep pink and purple. Even without looking directly in the mirror I could see them reflected at me – a big blur of scorched skin.

"Camille," my mother spat.

"Why won't she just show us?"

"Camille."

"Momma, you saw the dresses, you know why they won't work," I urged.

"Just let me see."

"I'll try one on, Momma," Amma wheedled.

"Camille . . ."

"Fine." I banged open the door. My mother, her face level with my neckline, winced.

"Oh, dear God." I could feel her breath on me. She held up a bandaged hand, as if about to touch my chest, then let it drop. Behind her Amma whined like a puppy. "Look what you've done to yourself," Adora said. "Look at it."

"I do."

"I hope you just loved it. I hope you can stand yourself."

She shut the door and I ripped at the dress, the zipper still jammed until my furious tugs yanked the teeth apart enough to get it to my hips, where I wriggled out, the zipper leaving a trail of pink scratches on my skin. I bunched the cotton of the dress over my mouth and screamed.

I could hear my mother's measured voice in the other room. When I came out, the saleswoman was wrapping a long-sleeved, high-collared lace blouse and a coral skirt that would come to my ankles. Amma stared at me, her eyes pink and darting, before leaving to stand by the car outside.

Back at the house I trailed Adora into the entryway, where Alan stood in a falsely casual pose, hands stuffed into his linen trouser pockets. She fluttered past him toward the stairs.

"How was your day out?" he called after her.

"Horrible," my mother whimpered. Upstairs I heard her door close. Alan frowned at me and went to tend to my mother. Amma had already disappeared.

I walked into the kitchen, to the cutlery drawer. I wanted to just look at the knives I once used on myself. I wasn't going to cut, just allow myself that sharp pressure. I could already feel the knifepoint gently pressing against the plump pads of my fingertips, that delicate tension right before the cut.

The drawer pulled out only an inch and then jammed. My mother had padlocked it. I pulled again and again. I could hear the silvery clink of all those blades sliding onto each other. Like petulant metal fish. My skin was hot. I was about to go call Curry when the doorbell insinuated itself with its polite tones.

Peering around the corner, I could see Meredith Wheeler and John Keene standing outside.

I felt like I'd been caught masturbating. Chewing the inside of my mouth, I opened the door. Meredith rolled in, assaying the rooms, letting out minty exclamations of how beautiful everything was and sending off waves of a dark perfume more suited to a society matron than a teenage girl in a green-and-white cheerleading outfit. She caught me looking.

"I know, I know. School days are over. This is my last time to wear this actually. We're having a cheer session with next year's girls. It's sort of a torch-passing thing. You were a cheerleader, right?"

"I was, if you can believe that." I hadn't been particularly good, but I looked nice in the skirt. Back in the days when I limited my cutting to my torso.

"I can believe it. You were the prettiest girl in the entire town. My cousin was a freshman when you were a senior. Dan Wheeler? He was always talking about you. Pretty and smart, pretty and smart. And nice. He'd kill me if he knew I was telling you this. He lives in Springfield now. But he's not married."

Her wheedling tone reminded me of just the kind of girls I was never comfortable with, the types who peddled a sort of plastic chumminess, who told me things about themselves only friends should know, who described themselves as "people persons."

"This is John," she said, as if surprised to see him beside her.

My first time seeing him up close. He was truly beautiful, almost androgynous, tall and slim with obscenely full lips and ice-colored eyes. He tucked a shock of black hair behind his ear and smiled at his hand as he held it out to me, as if it were a beloved pet performing a new trick.

"So, where do you guys want to talk?" Meredith asked. I debated for a second about ridding myself of the girl, worried she might not know when, or how, to shut up. But he seemed in need of company, and I didn't want to scare him off.

"You guys grab a seat in the living room," I said. "I'll get us some sweet tea."

I first bounded up the stairs, slammed a new cassette into my minirecorder, and listened at my mother's door. Silence except for the whir of a fan. Was she sleeping? If so, was Alan curled up next to her or perched on her vanity chair, just watching? Even after all this time, I hadn't even a guess as to the private life of Adora and her husband. Walking past Amma's room, I saw her sitting very properly on the edge of a rocking chair, reading a book called *Greek Goddesses*. Since I'd been here, she'd played at being Joan of Arc and Bluebeard's wife and Princess Diana – all martyrs, I realized. She'd find even unhealthier role models among the goddesses. I left her to it.

In the kitchen I poured out the drinks. Then, counting out a full ten seconds, I pressed the tines of a fork into the palm of my hand. My skin began to quiet down.

I entered the living room to see Meredith with her legs dangled over John's lap, kissing his neck. When I clanked the tea tray down on a table, she didn't stop. John looked at me and peeled himself slowly away.

"You're no fun today," she pouted.

"So, John, I'm really glad you decided to talk to me," I began. "I know your mom has been reluctant."

"Yes. She doesn't want to talk to much of anyone, but especially not . . . press. She's very private."

"But you're okay with it?" I prompted. "You're eighteen, I assume?"

"Just turned." He sipped his tea formally, as if he was measuring tablespoons in his mouth.

"Because what I really want is to be able to describe your sister to our readers," I said. "Ann Nash's father is speaking about her, and I don't want Natalie to get lost in this story. Does your mother know you're speaking to me?"

"No, but it's okay. I think we'll have to agree to disagree about this." His laugh came in a quick stutter.

"His mom is kind of a freak about the media," Meredith said, drinking from John's glass. "She's an extremely private person. I mean, I hardly think she even knows who I am, and we've been together for over a year, right?" He nodded. She frowned, disappointed, I assumed, that he didn't add to the story of their romance. She removed her legs from his lap, crossed them, and began picking at the edge of the couch.

"And I hear you're living over with the Wheelers now?"

"We have a place out back, a carriage house from the old days," Meredith said. "My little sister's pissed; it used to be the hangout for her and her nasty friends. Except for your sister. Your sister's cool. You know my sister, right? Kelsey?"

Of course, this piece of work would have connections to Amma.

"Kelsey tall or Kelsey small?" I asked.

"Totally. This town has way too many Kelseys. Mine's the tall one."

"I've met her. They seem close."

"They'd better be," Meredith said tightly. "Little Amma runs that school. Be a fool that got on her bad side."

Enough about Amma, I thought, but images of her teasing lesser girls by those lockers bumped around in my head. Junior high is an ugly time.

"So, John, are you adjusting all right over there?"

"He's fine," Meredith snipped. "We put together a little care basket of guy stuff for him – my mom even got him a CD player."

"Oh, really?" I looked pointedly at John. *Time to speak up, buddy. Don't be pussy whipped on my time.*

"I just need to be away from home right now," he said. "We're all a little on edge, you know, and Natalie's stuff is everywhere, and my mom won't let anyone touch it. Her shoes are in the hallway and her swimming suit is hanging in the bathroom we share so I have to see it every morning I shower. I can't deal."

"I can imagine." I could: I remember Marian's tiny pink coat hanging in the hall closet till I left for college. Might still be there.

I turned on the tape recorder, pushed it across the table toward the boy.

"Tell me what your sister was like, John."

"Uh, she was a nice kid. She was extremely smart. Just unbelievable."

"Smart how? Like good in school, or just bright?"

"Well, she didn't do that well in school. She had a bit of a discipline problem," he said. "But I think it was just because she got bored. She should have skipped a grade or two, I think."

"His mom thought it would stigmatize her," Meredith interjected. "She was always worried about Natalie sticking out."

I raised my eyebrows at him.

"That's true. My mom really wanted Natalie to fit in. She was this sort of goofy kid, kind of a tomboy, and just kind of a weirdo." He laughed, staring at his feet.

"Are you thinking of a particular story?" I asked. Anecdotes are Curry's coin of the realm. Plus, I was interested.

"Oh, like once, she invented this whole other language, you know? And a regular kid, I mean it'd be gibberish. But Natalie had the whole alphabet figured out – looked like Russian. And she actually taught it to me. Or tried. She got frustrated with me pretty quickly." He laughed again, that same croak, like it was coming up from underground.

"Did she like school?"

"Well it's hard to be the new kid, and the girls here . . . well I guess the girls anywhere can be a little bit snotty."

"Johnny! Rude!" Meredith pretended to push him. He ignored her.

"I mean, your sister . . . Amma, right?" I nodded to him. "She was actually friends with her for a little bit. They'd run around in the woods, Natalie'd come back all scraped up and daffy."

"Really?" Considering the scorn with which she'd mentioned Natalie's name, I couldn't picture it.

"They were real intense for a little bit. But I think Amma got bored with her, Natalie being a few years younger. I don't know. They had some sort of falling out." Amma learned that from her mother – the glib discarding of friends. "It was okay, though," John said, as if to reassure me. Or him. "She had one kid she played with a lot, James Capisi. Farm kid a year or so younger that no one else talked to. They seemed to get along though."

"He says he's the last one to see Natalie alive," I said.

"He's a liar," Meredith said. "I heard that story, too. He's always made stuff up. I mean, his mom's dying of cancer. He's got no dad. He has no one to pay any attention to him. So he throws out that wild story. Don't listen to anything he says."

Again I looked at John, who shrugged.

"It is sort of a wild story, you know? A crazy lady snatches Natalie in broad daylight," he said. "Besides, why would a woman do something like that?"

"Why would a man do something like that?" I asked.

"Who knows why men do such freaky stuff," Meredith added. "It's a gene thing."

"I have to ask you John, have you been questioned by the police?"

"Along with both my parents."

"And you have an alibi for the nights of both killings?" I waited for a reaction, but he continued to sip his tea calmly.

"Nope. I was out driving around. I just need to get

out of here sometimes, you know?" He darted a quick glance at Meredith, whose lips pursed when she caught him looking. "It's just a smaller town than I'm used to. Sometimes you need to get lost for a little. I know you don't get it, Mer." Meredith stayed silent.

"I get it," I offered. "I remember getting very claustrophobic growing up here, I can't imagine what it must be like to move here from somewhere else."

"Johnny's being noble," Meredith interrupted. "He was with me both those nights. He just doesn't want to get me in trouble. Print that." Meredith was wobbling on the edge of the sofa, stiff and upright and slightly disconnected, as if she were speaking in tongues.

"Meredith," John murmured. "No."

"I'm not going to have people thinking my boyfriend is a fucking baby killer, thank you very much, John."

"You tell that story to the police, and they'll know the truth in an hour. It will look even worse for me. No one really thinks I'd kill my own sister." John took a single lock of Meredith's hair and pulled his fingers gently from the roots to the end. The word *tickle* flashed randomly from my right hip. I believed the boy. He cried in public and told silly stories about his sister and played with his girlfriend's hair and I believed him. I could almost hear Curry snort at my naiveté.

"Speaking of stories," I started. "I need to ask you about one. Is it true Natalie hurt one of her classmates back in Philadelphia?"

John froze, turned to Meredith, and for the first time he looked unpleasant. He gave me a true image for the phrase *curled lips*. His whole body jolted and I thought he'd bolt for the door, but then he leaned back and took a breath.

"Great. This is why my mom hates the media," he grumbled. "There was an article about that in the paper back home. It was just a few paragraphs. It made Natalie sound like an animal."

"So tell me what happened."

He shrugged. Picked at a nail. "It was in art class, and the kids were cutting and painting, and a little girl got hurt. Natalie was a little kid with a temper, and this girl was sort of always bossing Natalie around. And one time Natalie happened to have scissors in her hand. It wasn't like a premeditated assault. I mean, she was nine at the time."

I had a flash of Natalie, that serious child from the Keene family photo, wielding blades at a little girl's eyes. An image of bright red blood mingling unexpectedly with pastel watercolors.

"What happened to the little girl?"

"They saved her left eye. Her right was, uh, ruined."

"Natalie attacked both her eyes?"

He stood up, pointing down at me from almost the same angle as his mother had. "Natalie saw a shrink for a year after, dealing with this. Natalie woke up with nightmares for months. She was nine. It was an accident. We all felt horrible. My dad set up a fund for the little girl. We had to leave so Natalie could start over. That's why we had to come here – Dad took the first job he could find. We moved in the middle of the night, like criminals. To this place. To this goddam town."

"Gee John, I didn't realize you were having such a horrible time," Meredith murmured.

He began to cry then, sitting back down, his head in his hands.

"I didn't mean that I was sorry I came here. I meant I'm sorry she came here, because now she's dead. And we were trying to help. And she's dead." He let out a quiet wail, and Meredith wrapped her arms grudgingly around him. "Someone killed my sister."

There would be no formal dinner that night, as Miss Adora wasn't feeling well, Gayla informed me. I assume it was my mother's affectation to request the *Miss* in front of her name, and I tried to imagine how the conversation might go. *Gayla, the best servants in the best households call their mistresses by their formal names. We want to be the best, don't we?* Something like that.

Whether it was my argument with my mother or Amma's that was the cause of the trouble, I wasn't sure. I could hear them bickering like pretty birds in my mother's room, Adora accusing Amma, correctly, of having driven the golf cart without permission. Like all rural towns, Wind Gap has an obsession with machinery. Most homes own a car and a half for every occupant (the half being an antique collectible, or an old piece of crap on blocks, depending on the income bracket), plus boats, Jet Skis, scooters, tractors, and, among the elite of Wind Gap, golf carts, which younger kids without licenses use to whip around town. Technically illegal, but no one

ever stops them. I guessed my mother had tried to with-
hold this bit of freedom from Amma after the murders.
I would have. Their fight squeaked on like an old see-
saw for nearly half an hour. *Don't lie to me, little girl. . . .*
The warning was so familiar it gave me an old feeling of
unease. So Amma did occasionally get caught.

When the phone rang, I picked up, just so Amma
wouldn't lose her momentum, and was surprised to hear
the cheerleader staccato of my old friend Katie Lacey.
Angie Papermaker was having the girls over for a Pity
Party. Drink a bunch of wine, watch a sad movie, cry,
gossip. I should come. Angie lived in the New Rich part
of town – huge mansions at the outskirts of Wind Gap.
Practically Tennessee. I couldn't tell from Katie's voice
if that made her jealous or smug. Knowing her, probably a bit of both. She'd always been one of those girls
who wanted what anyone else had, even if she didn't
want it.

I knew when I saw Katie and her friends at the
Keenes' home that I'd have to submit to at least one
evening out. It was this or finish transcribing my talk
with John, which was making me dangerously sad. Plus,
like Annabelle, Jackie, and that catty group of my
mother's friends, this gathering was likely to yield more
information than I'd get through a dozen formal inter-
views.

As soon as she pulled up in front of the house I realized that Katie Lacey, now Katie Brucker, had, predictably, done well for herself. I knew this both from the
fact it took her just five minutes to pick me up (turns

out her home was but a block away) and what she picked me up in: one of those huge, stupid SUVs that cost more than some people's homes and provide just as many comforts. Behind my head, I could hear the DVD player tittering with some kids' show, despite the absence of kids. In front of me, the dashboard navigator was providing unnecessary play-by-play directions.

Her husband, Brad Brucker, was studying at her father's feet, and when Daddy retired, he'd take over the business himself. They peddled a controversial hormone used to bulk up chickens with horrific rapidity. My mother always sniffed at this – she'd never use anything that put such a stunning rush on the growing process. That didn't mean she eschewed hormones: My mother's pigs were pricked with chemicals till they plumped and reddened like squirting cherries, till their legs couldn't support their juicy girth. But it was done at a more leisurely pace.

Brad Brucker was the type of husband to live where Katie said, impregnate Katie when she asked, buy Katie the Pottery Barn sofa she wanted, and otherwise shut up. He was good-looking if you looked at him long enough, and he had a dick the size of my ring finger. This I knew firsthand, thanks to a slightly mechanical exchange my freshman year. But apparently the tiny thing worked fine: Katie was at the end of her first trimester for her third kid. They were going to keep trying till she had a boy. *We really want a little rascal running around.*

Talk of me, Chicago, no husband yet but fingers crossed! Talk of her, her hair, her new vitamin program,

Brad, her two girls, Emma and Mackenzie, Wind Gap ladies' auxiliary, and the horrible job they did with the St. Patrick's Day Parade. Then sigh: *those poor little girls.* Yes, sigh: my story on those poor little girls. Apparently she didn't care that much, because she was quickly back to the ladies' auxiliary and how scattered it had become now that Becca Hart (née Mooney) was activities director. Becca was a girl of midtier popularity from our days, who shot to social stardom five years ago when she snagged Eric Hart, whose parents owned a sprawling Go-Kart, waterslide, mini-golf tourist trap in the ugliest part of the Ozarks. The situation was quite reproachable. She'd be there tonight and I could see for myself. She just didn't fit in.

Angie's house looked like a child's drawing of a mansion: It was so generic it was barely three-dimensional. When I entered the room I realized how much I didn't want to be there. There was Angie, who'd unnecessarily dropped ten pounds since high school, and who smiled demurely at me and went back to setting out a fondue. There was Tish, who'd been the little mommy of the group even back then, the one who held your hair when you threw up, and who had occasional dramatic crying jags about feeling unloved. She'd married a guy from Newcastle, I learned, a slightly dorky man (this in hushed tones from Katie) who made a solid living. Mimi draped herself over a chocolate-leather couch. A dazzling adolescent, her looks didn't translate into adulthood. No one else seemed to notice. Everyone still referred to her as "the hot one." Backing this up: the giant rock on her hand, courtesy of Joey Johansen, a gangly, sweet boy who'd sprouted into a linebacker junior year, and suddenly demanded to be called Jo-ha. (That's truly all I remember of him.) Poor Becca sat amidst them, looking eager and awkward, dressed almost comically similar to her hostess (Had Angie taken Becca shopping?). She flashed smiles to anyone who caught her eye, but no one talked to her.

We watched *Beaches*.

Tish was sobbing when Angie turned the lights on.

"I've gone back to work," she announced in a wail, pressed coral pink fingernails across her eyes. Angie poured wine and patted her knee, stared at her with a showy concern.

"Good God, sweetie, why?" Katie murmured. Even her murmur was girlish and clicky. Like a thousand mice nibbling crackers.

"With Tyler in preschool, I thought I wanted to," Tish said between sobs. "Like I needed a purpose." She spat the last word out as if it were contaminated.

"You have a purpose," said Angie. "Don't let society tell you how to raise your family. Don't let feminists" – here she looked at me – "make you feel guilty for having what they can't have."

"She's right, Tish, she's completely right," offered Becca. "Feminism means allowing women to make whatever kind of choices they want."

The women were looking dubiously at Becca when suddenly Mimi's sobs popped up from her corner, and the attention, and Angie-with-the-wine, turned to her.

"Steven doesn't want to have any more kids," she wept.

"Why not?" Katie said with impressively strident outrage.

"He says three's enough."

"Enough for him or for you?" Katie snapped.

"That's what I said. I want a girl. I want a daughter." The women pet her hair. Katie pet her belly. "And I want a son," she whimpered, staring pointedly at the photo of Angie's three-year-old boy on the mantel.

The weeping and fretting went back and forth between Tish and Mimi – *I miss my babies . . . I've always dreamed of a big houseful of kids, that's all I've ever wanted . . . what's so wrong with just being a mommy?* I felt sorry for them – they seemed truly distraught – and I certainly could sympathize with a life that didn't turn out as planned. But after much head nodding and murmurs of assent, I could think of nothing useful to say and I ducked into the kitchen to slice some cheese and stay out of the way. I knew this ritual from high school, and I knew it didn't take much for it to turn nasty. Becca soon joined me in the kitchen, began washing dishes.

"This happens pretty much every week," she said and half rolled her eyes, pretending to be less annoyed than bemused.

"Cathartic, I guess," I offered. I could sense her wanting me to say more. I knew the feeling. When I'm on the edge of getting a good quote, it seems like I can almost reach inside the person's mouth and pluck it off their tongue.

"I had no idea my life was so miserable until I started coming to Angie's little get-togethers," Becca whispered, taking a newly clean knife to slice some Gruyere. We had enough cheese to feed all of Wind Gap quite prettily.

"Ah, well, being conflicted means you can live a shallow life without copping to being a shallow person."

"Sounds about right," Becca said. "Was it like this with you guys in high school?" she asked.

"Oh pretty much, when we weren't stabbing each other in the back."

"Guess I'm glad I was such a loser," she said, and laughed. "Wonder how I can be less cool now?" I laughed then too, poured her a glass of wine, slightly giddy at the absurdity of finding myself plopped right back in my teenage life.

By the time we returned, still lightly giggling, every woman in the room was crying, and they all stared up at us simultaneously, like a gruesome Victorian portrait come to life.

"Well, I'm glad you two are having such fun," Katie snapped.

"Considering what's going on in our town," Angie added. The subject had clearly widened.

"What's wrong with the world? Why would someone hurt little girls?" Mimi cried. "Those poor things."

"And to take their teeth, that's what I can't get over," Katie said.

"I just wish they'd been treated nicer when they

were alive," Angie sobbed. "Why are girls so cruel to each other?"

"The girls picked on them?" Becca asked.

"They cornered Natalie in the bathroom after school one day . . . and cut her hair off," Mimi sobbed. Her face was wrecked, swollen and splotchy. Dark rivulets of mascara marked her blouse.

"They made Ann show her . . . privates to the boys," said Angie.

"They always picked on those girls, just because they were a little different," Katie said, wiping her tears delicately on a cuff.

"Who's 'they'?" Becca asked.

"Ask Camille, she's the one *reporting* this whole thing," Katie said, lifting her chin up, a gesture I remembered from high school. It meant she was turning on you, but feeling quite justified. "You know how awful your sister is, right, Camille?"

"I know girls can be miserable."

"So you're defending her?" Katie glowered. I could feel myself getting pulled into Wind Gap politics and I panicked. *Catfight* began thumping on my calf.

"Oh, Katie, I don't even know her well enough to defend or not defend her," I said, faking weariness.

"Have you even cried once about those little girls?" Angie said. They were all in a bunch now, staring me down.

"Camille doesn't have any children," Katie said piously. "I don't think she can feel that hurt the way we do."

"I feel very sad about those girls," I said, but it

sounded artificial, like a beauty contestant pledging world peace. I did feel sad, but articulating it seemed cheap to me.

"I don't mean this to sound cruel," Tish began, "but it seems like part of your heart can never work if you don't have kids. Like it will always be shut off."

"I agree," Katie said. "I didn't really become a woman until I felt Mackenzie inside me. I mean, there's all this talk these days of God versus science, but it seems like, with babies, both sides agree. The Bible says be fruitful and multiply, and science, well, when it all boils down, that's what women were made for, right? To bear children."

"Girl power," Becca muttered under her breath.

Becca took me home because Katie wanted a sleepover at Angie's. Guess the nanny would deal with her darling girls in the morning. Becca made a few game jokes about the women's obsession with mothering, which I acknowledged with small croaks of laughter. *Easy for you to say, you have two kids.* I was feeling desperately sulky.

I put on a clean nightgown and sat squarely in the center of my bed. No more booze for you tonight, I whispered. I patted my cheek and unclenched my shoulders. I called myself sweetheart. I wanted to cut: *Sugar* flared on my thigh, *nasty* burned near my knee. I wanted to slice *barren* into my skin. That's how I'd stay, my insides unused. Empty and pristine. I pictured my pelvis split open, to reveal a tidy hollow, like the nest of a vanished animal.

Those little girls. *What's wrong with the world?* Mimi had cried, and it had barely registered, the lament was so commonplace. But I felt it now. Something was wrong, right here, very horribly wrong. I could picture Bob Nash sitting on the edge of Ann's bed, trying to remember the last thing he said to his daughter. I saw Natalie's mother, crying into one of her old T-shirts. I saw me, a despairing thirteen-year-old sobbing on the floor of my dead sister's room, holding a small flowered shoe. Or Amma, thirteen herself, a woman-child with a gorgeous body and a gnawing desire to be the baby girl my mother mourned. My mother weeping over Marian. Biting that baby. Amma, asserting her power over lesser creatures, laughing as she and her friends cut through Natalie's hair, the curls falling to the tile floor. Natalie, stabbing at the eyes of a little girl. My skin was screaming, my ears banged with my heartbeat. I closed my eyes, wrapped my arms around myself, and wept.

After ten minutes of sobbing in my pillow, I started pulling out of the crying jag, mundane thoughts bobbing into my head: the quotes from John Keene I might use in my article, the fact that my rent was due next week back in Chicago, the smell of the apple going sour in the trash basket by my bed.

Then, outside my door, Amma quietly whispered my name. I buttoned up the top of my nightgown, pulled my sleeves down, and let her in. She was wearing a pink flowered nightgown, her blonde hair flowing over her shoulders, her feet bare. She looked truly adorable, no better word.

"You've been crying," she said, slightly astounded.

"A little."

"Because of her?" The final word was weighted, I could picture it round and heavy, making a deep thump in a pillow.

"A little, I guess."

"Me, too." She stared at my edges: the collar of my nightgown, the ends of my sleeves. She was trying to glimpse my scars. "I didn't know you hurt yourself," she said finally.

"Not anymore."

"That's good, I guess." She wavered at the edge of my bed. "Camille, do you ever feel like bad things are going to happen, and you can't stop them? You can't do anything, you just have to wait?"

"Like an anxiety attack?" I couldn't stop staring at her skin, it was so smooth and tawny, like warm ice cream.

"No. Not really." She sounded like I'd disappointed her, failed to solve a clever riddle. "But, anyway. I brought you a present." She held out a square of wrapping paper and told me to open it carefully. Inside: a tidily rolled joint.

"It's better than that vodka you drink," Amma said, automatically defensive. "You drink a lot. This is better. It won't make you as sad."

"Amma, really . . ."

"Can I see your cuts again?" She smiled shyly.

"No." A silence. I held up the joint. "And Amma, I don't think you should . . ."

"Well I do, so take it or don't. I was just trying to be nice." She frowned and twisted a corner of her nightgown.

"Thank you. It's sweet that you'd like to help me feel better."

"I can be nice, you know?" she said, her brow still furrowed. She seemed on the edge of tears herself.

"I know. It's just that I'm wondering why you've decided to be nice to me now."

"Sometimes I can't. But right now, I can. When everyone's asleep and everything's quiet, it's easier." She reached out, her hand like a butterfly before my face, then dropped it, patted me on the knee, and left.

Chapter Ten

"I'm sorry she came here, because now she's dead," said a weeping John Keene, 18, of his younger sister Natalie, 10. "Someone killed my little sister." Natalie Keene's body was discovered on May 14, jammed upright in a space between Cut-N-Curl Beauty Parlor and Bifty's Hardware in the small town of Wind Gap, Mo. She is the second young girl murdered here in the past nine months: Ann Nash, nine, was discovered in a nearby creek last August. Both girls had been strangled; both had their teeth removed by the killer.

"She was this goofy kid," John Keene said, crying softly, "kind of a tomboy." Keene, who moved here from Philadelphia with his family two years ago, and who recently graduated from high school, described his younger sister as a bright, imaginative girl. She once even invented her own language, complete with a working alphabet. "A regular kid, it'd be gibberish," Keene said, laughing ruefully.

What is gibberish is the police case so far: Wind Gap police officials and Richard Willis, a homicide detective on loan from Kansas City, admit there are few leads. "We have not ruled anyone out," Willis said. "We are looking very closely at potential suspects within the community, but are also carefully considering the possibility that these killings may be the work of an outsider."

The police refuse to comment on one potential witness, a young boy who claims he saw the person who abducted Natalie Keene: a woman. A source close to the police say they believe the killer is, in fact, likely to be a man within the local community. Wind Gap dentist James L. Jellard, 56, concurs, adding that removing teeth "would take some strength. They don't just pop right out."

While the police work the case, Wind Gap has seen a run on security locks and firearms. The local hardware store has sold three dozen security locks; the town's gun and rifle dealer has processed more than 30 firearms permits since Keene's killing. "I thought most folks around here already had rifles, for hunting," says Dan R. Sniya, 35, who owns the town's largest firearms store. "But I think anyone who didn't have a gun – well, they will."

One Wind Gap resident who's increased his arsenal is Ann Nash's father, Robert, 41. "I have two other daughters and a son, and they're going to be protected," he said. Nash described his late daughter as quite bright. "Sometimes I thought she was smarter than her old man. Sometimes *she* thought she was smarter than her old man." He said his daughter was a tomboy like Natalie, a girl who liked to climb trees and ride her bike, which is what she was doing when she was abducted last August.

Father Louis D. Bluell, of the local Catholic parish, says he's seen the effect of the murders on residents: Sunday mass attendance has increased noticeably, and many members of his church have come for spiritual advice. "When something like this happens, people feel a real yearning for spiritual nourishment," he says. "They want to know how something like this could have happened."

So, too, do the police.

Before we hit press, Curry made fun of all the middle initials. *Good God, Southerners love their formalities.* I pointed out Missouri was technically the Midwest and he snickered at me. *And I'm technically middle-aged, but tell that to poor Eileen when she has to deal with my bursitis.* He also excised all but the most general details from my interview with James Capisi. Makes us look like suckers if we pay too much attention to the kid, especially if the police aren't biting. He also cut a lame quote about John from his mother: "He's a kind, gentle boy." It was the only comment I got from her before she kicked me out of the house, the only thing that made that miserable visit near worthwhile, but Curry thought it was distracting. He was probably right. He was quite pleased that we finally had a suspect to focus on, my "man within the local community." My "source close to the police" was a fabrication, or more euphemistically, an amalgam – everyone from Richard to the priest thought a local guy did it. I didn't tell Curry about my lie.

The morning my story came out, I stayed in bed and stared at the white rotary phone, waited for it to ring with rebukes. It would be John's mom, who'd be plenty angry when she discovered I got to her son. Or Richard, for my leak about the suspect being local.

Several silent hours went by as I got progressively more sweaty, the horseflies buzzing around my window screen, Gayla hovering outside my door, anxious for access to my room. Our bedclothes and bath towels have always been changed daily; the laundry is forever churning down in the basement. I think this is a lingering habit from Marian's lifetime. Crisp clean clothes to make us forget all the drips and dank smells that come from our bodies. I was in college by the time I realized I liked the smell of sex. I came into my friend's bedroom one morning after a boy darted past me, smiling sideways and tucking his socks into his back pocket. She was lazing in bed, splotchy and naked, with one bare leg dangling out from under the sheets. That sweet muddy smell was purely animal, like the deepest corner of a bear's cave. It was almost foreign to me, this lived-in, overnight odor. My most evocative childhood scent was bleach.

As it turned out, my first angry caller was not anyone I'd guessed.

"I can't believe you left me completely out of the story," Meredith Wheeler's voice clanged into the phone. "You didn't use one thing I said. You'd never even know I was there. I was the one who got you John, remember?"

"Meredith, I never told you I'd use your comments," I said, irritated at her pushiness. "I'm sorry if you got that impression." I jammed a floppy blue teddy bear under my head, then felt guilty and returned him to the foot of the bed. One should have allegiance to one's childhood things.

"I just don't know why you wouldn't include me," she continued. "If the whole thing was to get an idea what Natalie was like, then you need John. And if you need John, you need me. I'm his girlfriend. I mean, I practically *own* him, ask anyone."

"Well, you and John, that wasn't really the focus of the story," I said. Behind Meredith's breathing, I could hear a country-rock ballad playing and a rhythmic thump and hiss.

"But you had other people from Wind Gap in the story. You had stupid Father Bluell. Why not me? John's in a lot of pain, and I've been really important to him, working through it all with him. He cries all the time. I'm the one keeping him together."

"When I do another story that needs more voices from Wind Gap, I'll interview you. If you have something to add to the story."

Thump. Hiss. She was ironing.

"I know a lot about that family, a lot about Natalie

that John wouldn't think of. Or say."

"Great, then. I'll be in touch. Soon." I hung up, not quite easy with what the girl was offering me. When I looked down, I realized I'd written "Meredith" in loopy girlish cursive across the scars on my left leg.

On the porch, Amma was swaddled in a pink silk comforter, a damp washcloth on her forehead. My mother had a silver tray with tea, toast, and assorted bottles on it, and was pressing the back of Amma's hand against her cheek in a circular motion.

"Baby, baby, baby," Adora murmured, rocking them both on the swing.

Amma lolled sleepy as a newborn in her blanket, smacking her lips occasionally. It was the first time I'd seen my mother since our trip to Woodberry. I hovered in front of her, but she wouldn't take her eyes off Amma.

"Hi, Camille," Amma finally whispered, and gave me a little curl of a smile.

"Your sister is sick. She's worried herself into a fever since you've been home," Adora said, still pressing Amma's hand in that circle. I pictured my mother's teeth gnashing against each other inside her cheek.

Alan, I realized, was sitting just inside, watching them through the window screen from the living-room loveseat.

"You need to make her feel more comfortable around you, Camille; she's just a little girl," my mother cooed to Amma.

A little girl with a hangover. Amma left my room last night and went down to drink a while in her own. That's the way this house worked. I left them whispering to each other, *favorite* buzzing on my knee.

"Hey, Scoop." Richard rolled along beside me in his sedan. I was walking to the space where Natalie's body had been discovered, to get specific details about the balloons and notes placed there. Curry wanted a "town in mourning" piece. That is, if there were no leads on the murders. Implication being there better be some lead, and soon.

"Hello, Richard."

"Nice story today." Damn Internet. "Glad to hear you've found a source close to the police." He was smiling when he said it.

"Me too."

"Get in, we've got some work to do." He pushed open the passenger door.

"I've got my own work to do. So far working with you has given me nothing but unusable, no-comment comments. My editor's going to pull me out soon."

"Well, we can't have that. Then I'll have no distractions," he said. "Come on with me. I need a Wind Gap tour guide. In return: I will answer three questions, completely and truthfully. Off record of course, but I'll give it to you straight. Come on, Camille. Unless you've got a date with your police source."

"Richard."

"No, truly, I don't want to interfere with a burgeoning love affair. You and this mysterious fellow must make quite a handsome pair."

"Shut up." I got in the car. He leaned over me, pulled down my seat belt and secured it, pausing for a second with his lips close to mine.

"I've got to keep you safe." He pointed over to a mylar balloon swaying in the gap where Natalie's body was found. It read *Get Well Soon*.

"That to me," Richard said, "perfectly sums up Wind Gap."

Richard wanted me to take him to all the town's secret places, the nooks that only locals know about. Places where people meet to screw or smoke dope, where teens drink, or folks go to sit by themselves and decide where their lives had unraveled. Everyone has a moment where life goes off the rails. Mine was the day Marian died. The day I picked up that knife is a tight second.

"We still haven't found a kill site for either girl," Richard said, one hand on the wheel, the other draped on the back of my seat. "Just the dumping areas, and those are pretty contaminated." He paused. "Sorry. 'Kill site' is an ugly phrase."

"More suited to an abattoir."

"Wow. Fifty-cent word there, Camille. Seventy-five cents in Wind Gap."

"Yeah, I forget how cultured you Kansas City folks are."

I directed Richard onto an unmarked gravel road, and we parked in the knee-length weeds about ten miles

Gillian Flynn

south of where Ann's body had been found. I fanned the back of my neck in the wet air, plucked at my long sleeves, stuck to my arms. I wondered if Richard could smell the booze of last night, now sitting in sweaty dots on my skin. We hiked into the woods, downhill and back up. The cottonwood leaves shimmered, as always, with imaginary breeze. Occasionally we could hear an animal skitter away, a bird suddenly take flight. Richard walked assuredly behind me, plucking leaves and slowly tearing them apart along the way. By the time we reached the spot, our clothes were soaked, my face dripping with sweat. It was an ancient one-room schoolhouse, tilting slightly to one side, vines weaving in and out of its slats.

Inside, half a chalkboard was nailed to the wall. It contained elaborate drawings of penises pushing into vaginas – no bodies attached. Dead leaves and liquor bottles littered the floor, some rusted beer cans from a time before pop tops. A few tiny desks remained. One was covered in a tablecloth, a vase of dead roses at its center. A pitiable place for a romantic dinner. I hoped it went well.

"Nice work," Richard said, pointing to one of the crayoned drawings. His light blue oxford clung to him. I could see the outline of a well-toned chest.

"This is mostly a kid hangout, obviously," I said. "But it's near the creek, so I thought you should see it."

"Mm-hmm." He looked at me in silence. "What do you do back in Chicago when you're not working?" He leaned on the desk, plucked a withered rose from the vase, began crumbling its leaves.

"What do I do?"

"Do you have a boyfriend? I bet you do."

"No. I haven't had a boyfriend in a long time."

He began pulling the petals off the rose. I couldn't tell if he was interested in my answer. He looked up at me and grinned.

"You're a tough one, Camille. You don't have a lot of *give* to you. You make me work. I like it, it's different. Most girls you can't get to shut up. No offense."

"I'm not trying to be difficult. It's just not the question I was expecting," I said, regaining my footing in the conversation. Small talk and banter. I can do that. "Do you have a girlfriend? I bet you have two. A blonde and brunette, to coordinate with your ties."

"Wrong on all counts. No girlfriend, and my last one was a redhead. She didn't match anything I owned. Had to go. Nice girl, too bad."

Normally, Richard was the kind of guy I disliked, someone born and raised plush: looks, charm, smarts, probably money. These men were never very interesting to me; they had no edges, and they were usually cowards. They instinctively fled any situation that might cause them embarrassment or awkwardness. But Richard didn't bore me. Maybe because his grin was a little crooked. Or because he made his living dealing in ugly things.

"You ever come here when you were a kid, Camille?" His voice was quiet, almost shy. He looked sideways, and the afternoon sun made his hair glimmer gold.

"Sure. Perfect place for inappropriate activities."

Richard walked over to me, handed me the last of the rose, ran a finger up my sweaty cheek.

"I can see that," he said. "First time I've ever wished I grew up in Wind Gap."

"You and I might have gotten along just fine," I said, and meant it. I was suddenly sad I'd never known a boy like Richard growing up, someone who'd at least give me a bit of a challenge.

"You know you're beautiful, right?" he asked. "I'd tell you, but it seems like the kind of thing that you'd brush off. Instead I thought . . ."

He tilted my head up to him and kissed me, first slowly and then, when I didn't pull away, he folded me into his arms, pushed his tongue into my mouth. It was the first time I'd been kissed in almost three years. I ran my hands between his shoulder blades, the rose crumbling down his back. I pulled his collar away from his neck and licked him.

"I think you are the most beautiful girl I have ever seen," he said, running a finger along my jawline. "The first time I saw you, I couldn't even think the rest of the day. Vickery sent me home." He laughed.

"I think you're very handsome, too," I said, holding his hands so they wouldn't roam. My shirt was thin, I didn't want him to feel my scars.

"*I think you're very handsome, too?*" He laughed. "Geez, Camille, you really don't do the romance stuff, huh?"

"I'm just caught off guard. I mean, first of all, this is a bad idea, you and me."

"Horrible." He kissed my earlobe.

"And, I mean, don't you want to look around this place?"

"*Miss* Preaker, I searched this place the second week I was here. I just wanted to go for a walk with you."

Richard also had covered the two other spots I had in mind, as it turned out. An abandoned hunting shed on the south part of the woods had yielded a yellow plaid hair ribbon that neither girl's parents could identify. The bluffs to the east of Wind Gap, where you could sit and watch the distant Mississippi River below, offered a child's sneaker print that matched shoes neither girl owned. Some dried blood was found dribbled over grass blades; but the type was the wrong match for both. Once again I was turning up useless. Then again, Richard didn't seem to care. We drove up to the bluffs anyway, grabbed a six-pack of beer and sat in the sun, watching the Mississippi River glimmer gray like a lazy snake.

This had been one of Marian's favorite places to go when she could leave her bed. For an instant, I could feel the weight of her as a child on my back, her hot giggles in my ears, skinny arms wrapped tight around my shoulders.

"Where would you take a little girl to strangle her?" Richard asked.

"My car or my home," I said, jolting back.

"And to pull out the teeth?"

"Somewhere that I could scrub down well. A basement. A bathtub. The girls were dead first, right?"

"Is that one of your questions?"

"Sure."

"They were both dead."

"Dead long enough there was no blood when the teeth came out?"

A barge floating down the river began turning sideways in the current; men appeared on board with long-poles to twist it back in the right direction.

"With Natalie there was blood. The teeth were removed immediately after the strangling."

I had the image of Natalie Keene, brown eyes frozen open, slumped down in a bathtub as someone pried her teeth from her mouth. Blood on Natalie's chin. A hand on pliers. A woman's hand.

"Do you believe James Capisi?"

"I truly don't know, Camille, and I'm not blowing smoke at you. The kid is scared out of his wits. His mom keeps calling us to put someone on guard. He's sure this woman is going to come get him. I sweated him a little bit, called him a liar, tried to see if he'd change his story. Nothing." He turned to face me. "I'll tell you this: James Capisi believes his story. But I can't see how it can be true. It doesn't fit any kind of profile I've ever heard of. It doesn't feel right to me. Cop's intuition. I mean, you talked to him, what did you think?"

"I agree with you. I wonder if he isn't just freaked out about his mom's cancer and projecting that fear somehow. I don't know. And what about John Keene?"

"Profilewise: right age, in the family of one of the victims, seems maybe too broken up over the whole thing."

"His sister was murdered."

"Right. But . . . I'm a guy and I can tell you teenage boys will sooner kill themselves than cry in public. And he's been weeping it up all over town." Richard blew a hollow toot with his beer bottle, a mating call to a passing tugboat.

The moon was out, the cicadas in full jungle pulse, when Richard dropped me at home. Their creaking matched the throbbing between my legs where I'd let him touch me. Zipper down, his hand guided by mine to my clitoris and held there lest he explore and bump into the raised outlines of my scars. We got each other off like a couple of schoolkids (*dumpling* thumping hard and pink on my left foot as I came) and I was sticky and smelling of sex as I opened the door to find my mother sitting on the bottom stair with a pitcher of amaretto sours.

She was wearing a pink nightgown with girlish puffed sleeves and a satin ribbon around the neckline. Her hands were unnecessarly repacked in that snowy gauze, which she'd managed to keep pristine despite being deeply in her cups. She swayed slightly as I came through the door, like a ghost debating whether to vanish. She stayed.

"Camille. Come sit." She beckoned her cloudy hands toward me. "No! Get a glass first from the back kitchen. You can have a drink with Mother. With your mother."

This should be miserable, I murmured as I grabbed a tumbler. But underneath that, a thought: time alone with *her!* A leftover rattle from childhood. Get that fixed.

My mother poured recklessly but perfect, capping off my glass just before it overflowed. Still, a trick to get it to my mouth without spilling. She smirked a little as she watched me. Leaned back against the newel post, tucked her feet under her, sipped.

"I think I finally realized why I don't love you," she said.

I knew she didn't, but I'd never heard her admit as much. I tried to tell myself I was intrigued, like a scientist on the edge of a breakthrough, but my throat closed up and I had to make myself breathe.

"You remind me of my mother. Joya. Cold and distant and so, so smug. My mother never loved me, either. And if you girls won't love me, I won't love you."

A wave of fury rattled through me. "I never said I didn't love you, that's just ridiculous. Just fucking ridiculous. You were the one who never liked me, even as a kid. I never felt anything but coldness from you, so don't you dare turn this on me." I began rubbing my palm hard on the edge of the stair. My mother gave a half smile at the action and I stopped.

"You were always so willful, never sweet. I remember when you were six or seven. I wanted to put your hair up in curlers for your school picture. Instead you cut it all off with my fabric shears." I didn't remember doing this. I remembered hearing about Ann doing this.

"I don't think so, Momma."

"Headstrong. Like those girls. I tried to be close with those girls, those dead girls."

"What do you mean be close with them?"

"They reminded me of you, running around town wild. Like little pretty animals. I thought if I could be close with them, I would understand you better. If I could like them, maybe I could like you. But I couldn't."

"No, I don't expect so." The grandfather clock chimed eleven. I wonder how many times my mother had heard that growing up in this house.

"When I had you inside of me, when I was a girl — so much younger than you are now — I thought you'd save me. I thought you'd love me. And then my mother would love me. That was a joke." My mother's voice swept high and raw, like a red scarf in a storm.

"I was a baby."

"Even from the beginning you disobeyed, wouldn't eat. Like you were punishing me for being born. Made me look like a fool. Like a child."

"You *were* a child."

"And now you come back and all I can think of is 'Why Marian and not her?'"

Rage flattened immediately into a dark despair. My fingers found a wood staple in the floorboard. I jabbed it under my fingernail. I would not cry for this woman.

"I'm not so pleased to be left here anyway, Momma, if it makes you feel any better."

"You're so hateful."

"I learned at your feet."

My mother lunged then, grabbed me by both arms. Then she reached behind me and, with one fingernail, circled the spot on my back that had no scars.

"The only place you have left," she whispered at me.

Her breath was cloying and musky, like air coming from a spring well.

"Yes."

"Someday I'll carve my name there." She shook me once, released me, then left me on the stairs with the warm remains of our liquor.

I drank the rest of the sours and had dark sticky dreams. My mother had cut me open and was unpacking my organs, stacking them in a row on my bed as my flesh flapped to either side. She was sewing her initials into each of them, then tossing them back into me, along with a passel of forgotten objects: an orange Day-Glo rubber ball I got from a gumball machine when I was ten; a pair of violet wool stockings I wore when I was twelve; a cheap gold-tinted ring a boy bought me when I was a freshman. With each object, relief that it was no longer lost.

When I woke, it was past noon, and I was disoriented and afraid. I took a gulp from my flask of vodka to ease the panic, then ran to the bathroom and threw it up, along with strings of sugary brown saliva from the amaretto sours.

Stripped naked and into the bathtub, the porcelain cool on my back. I lay flat, turned on the water, and let it creep up over me, fill my ears until they submerged with the satisfying *whulp!* of a sinking ship going under. Would I ever have the discipline to let the water cover my face, drown with my eyes open? Just refuse to lift yourself two inches, and it will be done.

The water stung at my eyes, covered my nose, and then enveloped me. I pictured myself from above: lashed skin and a still face flickering under a film of water. My body refused the quiet. *Bodice, dirty, nag, widow!* it screamed. My stomach and throat were convulsing, desperate to pull in air. *Finger, whore, hollow!* A few moments of discipline. What a pure way to die. *Blossom, bloom, bonny.*

I jerked to the surface, gulped in air. Panting, my head tilted toward the ceiling. Easy, easy, I told myself. Easy, sweet girl, you'll be okay. I petted my cheek, baby-talked myself – how pitiful – but my breathing hushed.

Then, a bolt of panic. I reached behind me to find the circle of skin in my back. Still smooth.

Black clouds were sitting low over the town, so the sun curled around the edges and turned everything a sickly yellow, as if we were bugs under fluorescents. Still weak from the encounter with my mother, the feeble glow seemed appropriate. I had an appointment at Meredith Wheeler's for an interview concerning the Keenes. Not sure it would yield much of import but I'd at least get a quote, which I needed, having not heard a word from the Keenes after my last article. Truth was, with John living behind Meredith's house now, I had no way of reaching him except through her. I'm sure she loved that.

I hiked over to Main Street to pick up my car where I'd abandoned it during yesterday's outing with Richard.

Weakly dropped into the driver's seat. I still managed to arrive at Meredith's a half hour early. Knowing the primping and plumping going on in preparation for my visit, I assumed she'd set me out back on the patio, and I'd have a chance to check in on John. As it turned out, she wasn't there at all, but I could hear music from behind the house, and I followed it to see the Four Little Blondes in fluorescent bikinis at one end of the pool, passing a joint between them, and John sitting in the shade at the other end, watching. Amma looked tan and blonde and delicious, not a trace of yesterday's hangover on her. She was as tiny and colorful as an appetizer.

Confronted with all that smooth flesh, I could feel my skin begin its chattering. I couldn't handle direct contact on top of my hangover panic. So I spied from the edge of the house. Anyone could have seen me, but none bothered. Amma's three friends were soon in a marijuana-and-heat spiral, splayed face down on their blankets.

Amma stayed up, staring down John, rubbing suntan oil on her shoulders, her chest, breasts, slipping her hands under her bikini top, watching John watching her. John gave no reaction, like a kid on his sixth hour of TV. The more lasciviously Amma rubbed, the less flicker he gave. One triangle of her top had fallen askew to reveal the plump breast beneath. Thirteen years old, I thought to myself, but I felt a spear of admiration for the girl. When I'd been sad, I hurt myself. Amma hurt other people. When I'd wanted attention, I'd submitted myself to boys: *Do what you want; just like me.* Amma's sexual offerings seemed a form of aggression. Long skinny legs and slim wrists and high, babied voice, all aimed like a gun. *Do what I want; I might like you.*

"Hey John, who do I remind you of?" Amma called.

"A little girl who's misbehaving and thinks it's cuter than it is," John called back. He sat at the pool's edge in shorts and a T-shirt, his feet dipped into the water. His legs had a thin, almost feminine coating of dark hair.

"Really? Why don't you stop watching me from your little hideaway then," she said, pointing a leg toward the carriage house, with its tiny attic window sporting blue checked curtains. "Meredith will be jealous."

"I like to keep an eye on you, Amma. Always know I have my eye on you."

My guess: My half sister had gone into his room without permission, rifled through his things. Or waited for him on his bed.

"You sure do now," she said, laughing, her legs spread wide. She looked gruesome in the dark light, the rays casting pockets of shadows on her face.

"It'll be your turn some day, Amma," he said. "Soon."

"Big man. I hear," Amma called back. Kylie looked up, focused her eyes on her friend, smiled, and lay back down.

"Patient, too."

"You'll need it." She blew him a kiss.

The amaretto sours were turning on me, and I was sick of this banter. I didn't like John Keene flirting with Amma, no matter how provocative she was being. She was still thirteen.

"Hello?" I called out, rousing Amma, who waggled her fingers at me. Two of the three blondes looked up, then lay back down. John cupped some pool water in his hands and rubbed it across his face before turning the corners of his mouth up at me. He was tracing back the conversation, guessing how much I'd heard. I was equidistant from each side, and walked toward John, sat a good six feet away.

"You read the story?" I asked. He nodded.

"Yeah, thanks, it was nice. The part about Natalie at least."

"I'm here to talk a little bit to Meredith today about Wind Gap; maybe Natalie will come up," I said. "Is that okay by you?"

He shrugged his shoulders.

"Sure. She's not home yet. Not enough sugar for the sweet tea. She freaked, ran off to the store without makeup."

"Scandalous."

"For Meredith, yes."

"How are things going here?"

"Oh, all right," he said. He began patting his right hand. Self-comfort. I felt sorry for him again. "I don't know that anything would be any good anywhere, so it's hard to gauge if this is better or worse, you know what I mean?"

"Like: This place is miserable and I want to die, but I can't think of any place I'd rather be," I offered. He turned and stared at me, blue eyes mirroring the oval pool.

"That's exactly what I mean." *Get used to it,* I thought.

"Have you thought about getting some counseling, seeing a therapist?" I said. "It might be really helpful."

"Yeah, John, might quell some of your *urges.* They can be *deadly*, you know? We don't want more little girls showing up without their teeth." Amma had slipped into the pool and was floating ten feet away.

John shot up, and for a second I thought he was going to dive into the pool and throttle her. Instead, he pointed a finger at her, opened his mouth, closed it, and walked to his attic room.

"That was really cruel," I said to her.

"But funny," said Kylie, floating by on a hot pink air mattress.

"What a freak," added Kelsey, paddling past.

Jodes was sitting in her blanket, knees pulled to her chin, eyes trained on the carriage house.

"You were so sweet with me the other night. Now you're so changed," I murmured to Amma. "Why?"

She looked caught off guard for a split second. "I don't know. I wish I could fix it. I do." She swam off toward her friends as Meredith appeared at the door and peevishly called me in.

The Wheelers' home looked familiar: an overstuffed plush sofa, a coffee table hosting a sailboat replica, a jaunty velvet ottoman in lime green, a black-and-white photo of the Eiffel Tower taken at a severe angle. Pottery Barn, spring catalog. Right down to the lemon yellow plates Meredith was now placing on the table, glazed berry tarts sitting in the center.

She was wearing a linen sundress the color of an unripe peach, her hair pulled down over her ears and held at the nape of her neck in a loose ponytail that had to have taken twenty minutes to get that perfect. She looked, suddenly, a lot like my mother. She could have been Adora's child more believably than I. I could feel a grudge coming, tried to keep it in check, as she poured us each a glass of sweet tea and smiled.

"I have no idea what my sister was saying to you, but I can only guess it was hateful or dirty, so I apologize," she said. "Although, I'm sure you know Amma's the real ringleader there." She looked at the tart but seemed disinclined to eat it. Too pretty.

"You probably know Amma better than I do," I said. "She and John don't seem to . . ."

"She's a very needy child," she said, crossing her legs, uncrossing them, straightening her dress. "Amma worries she'll shrivel up and blow away if attention isn't always on her. Especially from boys."

"Why doesn't she like John? She was implying he was the one who hurt Natalie." I took out my tape recorder and pressed the On button, partly because I didn't want to waste time with ego games, and partly because I hoped she'd say something about John worth printing. If he was the prime suspect, at least in Wind Gap minds, I needed comment.

"That's just Amma. She has a mean streak. John likes me and not her, so she attacks him. When she's not trying to steal him away from me. Like that's going to happen."

"It seems a lot of people have been talking, though, saying they think John may have something to do with this. Why do you think that is?"

She shrugged, stuck her lower lip out, watched the tape whir a few seconds.

"You know how it is. He's from out of town. He's smart and worldly and eight times better looking than anyone else around here. People would like it to be him, because then that means this . . . *evilness* didn't come from Wind Gap. It came from outside. Eat your tart."

"Do you believe he's innocent?" I took a bite, the glaze dripping off my lip.

"Of course I do. It's all idle gossip. Just because someone goes for a drive . . . lots of people do that around here. John just had bad timing."

"And what about the family? What can you tell me about either of the girls?"

"They were darling girls, very well behaved and sweet little things. It's like God plucked the best girls from Wind Gap to take to heaven for his own." She'd been practicing, the words had a rehearsed rhythm. Even her smile seemed measured: Too small is stingy, too big is inappropriately pleased. This smile just right. Brave and hopeful, it said.

"Meredith, I know that's not what you thought about the girls."

"Well, what kind of quote do you want?" she snapped.

"A truthful one."

"I can't do that. John would hate me."

"I wouldn't have to name you in the article."

"Then what would be the point of me doing the interview?"

"If you know something about the girls that people aren't saying, you should tell me. It could direct attention away from John, depending on what the information is."

Meredith took a demure sip of tea, dabbed at the corner of her strawberry lips with her napkin.

"But could I still get my name in the article somewhere?"

"I can quote you elsewhere by name."

"I want the stuff about God plucking them to heaven," Meredith baby-talked. She wrung her hands and smiled at me sideways.

"No. Not that. I'll use the quote about John being from out of town and that's why people are so gossipy about him."

"Why can't you use the one I want?" I could see Meredith as a five-year-old, dressed as a princess and bitching because her favorite doll didn't like her imaginary tea.

"Because it goes against a lot of things I've heard, and because no one really talks that way. It sounds fake."

It was the most pathetic showdown I've ever had with a subject, and a completely unethical way to do my work. But I wanted her fucking story. Meredith twirled the silver chain around her neck, studied me.

"You could have been a model, you know?" she said suddenly.

"I doubt that," I snapped. Every time people said I was pretty, I thought of everything ugly swarming beneath my clothes.

"You could have. I always wanted to be you when I grew up. I think about you, you know? I mean, our moms are friends and all, so I knew you were in Chicago and I pictured you in this big mansion with a few little curly tops and some stud husband investment banker. You all in the kitchen drinking orange juice and him getting in his Jag and going to work. But I guess I imagined wrong."

"You did. Sounds nice, though." I took another bite of tart. "So tell me about the girls."

"All business, huh? You never were the friendliest. I know about your sister. That you had a sister who died."

"Meredith, we can talk some time. I'd like that. After this. But let's get this story, and then maybe we can enjoy ourselves." I didn't intend on staying more than a minute after the interview wrapped.

"Okay . . . So, here it is. I think I know why . . . the teeth . . ." she pantomimed extraction.

"Why?"

"I can't believe everyone refuses to acknowledge this," she said.

Meredith glanced around the room.

"You didn't hear this from me, okay?" she continued. "The girls, Ann and Natalie, they were biters."

"What do you mean, biters?"

"Both of them. They had serious tempers. Like scary-time tempers. Like boy tempers. But they didn't hit. They bit. Look."

She held out her right hand. Just below the thumb were three white scars that shone in the afternoon light.

"That's from Natalie. And this." She pulled back her hair to reveal a left ear with only half an earlobe. "My hand she bit when I was painting her fingernails. She decided halfway through that she didn't like it, but I told her to let me finish, and when I held her hand down, she sunk her teeth into me."

"And the earlobe?"

"I stayed over there one night when my car wouldn't start. I was asleep in the guest room and the next thing I knew, blood all over the sheets and my ear just felt like it was on fire, like I wanted to run away from it but it was attached to my head. And Natalie was screaming like *she* was on fire. That screaming was scarier than the biting. Mr. Keene had to hold her down. The kid had serious problems. We looked for my earlobe, see if it could be stitched back on, but it was gone. I guess she swallowed it." She gave a laugh that sounded like the reverse of a gulp of air. "I mostly just felt sorry for her."

Lie.

"Ann, was she as bad?" I asked.

"Worse. There are people all over this town with her teeth marks in them. Your mother included."

"What?" My hands began to sweat and the back of my neck went cold.

"Your mom was tutoring her and Ann didn't understand. She completely lost it, pulled some of your momma's hair out, and bit into her wrist. Hard. I think there had to be stitches." Images of my mother's thin arm caught between tiny teeth, Ann shaking her head like a dog, blood blossoming on my mother's sleeve, on Ann's lips. A scream, a release.

A little circle of jagged lines, and within, a ring of perfect skin.

Chapter Eleven

Phone calls back in my room, no sign of my mother. I could hear Alan downstairs, snapping at Gayla for cutting the filets wrong.

"I know it seems trivial, Gayla, but think of it like this: Trivial details are the difference between a good meal and a dining experience." Gayla emitted an assenting sound. Even her mm-hhmms have a twang.

I phoned Richard on his cell, one of the few people in Wind Gap to own one, though I shouldn't snipe, since I'm one of the only holdouts in Chicago. I just never want to be that reachable.

"Detective Willis." I could hear a loudspeaker calling a name in the background.

"You busy, Detective?" I blushed. Levity felt like flirting felt like foolishness.

"Hi there," came his formal voice. "I'm wrapping things up here; can I give a call back?"

"Sure, I'm at . . ."

"The number shows up on my display."

"Fancy."

"Very true."

Twenty minutes later: "Sorry, I was at the hospital in Woodberry with Vickery."

"A lead?"

"Of sorts."

"A comment?"

"I had a very nice time last night."

I'd written *Richard cop Richard cop* twelve times down my leg, and had to make myself stop because I was itching for a razor.

"Me, too. Look, I need to ask you something straight and I need you to tell me. Off record. Then I need a comment I can print for my next piece."

"Okay, I'll try to help you, Camille. What do you need to ask me?"

"Can we meet at that cheesy bar we first had a drink at? I need to do this in person, and I need to get out of the house and, yes, I'll say it: I need a drink."

Three guys from my class were at Sensors when I got there, nice guys, one of whom had famously won a State Fair blue ribbon for his obscenely big, milk-dripping sow one year. A folksy stereotype Richard would have loved. We exchanged niceties – they bought me my first two rounds – and photographs of their kids, eight in all. One of them, Jason Turnbough, was still as blond and round-faced as a kid. Tongue just peeking out the corner of his mouth, pink cheeks, round blue eyes darting between my face and my breasts for most of the conversation. He stopped once I pulled out my tape recorder and asked about the murders. Then it was those whirling wheels that had his full attention. People got such a charge from seeing their names in print. Proof of existence. I could picture a squabble of ghosts ripping through piles of newspapers. Pointing at a name on the page. *See, there I am. I told you I lived. I told you I was.*

"Who'd have thought when we were kids back in school, we'd be sitting here talking about murders in Wind Gap?" marveled Tommy Ringer, now grown into a dark-haired fellow with a rangy beard.

"I know, I mean I work in a supermarket, for Chrissakes," said Ron Laird, a kindly, mouse-faced guy with a booming voice. The three glowed with misplaced civic pride. Infamy had come to Wind Gap, and they'd take it. They could keep working at the supermarket, the drugstore, the hatchery. When they died, this – along with getting married and having kids – would be on their list of things they'd done. And it was something that merely happened to them. No, more accurately, it was something that happened in their town. I wasn't entirely sure about Meredith's assessment. Some people would love to have the killer be a guy born and raised in Wind Gap. Someone they went fishing with once, someone they were in Cub Scouts with. Makes a better story.

Richard flung open the door, which was surprisingly light for its looks. Any customer who wasn't a regular used too much force, so every few minutes the door banged into the side of the building. It offered an interesting punctuation to conversation.

As he walked in, pitching his jacket over his shoulder, the three men groaned.

"This guy."

"I'm so fucking impressed, dude."

"Save some brain cells for the case, buddy. You need 'em."

I hopped off the stool, licked my lips, and smiled.

"Well fellows, got to go to work. Interview time. Thanks for the drinks."

"We'll be over here when you get bored," Jason called out. Richard just smiled at him, muttering *idiot* through his teeth.

I slugged back my third bourbon, grabbed the waitress to set us up, and once we had our drinks in front of us, I rested my chin on my hands and wondered if I really wanted to talk business. He had a scar just above his right eyebrow and a tiny dimple in his chin. He tapped his foot on top of mine twice, where no one could see.

"So what gives, Scoop?"

"Look, I need to know something. I really need to know it, and if you can't tell me, then you can't tell me, but please think hard." He nodded.

"When you think of the person who did these killings, do you have a specific person in your mind?" I asked.

"I have a few."

"Male or female?"

"Why are you asking me this with such urgency right now, Camille?"

"I just need to know."

He paused, sipped his drink, rubbed his hand over stubble on his chin.

"I don't believe a woman would have done these girls this way." He tapped my foot again. "Hey, what's going on? You tell me the truth now."

"I don't know, I'm just freaking out. I just needed to know where to point my energies."

"Let me help."

"Did you know the girls were known for biting people?"

"I understood from the school there had been an incident involving Ann hurting a neighbor's bird," he said. "Natalie was on a pretty tight leash, though, because of what happened at her last school."

"Natalie bit the earlobe off of someone she knew."

"No. I have no incident reports filed against Natalie since she came here."

"Then they didn't report it. I saw the ear, Richard, there was no lobe, and there was no reason for this person to lie. And Ann attacked someone, too. Bit someone. But I wonder more and more if these girls got tangled up with the wrong person. It's like they were put down. Like a bad animal. Maybe that's why their teeth were taken."

"Let's begin slowly. First, who did each of the girls bite?"

"I can't say."

"Goddam it, Camille, I'm not fucking around. Tell me."

"No." I was surprised at his anger. I'd expected him to laugh and tell me I was pretty when defiant.

"This is a fucking murder case, okay? If you have information, I need it."

"So do your job."

"I'm trying, Camille, but your screwing around with me doesn't help."

"Now you know how it feels," I muttered childishly.

"Fine." He rubbed at his eyes. "I've had a real long day, so . . . good night. I hope I was helpful to you." He stood up, nudged his half-full glass over to me.

"I need an on-record quote."

"Later. I need to get a little perspective. You may have been right about us being a horrible idea." He left, and the guys called me to come back and join them. I shook my head, finished my drink, and pretended to take notes until they left. All I did was write *sick place sick place* over and over for twelve pages.

This time it was Alan waiting for me when I got home. He was sitting on the Victorian love seat, white brocade and black walnut, dressed in white slacks and a silk shirt, dainty white silk slippers on his feet. If he'd been in a photograph, it would be impossible to place him in time – Victorian gentleman, Edwardian dandy, '50s fop? Twenty-first-century househusband who never worked, often drank, and occasionally made love to my mother.

Very rarely did Alan and I talk outside of my mother's presence. As a child, I'd once bumped into him in the hallway, and he'd bent down stiffly, to my eye level, and said, "Hello, I hope you're well." We'd been living in the same house for more than five years, and that's all he could come up with. "Yes, thank you," was all I could give in return.

Now, though, Alan seemed ready to take me on. He didn't say my name, just patted the couch beside him. On his knee he balanced a cake plate with several large silvery sardines. I could smell them from the entryway.

"Camille," he said, picking at a tail with a tiny fish fork, "you're making your mother ill. I'm going to have to ask you to leave if conditions don't improve."

"How am I making her ill?"

"By tormenting her. By constantly bringing up Marian. You can't speculate to the mother of a dead child how that child's body might look in the ground right now. I don't know if that's something you can feel detached from, but Adora can't." A glob of fish tumbled down his front, leaving a row of greasy stains the size of buttons.

"You can't talk to her about the corpses of these two dead little girls, or how much blood must have come out of their mouths when their teeth were pulled, or how long it took for a person to strangle them."

"Alan, I never said any of those things to my mother. Nothing even close. I truly have no idea what she's talking about." I didn't even feel indignant, just weary.

"Please, Camille, I know how strained your relationship is with your mother. I know how jealous you've always been of anyone else's well-being. It's true, you know, you really are like Adora's mother. She'd stand guard over this house like a . . . witch, old and angry. Laughter offended her. The only time she ever smiled was when you refused to nurse from Adora. Refused to take the nipple."

That word on Alan's oily lips lit me up in ten different places. *Suck, bitch, rubber* all caught fire.

"And you know this from Adora," I prompted.

He nodded, lips pursed beatifically.

"Like you know that I said horrible things about Marian and the dead girls from Adora."

"Exactly," he said, the syllables precisely cut.

"Adora is a liar. If you don't know that, you're an idiot."

"Adora's had a hard life."

I forced out a laugh. Alan was undaunted. "Her mother used to come into her room in the middle of the night and pinch her when she was a child," he said, eyeing the last slab of sardine pitifully. "She said it was because she was worried Adora would die in her sleep. I think it was because she just liked to hurt her."

A jangle of memory: Marian down the hall in her pulsing, machine-filled invalid's room. A sharp pain on my arm. My mother standing over me in her cloudy nightgown, asking if I was okay. Kissing the pink circle and telling me to go back to sleep.

"I just think you should know these things," Alan said. "Might make you be a bit kinder to your mother."

I had no plans for being kinder to my mother. I just wanted the conversation to end. "I'll try to leave as soon as I can."

"Be a good idea, if you can't make amends," Alan said. "But you might feel better about yourself if you tried. Might help you heal. Your mind at least."

Alan grabbed the last floppy sardine and sucked it into his mouth whole. I could picture the tiny bones snapping as he chewed.

A tumbler full of ice and an entire bottle of bourbon purloined from the back kitchen, then up to my room to drink. The booze hit me fast, probably because that was how I was drinking it. My ears were hot and my skin had stopped its blinking. I thought about that word at the back of my neck. *Vanish. Vanish* will banish my woes, I thought loopily. *Vanish* will banish my troubles. Would we have been this ugly if Marian hadn't died? Other families got over such things. Grieve and move on. She still hovered over us, a blonde baby girl maybe a hair too cute for her own good, maybe just a bit too doted on. This before she got sick, really sick. She had an invisible friend, a giant stuffed bear she called Ben. What kind of kid has an imaginary friend that's a stuffed animal? She collected hair ribbons and arranged them in alphabetical order by color name. She was the kind of girl who exploited her cuteness with such joy you couldn't begrudge her. Batting of the eyes, tossings of the curls. She called my mother Mudder and Alan . . . hell, maybe she called Alan Alan, I can't place him in the room in these memories. She always cleaned her plate, kept a remarkably tidy room, and refused to wear anything but dresses and Mary Janes.

She called me Mille and she couldn't keep her hands off me.

I adored her.

Drunk but still drinking, I took a tumbler of liquor and crept down the hallway to Marian's room. Amma's door, just one room down, had been closed for hours. What was it like growing up next to the room of a dead sister you never met? I felt a pang of sorrow for Amma. Alan and my mother were in their big corner bedroom, but the light was out and the fan whirring. No such thing as central air in these old Victorians, and my mother finds room units tacky, so we sweat the summers out. Ninety degrees but the heat made me feel safe, like walking underwater.

The pillow on her bed still had a small indentation. A set of clothes was laid out as if covering a living child. Violet dress, white tights, shiny black shoes. Who'd done that – my mother? Amma? The IV stand that had tailed Marian so relentlessly in her last year was standing, alert and shiny, next to the rest of the medical equipment: the bed that was two feet taller than standard, to allow patient access; the heart monitor; the bedpan. I was disgusted my mother hadn't purged this stuff. It was a clinical and utterly lifeless room. Marian's favorite doll had been buried with her, a massive rag doll with blonde yarn curls to match my sister's. Evelyn. Or Eleanor? The rest were lined against the wall on a set of stands, like fans in bleachers. Twenty or so with white china faces and deep glassy eyes.

I could see her so easily here, sitting cross-legged on

that bed, small and sweat dotted, her eyes ringed with purple. Shuffling cards or combing her doll's hair or coloring angrily. I could hear that sound: a crayon running in hard lines across a paper. Dark scribbles with the crayon pushed so hard it ripped the paper. She looked up at me, breathing hard and shallow.

"I'm tired of dying."

I skitted back to my room as if I were being chased.

The phone rang six times before Eileen picked up. Things the Currys don't have in their home: a microwave, a VCR, a dishwasher, an answering machine. Her hello was smooth but tense. Guess they don't get many calls after eleven. She pretended they hadn't been asleep, that they simply hadn't heard the phone, but it took another two minutes to get Curry on the line. I pictured him, shining his glasses on the corner of pajamas, putting on old leather slippers, looking at the glowing face of an alarm clock. A soothing image.

Then I realized I was remembering a commercial for an all-night pharmacy in Chicago.

It had been three days since I'd last talked to Curry. Nearly two weeks since I'd been in Wind Gap. Any other circumstance and he'd have been phoning me three times a day for updates. But he couldn't bring himself to ring me at a civilian's, at my mother's house no less, down in Missouri, which in his Windy City mind he equated with the Deep South. Any other circumstances and he'd be rumbling into the phone at me for not staying in pocket, but not tonight.

"Cubby, you okay? What's the story?"

"Well, I haven't gotten this on record, but I will. The police definitely think the killer is male, definitely from Wind Gap, and they have no DNA, no kill site; they really have very little. Either the killer is a mastermind or an accidental genius. The town seems to be focusing on Natalie Keene's brother, John. I have his girlfriend on record protesting his innocence."

"Good, good stuff, but I really meant . . . I was asking about you. You doing okay down there? You have to tell me, because I can't see your face. Don't do the stoic thing."

"I'm not so good, but what does that matter?" My voice came out higher and more bitter than I'd planned. "This is a good story, and I think I'm on the edge of something. I feel like another few days, a week, and . . . I don't know. The little girls bit people. That's what I got today, and the cop I've been working with, he didn't even know."

"You told him that? What was his comment?"

"Nothing."

"Why the hell didn't you get a comment, girl?"

See, Curry, Detective Willis felt I was holding back some information and so he sulked off, like all men do when they don't get their way with women they've fooled around with.

"I screwed up. I'll get it, though. I need a few more days before I file, Curry. Get a little more local color, work on this cop. I think they're almost convinced a little press would help juice things. Not that anyone reads our paper down here." Or up there.

"They will. You'll get some serious notice for this, Cubby. Your stuff is getting close to good. Push harder. Go talk to some of your old friends. They might be more open. Plus it's good for the piece – that Texas floods series that won the Pulitzer had a whole story on the guy's perspective about coming home during a tragedy. Great read. And a friendly face, a few beers might do you good. Sounds like you've already had a few tonight?"

"A few."

"Are you feeling . . . like this is a bad situation for you? With the recovery?" I heard a lighter strike, the scratch of a kitchen chair across linoleum, a grunt as Curry sat down.

"Oh, it's not for you to worry about."

"Of course it is. Don't play martyr, Cubby. I'm not going to penalize you if you need to leave. You've got to take care of yourself. I thought being home might do you good, but . . . I forget sometimes parents aren't always . . . good for their kids."

"Whenever I'm here," I stopped, tried to pull it together. "I just always feel like I'm a bad person when I'm here." Then I started crying, silent sobbing as Curry stammered on the other end. I could picture him panicking, waving Eileen over to handle this weeping *girl*. But no.

"Ohhh, Camille," he whispered. "You are one of the most decent people I know. And there aren't that many decent people in this world, you know? With my folks gone, it's basically you and Eileen."

"I'm not decent." The tip of my pen was scribbling deep, scratchy words into my thigh. *Wrong, woman, teeth.*

"Camille, you are. I see how you treat people, even the most worthless pieces of crap I can think of. You give them some . . . dignity. Understanding. Why do you think I keep you around? Not because you're a great reporter." Silence and thick tears on my end. *Wrong, woman, teeth.*

"Was that funny at all? I meant it to be funny."

"No."

"My grandfather was in vaudeville. But I guess that gene missed me."

"He was?"

"Oh yeah, straight off the boat from Ireland in New York City. He was a hilarious guy, played four instruments. . . ." Another spark of a lighter. I pulled the thin covers up over me and closed my eyes, listened to Curry's story.

Chapter Twelve

Richard was living in Wind Gap's only apartment building, an industrial box built to house four tenants. Only two apartments were filled. The stumpy columns holding up the carport had been spray painted red, four in a row, reading: "Stop the Democrats, Stop the Democrats, Stop the Democrats," then, randomly, "I like Louie."

Wednesday morning. The storm still sitting in a cloud above town. Hot and windy, piss-yellow light. I banged on his door with the corner of a bourbon bottle. Bear gifts if you can't bear anything else. I'd stopped wearing skirts. Makes my legs too accessible to someone prone to touching. If he was anymore.

He opened the door smelling of sleep. Tousled hair, boxers, a T-shirt inside out. No smile. He kept the place frigid. I could feel the air from where I was standing.

"You want to come in, or you want me to come out?" he asked, scratching his chin. Then he spotted the bottle. "Ah, come in. I guess we're getting drunk?"

The place was a mess, which surprised me. Pants strewn over chairs, a garbage can near overflowing, boxes of papers piled up in awkward spots in the hallways, forcing you to turn sideways to pass. He motioned me to a cracked leather sofa and returned with a tray of ice and two glasses. Poured fat portions.

"So, I shouldn't have been so rude last night," he said.

"Yeah. I mean, I feel like I'm giving you a fair amount of information, and you're not giving me any."

"I'm trying to solve a murder. You're trying to report about that. I think I get priority. There are certain things, Camille, that I'm just not able to tell you."

"And vice versa – I have a right to protect my sources."

"Which in turn could help protect the person doing these killings."

"You can figure it out, Richard. I gave you almost everything. Jeez, do a little work on your own." We stared at each other.

"I love it when you get all tough reporter on me." Richard smiled. Shook his head. Poked me with his bare foot. "I actually really kind of do."

He poured us each another glass. We'd be smashed before noon. He pulled me to him, kissed me on my lobe, stuck his tongue in my ear.

"So Wind Gap girl, how bad exactly were you?" he whispered. "Tell me about the first time you did it." The first time was the second time was the third was the fourth, thanks to my eighth-grade encounter. I decided to leave it at the first.

"I was sixteen," I lied. Older seemed more appropriate

for the mood. "I fucked a football player in the bathroom at this party."

My tolerance was better than Richard's, he was already looking glazed, twirling a finger around my nipple, hard beneath my shirt.

"Mmmm . . . did you come?"

I nodded. I remember pretending to come. I remember a murmur of an orgasm, but that wasn't until they'd passed me over to the third guy. I remember thinking it was sweet that he kept panting in my ear, "Is this all right? Is this all right?"

"Do you want to come now? With me?" Richard whispered.

I nodded and he was on me. Those hands everywhere, trying to go up my shirt, then struggling to unbutton my pants, tug them down.

"Hold on, hold on. My way," I whispered. "I like it with my clothes on."

"No. I want to touch you."

"No, baby, my way."

I pulled my pants down just a little bit, kept my stomach covered with my shirt, kept him distracted with well-placed kisses. Then I guided him into me and we fucked, fully clothed, the crack on the leather couch scratching my ass. *Trash, pump, little, girl.* It was the first time I'd been with a man in ten years. *Trash, pump, little, girl!* His groaning was soon louder than my skin. Only then could I enjoy it. Those last few sweet thrusts.

He lay half beside me, half on top of me and panted

when it was done, still holding the neck of my shirt in his fist. The day had gone black. We were trembling on the edge of a thunderstorm.

"Tell me who you think did it," I said. He looked shocked. Was he expecting "I love you"? He twirled my hair for a minute, poked his tongue in my ear. When denied access to other body parts, men become fixated on the ear. Something I'd learned in the last decade. He couldn't touch my breasts or my ass, my arms or my legs, but Richard seemed content, for now, with my ear.

"Between you and me, it's John Keene. The kid was very close to his sister. In an unhealthy way. He has no alibi. I think he's got a thing for little girls that he's trying to fight, ends up killing them and pulling the teeth for a thrill. He won't be able to hold out much longer, though. This is going to accelerate. We're checking for any weird behavior back in Philly. Could be Natalie's problems weren't the only reason they moved."

"I need something on record."

"Who told you about the biting, and who did the girls bite?" he whispered hot in my ear. Outside, the rain began hitting the pavement like someone pissing.

"Meredith Wheeler told me Natalie bit her earlobe off."

"What else?"

"Ann bit my mother. On her wrist. That's it."

"See, that wasn't so hard. Good girl," he whispered, stroking my nipple again.

"Now give me something on record."

"No." He smiled at me. "My way."

Richard fucked me another time that afternoon, finally gave me a grudging quote about a break in the case, and an arrest likely. I left him asleep in his bed and ran through the rain to my car. A random thought clanged in my head: Amma would have gotten more from him.

I drove to Garrett Park and sat in my car staring at the rain, because I didn't want to go home. Tomorrow this spot would be filled with kids beginning their long, lazy summer. Now it was just me, feeling sticky and stupid. I couldn't decide if I'd been mistreated. By Richard, by those boys who took my virginity, by anyone. I was never really on my side in any argument. I liked the Old Testament spitefulness of the phrase *got what she deserved*. Sometimes women do.

Silence and then not. The yellow IROC rumbled up next to me, Amma and Kylie sharing the front passenger's seat. A scraggly haired boy wearing gas-station shades and a stained undershirt was in the driver's seat; his skinny doppelgänger in back. Smoke rolled out of the car, along with the smell of citrus-flavored liquor.

"Get in, we're going to party a little," Amma said. She was proffering a bottle of cheap orange-flavored vodka. She stuck her tongue out and let a raindrop splash on it. Her hair and tank top were already dripping.

"I'm fine, thanks."

"You don't look it. Come on, they're patrolling the park. You'll get a DUI for sure. I can *smell* you."

"Come on, chiquita," Kylie called. "You can help us keep these boys in line."

I thought about my options: Go home, drink by myself. Go to a bar, drink with whatever guys floated over. Go with these kids, maybe hear some interesting gossip at the very least. An hour. Then home to sleep it off. Plus, there was Amma and her mysterious friendliness toward me. I hated to admit it, but I was becoming obsessed with the girl.

The kids cheered as I got in the backseat. Amma passed around a different bottle, hot rum that tasted like suntan lotion. I worried they'd ask me to buy them liquor. Not because I wouldn't. Pathetically, I wanted them to just want me along. Like I was popular once again. Not a freak. Approved of by the coolest girl in school. The thought was almost enough to make me jump out of the car and walk home. But then Amma passed the bottle again. The rim was ringed with pink lip gloss.

The boy next to me, introduced only as Nolan, nodded and wiped sweat off his upper lip. Skinny arms with scabs and a face full of acne. Meth. Missouri is the second-most addicted state in the Union. We get bored down here, and we have a lot of farm chemicals. When I grew up, it was mostly the hard cores that did it. Now it was a party drug. Nolan was running his finger up and down the vinyl ribbing of the driver's seat in front of him, but he looked up at me long enough to say, "You're like my mom's age. I like it."

"I doubt I'm quite your mom's age."

"She's like, thirty-three, thirty-four?" Close enough.

"What's her name?"

"Casey Rayburn." I knew her. Few years older than me. Factory side. Too much hair gel and a fondness for the Mexican chicken killers down on the Arkansas border. During a church retreat, she told her group she'd tried to commit suicide. The girls at school started calling her Casey Razor.

"Must have been before my time," I said.

"Dude, this chick was too cool to hang with your druggie whore momma," the driver said.

"Fuck you," Nolan whispered.

"Camille, look what we got," Amma leaned over the passenger's seat, so her rear was bumping Kylie's face. She shook a bottle of pills at me. "OxyContin. Makes you feel real good." She stuck out her tongue and placed three in a row like white buttons, then chewed and swallowed with a gulp of vodka. "Try."

"No thanks, Amma." OxyContin is good stuff. Doing it with your kid sister isn't.

"Oh, come on, Mille, just one," she wheedled. "You'll feel lighter. I feel so happy and good right now. You have to, too."

"I feel fine, Amma." Her calling me Mille took me back to Marian. "I promise."

She turned back around and sighed, looking irretrievably glum.

"Come on, Amma, you can't care that much," I said, touching her shoulder.

"I did." I couldn't take it, I was losing ground, feeling that dangerous need to please, just like the old days.

And really, one wasn't going to kill me.

"Okay, okay, give me one. One."

She immediately brightened and flung herself back to face me.

"Put out your tongue. Like communion. Drug communion."

I put out my tongue and she set the pill on the tip, and squealed.

"Good girl." She smiled. I was getting tired of that phrase today.

We pulled up outside one of Wind Gap's great old Victorian mansions, completely renovated and repainted in ludicrous blues and pinks and greens that were supposed to be funky. Instead the place looked like the home of a mad ice-cream man. A boy with no shirt was throwing up in the bushes to the side of the house, two kids were wrestling in what was left of a flower garden, and a young couple was in full spider embrace on a child's swing. Nolan was abandoned in the car, still running his fingers up and down that piping. The driver, Damon, locked him in "so no one fucks with him." I found it a charming gesture.

Thanks to the OxyContin, I was feeling quite game, and as we walked into the mansion, I caught myself looking for faces from my youth: boys in buzz cuts and letter jackets, girls with spiral perms and chunky gold earrings. The smell of Drakkar Noir and Georgio.

All gone. The boys here were babies in loose skater shorts and sneakers, the girls in halters and mini skirts and belly rings, and they were all staring at me as if I might be a cop. *No, but I fucked one this afternoon.* I smiled and nodded. *I am terribly chipper,* I thought mindlessly.

In the cavernous dining room, the table had been pushed to one side to make room for dancing and coolers. Amma bopped into the circle, grinded against a boy until the back of his neck turned red. She whispered into his ear, and with his nod, opened up a cooler and plucked out four beers, which she held against her wet bosom, pretending to have a hard time juggling them as she jiggled past an appreciative group of boys.

The girls were less so. I could see the sniping zip through the party like a line of firecrackers. But the little blondes had two things going for them. First, they were with the local drug dealer, who was sure to swing some clout. Second, they were prettier than almost any other female there, which meant the boys would refuse to boot them. And this party was hosted by a boy, as I could tell by the photos on the living-room mantel, a dark-haired kid, blandly handsome, posing in cap and gown for his senior photo; nearby, a shot of his proud father and mother. I knew Mom: She was the older sister of one of my high-school friends. The idea that I was at her child's party gave me my first wave of nerves.

"Ohmigodohmigodohmigod." A brunette with frog-eyes and a T-shirt proudly blaring *The Gap* ran past us and grabbed a similarly amphibious-looking girl. "They came. They totally came."

"Shit," replied her friend. "This is too good. Do we say hello?"

"I think we wait and see what happens. If J.C. doesn't want them here, then we got to stay out of it."

"Totally."

I knew before I saw him. Meredith Wheeler entered the living room, tugging John Keene behind. A few guys gave him nods, a few offered pats on the shoulder. Others pointedly turned their backs and closed their circles. Neither John nor Meredith noticed me, for which I was relieved. Meredith spotted a circle of skinny bow-legged girls, fellow cheerleaders, I assumed, standing at the door of the kitchen. She squealed and hopped over to them, stranding John in the living room. The girls were even chillier than the guys had been. "Hiiiii," said one without smiling. "I thought you said you weren't coming."

"I decided that was just stupid. Anyone with a brain knows John's cool. We're not going to be fucking outcasts just because of all this . . . crap."

"It's not cool, Meredith. J.C. is not cool with this," said a redhead who was either J.C.'s girlfriend or wanted to be.

"I'll talk to him," Meredith whined. "Let me talk to him."

"I think you should just go."

"Did they really take John's clothes?" asked a third tiny girl who had a maternal air about her. The one who ended up holding hair while her friends threw up.

"Yes, but that's to completely *eliminate* him. It's not because he's in trouble."

"Whatever," said the redhead. I hated her.

Meredith scanned the room for more friendly faces and spotted me, looked confused, spotted Kelsey, looked furious.

Leaving John by the door, pretending to check his watch, tie his shoe, look nonchalant as the crowds kicked into full scandal buzz, she strode over to us.

"What are you doing here?" Her eyes were full of tears, beads of sweat on her forehead. The question seemed to be addressed to neither of us. Maybe she was asking herself.

"Damon brought us," Amma chirped. She hopped twice on the tips of her feet. "I can't believe *you're* here. And I definitely can't believe *he's* showing his face."

"God, you're such a little bitch. You know nothing, you fucking druggie fucker." Meredith's voice was quivering, like a top twirling toward the edge of a table.

"Better than what you're fucking," Amma said. "Hiiii, murderer." She waved at John, who seemed to notice her for the first time and suddenly looked like he'd been smacked.

He was about to walk over when J.C. appeared from another room and took John aside. Two tall boys discussing death and house parties. The room tuned to a low whisper, watching. J.C. patted John on the back, in a way that aimed him directly for the door. John nodded to Meredith and headed out. She followed quickly, her head bowed, hands up to her face. Just before John made it to the door, some boy blurted in a high teasing voice, "Babykiller!" Nervous laughs and eye rolling. Meredith screeched once, wildly, turned around, teeth bared, yelled, "Fuck y'all" and slammed the door.

The same boy mimicked it for the crowd, a coy, girlish *Fuck y'all*, jutting his hip out to one side. J.C. turned the music back up, a teenage girl's synthesized pop voice teasing about blow jobs.

I wanted to follow John and just put my arms around him. I'd never seen anyone look so lonesome, and Meredith seemed unlikely to be of solace. What would he do, back by himself in that empty carriage house? Before I could run after him, Amma grabbed my hand and pulled me upstairs to "The VIP Room," where she and the blondes and two high-school boys with matching shaved heads rifled through J.C.'s mom's closet, flinging her best clothes off the hangers to make a nest. They clambered on the bed in the circle of satin and furs, Amma pulling me next to her and producing a button of Ecstasy from her bra.

"You ever played a game of Rolling Roulette?" she asked me. I shook my head. "You pass the X around from tongue to tongue, and the tongue it dissolves on last is the lucky winner. This is Damon's best shit, though, so we'll all roll a little."

"No thanks, I'm good," I said. I'd almost agreed until I saw the alarmed look on the boys' faces. I must have reminded them of their mothers.

"Oh, come on, Camille, I won't tell, for Chrissakes," Amma whined, picking at a fingernail. "Do it with me. Sisters?"

"Pleeease, Camille!" moaned Kylie and Kelsey. Jodes watched me silently.

The OxyContin and the booze and the sex from earlier and the storm that still hung wet outside and my wrecked skin (*icebox* popping eagerly on one arm) and the stained thoughts of my mother. I don't know which hit hardest but suddenly I was allowing Amma to kiss my cheek excitedly. I was nodding yes, and Kylie's tongue hit one boy, who nervously passed the pill to Kelsey, who licked the second boy, his tongue big as a wolf's, who slopped over Jodes, who wobbled her tongue hesitantly out to Amma – who lapped the pill up, and, tongue soft and little and hot, passed the X into my mouth, wrapping her arms around me and pushing the pill down hard on my tongue until I could feel it crumble in my mouth. It dissolved like cotton candy.

"Drink lots of water," she whispered to me, then giggled loudly at the circle, flinging herself back on a mink.

"Fuck, Amma, the game hadn't even started," the wolf boy snapped, his cheeks flushed red.

"Camille is my guest," Amma said mock haughtily. "Plus, she could use a little sunshine. She's had a pretty shitty life. We have a dead sister just like John Keene. She's never dealt with it." She announced it as if she were helping break the ice between cocktail party guests: *David owns his own dry-goods store, James just returned from an assignment in France, and, oh, yes, Camille has never gotten over her dead sister. Can I refresh anyone's drink?*

"I've got to go," I said, standing too abruptly, a red satin halter clinging to my backside. I had about fifteen minutes till I really started rolling, and this wasn't where

I wanted to be when it happened. Again, though, the problem: Richard, while a drinker, wasn't likely to condone anything more serious, and I sure as hell didn't want to sit in my steamy bedroom, alone and high, listening for my mother.

"Come with me," Amma offered. She slipped a hand into her overpadded bra and pulled a pill from its lining, popping it in her mouth and smiling huge and cruel at the rest of the kids, who looked hopeful but daunted. None for them.

"We'll go swimming, Mille, it'll feel so outrageous when we start rolling," she grinned, flashing perfect square white teeth. I had no fight left – it seemed easier to go along. We were down the stairs, into the kitchen (peach-faced young boys assessing us with confusion – one a shade too young, one definitely too old). We were grabbing bottled water from the icebox (that word suddenly panting again on my skin, like a puppy spotting a bigger dog), which was jammed with juices and casseroles, fresh fruit and white bread, and I was suddenly touched by this innocent, healthy family refrigerator, so oblivious to the debauchery occurring elsewhere in the house.

"Let's go, I'm so excited to swim," Amma declared wildly, pulling at my arm like a child. Which she was. *I am doing drugs with my thirteen-year-old sister,* I whispered to myself. But a good ten minutes had passed, and the idea brought only a flutter of happiness. She was a fun girl, my little sister, the most popular girl in Wind Gap, and she wanted to hang out with me. *She loves me like*

Marian did. I smiled. The X had released its first wave of chemical optimism, I could feel it float up inside me like a big test balloon and splatter on the roof of my mouth, spraying good cheer. I could almost taste it, like a fizzy pink jelly.

Kelsey and Kylie began following us to the door, and Amma swung around laughing. "I don't want you guys to come," she cackled. "You guys get to stay here. Help Jodes get laid, she needs a good fuck."

Kelsey scowled back at Jodes, who hung nervously on the stairs. Kylie looked at Amma's arm around my waist. They glanced at each other. Kelsey snuggled into Amma, put her head on her shoulder.

"We don't want to stay here, we want to come with you," she whined. "Please."

Amma shrugged her away, smiled at her like she was a dumb pony.

"Just be a sweetie and fuck off, okay?" Amma said. "I'm so tired of all of you. You're such bores."

Kelsey hung back, confused, her arms still half outstretched. Kylie shrugged at her and danced back into the crowd, grabbing a beer from an older boy's hands and licking her lips at him – looking back over to see if Amma was watching. She wasn't.

Instead, Amma was steering me out the door like an attentive date, down the stairs and onto the sidewalk, where tiny yellow oxalis weeds spurted from the cracks.

I pointed. "Beautiful."

Amma pointed at me and nodded. "I love yellow when I'm high. You feeling something?" I nodded back, her face flicking on and off as we walked past street-lamps, swimming forgotten, on autopilot in the direction of Adora's. I could feel the night hanging on me like a soft, damp bedgown and I had a flash of the Illinois hospital, me waking up wet with sweat, a desperate whistle in my ear. My roommate, the cheerleader, on the floor purple and twitching, the bottle of Windex next to her. A comedic squeaking sound. Postmortem gas. A burst of shocked laughter from me, here now, in Wind Gap, echoing the one I'd loosed in that miserable room in the pale yellow morning.

Amma put her hand in mine. "What do you think of . . . Adora?"

I felt my high wobble, then regain its spin.

"I think she's a very unhappy woman," I said. "And troubled."

"I hear her calling out names when she takes her naps: Joya, Marian . . . you."

"Glad I don't have to hear that," I said, patting Amma's hand. "But I'm sorry you do."

"She likes to take care of me."

"Great."

"It's weird," Amma said. "After she takes care of me, I like to have sex."

She flipped up her skirt from behind, flashed me a hot pink thong.

"I don't think you should let boys do things to you, Amma. Because that's what it is. It's not reciprocal at your age."

"Sometimes if you let people do things to you,

you're really doing it to them," Amma said, pulling another Blow Pop from her pocket. Cherry. "Know what I mean? If someone wants to do fucked-up things to you, and you let them, you're making them more fucked up. Then you have the control. As long as you don't go crazy."

"Amma, I just . . ." But she was already burbling ahead.

"I like our house," Amma interrupted. "I like her room. The floor is famous. I saw it in a magazine one time. They called it 'The Ivory Toast: Southern Living from a Bygone Time.' Because now of course you can't get ivory. Too bad. Really too bad."

She stuck the sucker in her mouth and snatched a firefly from the air, held it between two fingers and ripped out its back end. Wiped the light around her finger to make a glowing ring. She dropped the dying bug into the grass and admired her hand.

"Did girls like you growing up?" she asked. "Because they're definitely not nice to me."

I tried to reconcile the idea of Amma, brash, bossy, sometimes scary (stepping on my heels at the park – what kind of thirteen-year-old taunts adults like that?) with a girl to whom anyone was openly rude. She saw my look and read my thoughts.

"I don't mean not *nice* to me, actually. They do whatever I tell them. But they don't like me. The second I fuck up, the second I do something uncool, they'll be the first to gang up against me. Sometimes I sit in my room before bed and I write down every single thing I did and said that day. Then I grade it, A for a perfect move, F for I should kill myself I'm such a loser."

When I was in high school, I kept a log of every outfit I wore each day. No repeating until a month went by.

"Like tonight, Dave Rard, who's a very hot junior, told me he didn't know if he could wait a year, you know, to get with me, like until I was in high school? And I said, 'So don't.' And walked away, and all the guys were like, 'Awwwww.' So that's an A. But yesterday, I tripped on Main Street in front of the girls and they laughed. That's an F. Maybe a D, because I was so mean to them the rest of the day Kelsey and Kylie both cried. And Jodes always cries so it's not really a challenge."

"Safer to be feared than loved," I said.

"Machiavelli," she crowed, and skipped ahead laughing – whether in a mocking gesture of her age or genuine youthful energy, I couldn't tell.

"How do you know that?" I was impressed, and liking her more every minute. A smart, fucked-up little girl. Sounded familiar.

"I know tons of things I shouldn't know," she said, and I began skipping alongside her. The X had me wired, and while I was aware that under sober circumstances I wouldn't be doing it, I was too happy to care. My muscles were singing.

"I'm actually smarter than most of my teachers. I took an IQ test. I'm supposed to be in tenth grade, but Adora thinks I need to be with kids my age. Whatever. I'm going away for high school. To New

England."

She said it with the slight wonder of someone who knew the region only through photos, of a girl harboring Ivy League–sponsored images: *New England's where the smart people go.* Not that I should judge, I've never been there either.

"I've got to get out of here," Amma said with the exhausted affectation of a pampered housewife. "I'm bored all the time. That's why I act out. I know I can be a little . . . off."

"With the sex you mean?" I stopped, my heart making rumba thumps in my chest. The air smelled of irises, and I could feel the scent float into my nose, my lungs, my blood. My veins would smell of purple.

"Just, you know, lashing out. You know. I *know* you know." She took my hand and offered me a pure, sweet smile, petting my palm, which might have felt better than any touch I'd ever experienced. On my left calf *freak* sighed suddenly.

"How do you lash out?" We were near my mother's house now, and my high was in full bloom. My hair swished on my shoulders like warm water and I swayed side to side to no particular music. A snail shell lay on the edge of the sidewalk and my eyes looped into its curlicue.

"You know. You know how sometimes you need to hurt."

She said it as if she were selling a new hair product.

"There are better ways to deal with boredom and claustrophobia than to hurt," I said. "You're a smart girl, you know that."

I realized her fingers were inside the cuffs of my shirt, touching the ridges of my scars. I didn't stop her.

"Do you cut, Amma?"

"I hurt," she squealed, and twirled out onto the street, spinning flamboyantly, her head back, her arms outstretched like a swan. "I love it!" she screamed. The echo ran down the street, where my mother's house stood watch on the corner.

Amma spun until she clattered to the pavement, one of her silver bangle bracelets dislodging and rolling down the street drunkenly.

I wanted to talk to her about this, be the grown-up, but the X swooped me up again, and instead I grabbed her from the street (laughing, her elbow split open and bleeding) and we swung each other in circles on the way to our mother's house. Her face was split in two with her smile, her teeth wet and long, and I realized how entrancing they might be to a killer. Square blocks of shiny bone, the front ones like mosaic tiles you might press into a table.

"I'm so happy with you," Amma laughed, her breath hot and sweetly boozy in my face. "You're like my soul mate."

"You're like my sister," I said. Blasphemy? Didn't care.

"I love you," Amma screamed.

We were spinning so fast my cheeks were flapping, tickling me. I was laughing like a kid. *I have never been happier than right now*, I thought. The streetlight was almost rosy, and Amma's long hair was feathering my shoulders, her high cheekbones jutted out like scoops of butter in her tanned skin. I reached out to touch one, releasing my hand from hers, and the unlinking of our circle caused us to spin wildly to the ground.

I felt my ankle bone crack against the curb – pop! – blood exploding, splattering up my leg. Red bubbles began sprouting onto Amma's chest from her own skid across the pavement. She looked down, looked at me, all glowing blue husky eyes, ran her fingers across the bloody web on her chest and shrieked once, long, then lay her head on my lap laughing.

She swiped a finger across her chest, balancing a flat button of blood on her fingertip, and before I could stop her, rubbed it on my lips. I could taste it, like honeyed tin. She looked up at me and stroked my face, and I let her.

"I know you think Adora likes me better, but it's not true," she said. As if on cue, the porch light of our house, way atop the hill, switched on.

"You want to sleep in my room?" Amma offered, a little quieter.

I pictured us in her bed under her polka-dot covers, whispering secrets, falling asleep tangled with each other, and then I realized I was imagining me and Marian. She, escaped from her hospital bed, asleep next to me. The hot purring sounds she made as she curled into my belly. I'd have to sneak her back to her room before my mother woke in the morning. High drama in a quiet house, those five seconds, pulling her down the hallway, near my mother's room, fearing the door might swing open right then, yet almost hoping. *She's not sick, Momma.* It's what I planned on yelling if we were ever caught. *It's okay she's out of bed because she's not really sick.* I'd forgotten how desperately, positively I believed it.

Thanks to the drugs, however, these were only happy recollections now, flipping past my brain like pages of a child's storybook. Marian took on a bunnylike aura in these memories, a little cottontail dressed as my sister. I was almost feeling her fur when I roused myself to discover Amma's hair brushing up and down my leg.

"So, wanna?" she asked.

"Not tonight, Amma. I'm dead tired and I want to sleep in my own bed." It was true. The drug was fast and hard and then gone. I felt ten minutes from sober, and I didn't want Amma around when I hit ground.

"Can I sleep over with you then?" She stood in the streetlight, her jean skirt hanging from her tiny hip bones, her halter askew and ripped. A smear of blood near her lips. Hopeful.

"Naw. Let's just sleep separate. We'll hang out tomorrow."

She said nothing, just turned and ran as fast as she could toward the house, her feet kicking up behind her like a cartoon colt's.

"Amma!" I called after. "Wait, you can stay with me, okay?" I began running after her. Watching her through the drugs and the dark was like trying to track someone while looking backward in a mirror. I failed to realize her bouncing silhouette had turned around, and that she was in fact running to me. At me. She smacked into me headlong, her forehead clanging into my jaw, and we fell again, this time on the sidewalk. My head made a sharp cracking noise as it hit the pavement, my lower teeth lit up in pain. I lay for a second on the ground, Amma's hair folded in my fist, a firefly overhead throbbing in time to my blood. Then Amma began cackling, grabbing her forehead and nudging the spot that was already a dark blue, like the outline of a plum.

"Shit. I think you dented my face."

"I think you dented the back of my head," I whispered. I sat up and felt woozy. A blurt of blood that had been stanched by the sidewalk now seeped down my neck. "Christ, Amma. You're too rough."

"I thought you liked it rough." She reached a hand and pulled me up, the blood in my head sloshing from back to front. Then she took a tiny gold ring with a pale green peridot from her middle finger and put it on my pinky finger. "Here. I want you to have this."

I shook my head. "Whoever gave that to you would want you to keep it."

"Adora sorta did. She doesn't care, trust me. She was going to give it to Ann but . . . well, Ann's gone now, so it was just sitting there. It's ugly, right? I used to pretend that she gave it to me. Which is unlikely since she hates me."

"She doesn't hate you." We began walking toward home, the porch light glaring from the top of the hill.

"She doesn't like you," Amma ventured.

"No, she doesn't."

"Well, she doesn't like me either. Just in a different

way." We climbed the stairs, squishing mulberries beneath our feet. The air smelled like icing on a child's cake.

"Did she like you more or less after Marian was dead?" she asked, looping her arm into mine.

"Less."

"So it didn't help."

"What?"

"Her dying didn't help things."

"No. Now keep quiet till we get to my room, okay?"

We padded up the stairs, me holding a hand under the crook of my neck to catch the blood, Amma trailing dangerously behind, pausing to smell a rose in the hall vase, cracking a smile at her reflection in the mirror. Silence as usual from Adora's bedroom. That fan whirring in the dark behind the closed door.

I shut the door of my own room behind us, peeled off my rain-drenched sneakers (checked with squares of newly cut grass), wiped smashed mulberry juice off my leg, and began pulling up my shirt before I felt Amma's stare. Shirt back down, I pretended to sway into bed, too exhausted to undress. I pulled the covers up and curled away from Amma, mumbling a good night. I heard her drop her clothes to the floor, and in a second the light was off and she was in bed curled behind me, naked except for her panties. I wanted to cry at the idea of being able to sleep next to someone without clothes, no worries about what word might slip out from under a sleeve or pantcuff.

"Camille?" Her voice quiet and girlish and unsure. "You know how people sometimes say they have to hurt because if they don't, they're so numb they won't feel anything?"

"Mmm."

"What if it's the opposite?" Amma whispered. "What if you hurt because it feels so good? Like you have a tingling, like someone left a switch on in your body. And nothing can turn the switch off except hurting? What does that mean?"

I pretended to be asleep. I pretended not to feel her fingers tracing *vanish* over and over on the back of my neck.

A dream. Marian, her white nightgown sticky with sweat, a blonde curl pasted across her cheek. She takes my hand and tries to pull me from bed. "It's not safe here," she whispers. "It's not safe for you." I tell her to leave me be.

Chapter Thirteen

It was past two when I woke, my stomach coiled in on itself, my jaw aching from grinding my teeth for five hours straight. Fucking X. Amma had problems, too, I guessed. She'd left a tiny pile of eyelashes on the pillow next to me. I swept them into the palm of my hand and stirred them around. Stiff with mascara, they left a dark blue smudge in the hollow of my palm. I dusted them off into a saucer on my bedside table. Then I went to the bathroom and threw up. I never mind throwing up. When I'd get sick as a child, I remember my mother holding my hair back, her voice soothing: *Get all that bad stuff out, sweetheart. Don't stop till it's all out.* Turns out I like that retching and weakness and spit. Predictable, I know, but true.

I locked my door, stripped off all my clothes, and got back in bed. My head ached from my left ear, through my neck, and down my spine. My bowels were shifting, I could barely move my mouth for the pain, and my ankle was on fire. And I was still bleeding, I could see from the blooms of red all over my sheets. Amma's side was bloody too: a light spray where she'd scraped her chest, a darker spot on the pillow itself.

My heart was beating too hard, and I couldn't catch my breath. I needed to see if my mother knew what had happened. Had she seen her Amma? Was I in trouble? I felt panicky sick. Something horrible was about to happen. Through my paranoia, I knew what was really going on: My serotonin levels, so jacked up from the drug the night before, had plummeted, and left me on the dark side. I told myself this even as I turned my face into the pillow and began sobbing. I had forgotten about those girls, hell, never really thought about them: dead Ann and dead Natalie. Worse, I had betrayed Marian, replaced her with Amma, ignored her in my dreams. There would be consequences. I wept in the same retching, cleansing way I'd vomited, until the pillow was wet and my face had ballooned like a drunk's. Then the door handle jiggled. I hushed myself, stroking my cheek, hoping silence would make it go away.

"Camille. Open up." My mother, but not angry. Coaxing. Nice, even. I remained silent. A few more jiggles. A knock. Then silence as she padded away again.

Camille. Open up. The image of my mother sitting on the edge of my bed, a spoonful of sour-smelling syrup hovering over me. Her medicine always made me feel sicker than before. Weak stomach. Not as bad as Marian's, but still weak.

My hands began sweating. *Please don't let her come back.* I had a flash of Curry, one of his crappy ties swinging wildly over his belly, busting into the room to save me. Carrying me off in his smoky Ford Taurus, Eileen stroking my hair on the way back to Chicago.

My mother slipped a key into the lock. I never knew she had a key. She entered the room smugly, her chin tilted high as usual, the key dangling from a long pink ribbon. She wore a powder blue sundress and carried a bottle of rubbing alcohol, a box of tissues, and a satiny red cosmetic bag.

"Hi baby," she sighed. "Amma told me about what happened to you two. My poor little ones. She's been purging all morning. I swear, and I know it will sound boastful, but except for our own little outfit, meat is getting completely unreliable these days. Amma said it was probably the chicken?"

"I guess so," I said. I could only run with whatever lie Amma told. It was clear she could maneuver better than I.

"I can't believe you both fainted right on our own stairs, while I was sleeping just inside. I hate that idea," Adora said. "Her bruises! You'd have thought she was in a catfight."

There's no way my mother bought that story. She was an expert in illness and injury, and she would not be taken in by that unless she wanted to be. Now she was going to tend to me, and I was too weak and desperate to ward her off. I began crying again, unable to stop.

"I feel sick, Momma."

"I know, baby." She stripped the sheet off me, flung it down past my toes in one efficient move, and when I instinctively put my hands across myself, she took them and placed them firmly to my side.

"I have to see what's wrong, Camille." She tilted my jaw from side to side and pulled my lower lip down, like she was inspecting a horse. She raised each of my arms slowly and peered into my armpits, jamming fingers into the hollows, then rubbed my throat to feel for swollen glands. I remembered the drill. She put a hand between my legs, quickly, professionally. It was the best way to feel a temperature, she always said. Then she softly, lightly drew her cool fingers down my legs, and jabbed her thumb directly into the open wound of my smashed ankle. Bright green splashes exploded in front of my eyes, and I automatically tucked my legs beneath me, turned on my side. She used the moment to poke at my head until she hit the smashed-fruit spot on its crown.

"Just another little bit, Camille, and we'll be all over." She wet her tissues with alcohol and scrubbed at my ankle until I couldn't see anything for my tears and snot. Then she wrapped it tight with gauze that she cut with tiny clippers from her cosmetic bag. The wound began bleeding through immediately so the wrapping soon looked like the flag of Japan: pure white with a defiant red circle. Next she tilted my head down with one hand and I felt an urgent tugging at my hair. She was cutting it off around the wound. I began to pull away.

"Don't you dare, Camille. I'll cut you. Lie back down and be a good girl." She pressed a cool hand on my cheek, holding my head in place against the pillow, and *snip snip snip*, sawed through a swath of my hair until I felt a release. An eerie exposure to air that my scalp was unused to. I reached back and felt a prickly patch the size of a half dollar on my head. My mother quickly pulled my hand away, tucked it against my side, and began rubbing alcohol onto my scalp. Again I lost my breath the pain was so stunning.

She rolled me onto my back and ran a wet washcloth over my limbs as if I were bedridden. Her eyes were pink where she'd been pulling at the lashes. Her cheeks had that girlish flush. She plucked up her cosmetic bag and began sifting through various pillboxes and tubes, finding a square of folded tissue from the bottom, wadded and slightly stained. From its center she produced an electric blue pill.

"One second, sweetheart."

I could hear her hit the steps urgently, and knew she was heading down to the kitchen. Then those same quick steps back into my room. She had a glass of milk in her hand.

"Here, Camille, drink this with it."

"What is *it*?"

"Medicine. It will prevent infection and clear up any bacteria you got from that food."

"What is it?" I asked again.

My mother's chest turned a blotchy pink, and her smile began flickering like a candle in a draft. On, off, on, off in the space of a second.

"Camille, I'm your mother, and you're in my house." Glassy pink eyes. I turned away from her and hit another streak of panic. Something bad. Something I'd done.

"Camille. Open." Soothing voice, coaxing. *Nurse* began throbbing near my left armpit.

I remember being a kid, rejecting all those tablets and medicines, and losing her by doing so. She reminded me of Amma and her Ecstasy, wheedling, needing me to take what she was offering. To refuse has so many more consequences than submitting. My skin was on fire from where she'd cleaned me, and it felt like that satisfying heat after a cut. I thought of Amma and how content she'd seemed, wrapped in my mother's arms, fragile and sweaty.

I turned back over, let my mother put the pill on my tongue, pour the thick milk into my throat, and kiss me.

Within a few minutes I was asleep, the stink of my breath floating into my dreams like a sour fog. My mother came to me in my bedroom and told me I was ill. She lay on top of me and put her mouth on mine. I could feel her breath in my throat. Then she began pecking at me. When she pulled away, she smiled at me and smoothed my hair back. Then she spit my teeth into her hands.

Dizzy and hot, I woke up at dusk, drool dried in a crusty line down my neck. Weak. I wrapped a thin robe around myself and began crying again when I remembered the circle at the back of my head. *You're just coming down from the X*, I whispered to myself, patting my cheek with my hand. *A bad haircut is not the end of the world. So you wear a ponytail.*

I shuffled down the hallway, my joints clicking in and out of place, my knuckles swollen for no reason I could think of. Downstairs my mother was singing. I knocked on Amma's door and heard a whimper of welcome.

She sat naked on the floor in front of her huge dollhouse, a thumb in her mouth. The circles beneath her eyes were almost purple, and my mother had pasted bandages to her forehead and chest. Amma had wrapped her favorite doll in tissue paper, dotted all over with red Magic Marker, and propped her up in bed.

"What'd she do to you?" she said sleepily, half smiling.

I turned around so she could see my crop circle.

"And she gave me something that made me feel really groggy and sick," I said.

"Blue?"

I nodded.

"Yeah, she likes that one," Amma mumbled. "You fall asleep all hot and drooly, and then she can bring her friends in to look at you."

"She's done this before?" My body went cold under the sweat. I was right: Something horrible was about to happen.

She shrugged. "I don't mind. Sometimes I don't take it – just pretend. Then we're both happy. I play with my dolls or I read, and when I hear her coming I pretend to be asleep."

"Amma?" I sat down on the floor next to her and stroked her hair. I needed to be gentle. "Does she give you pills and stuff a lot?"

"Only when I'm about to be sick."

"What happens then?"

"Sometimes I get all hot and crazy and she has to give me cold baths. Sometimes I need to throw up. Sometimes I get all shivery and weak and tired and I just want to sleep."

It was happening again. Just like Marian. I could feel the bile in the back of my throat, the tightening. I began weeping again, stood up, sat back down. My stomach was churning. I put my head in my hands. Amma and I were sick *just like Marian*. It had to be made that obvious to me before I finally understood – nearly twenty years too late. I wanted to scream in shame.

"Play dolls with me, Camille." She either didn't notice or ignored my tears.

"I can't, Amma. I have to work. Remember to be asleep when Momma comes back."

I dragged on clothes over my aching skin and looked at myself in the mirror. *You are thinking crazy thoughts. You are being unreasonable. But I'm not. My mother killed Marian. My mother killed those little girls.*

I stumbled to the toilet and threw up a stream of salty, hot water, the backsplashes from the toilet freckling my cheeks as I kneeled. When my stomach unclenched, I realized I wasn't alone. My mother was standing behind me.

"Poor sweetness," she murmured. I started, scrambled away from her on all fours. Propped myself against the wall and looked up at her.

"Why are you dressed, darling?" she said. "You can't go anywhere."

"I need to go out. I need to do some work. Fresh air will be good."

"Camille, get back in bed." Her voice was urgent and shrill. She marched to my bed, pulled down the covers, and patted it. "Come on sweetness, you need to be smart about your health."

I stumbled to my feet, grabbed my car keys from the table, and darted past her.

"Can't, Momma; I won't be gone long."

I left Amma upstairs with her sick dolls and slammed down the driveway so quickly I dented my front bumper where the hill abruptly evened out at street level. A fat woman pushing a stroller shook her head at me.

I started driving nowhere, trying to assemble my thoughts, running through the faces of people I knew in Wind Gap. I needed someone to tell me plainly I was wrong about Adora, or else that I was right. Someone who knew Adora, who'd had a grown-up's view of my childhood, who'd been here while I was away. I suddenly thought of Jackie O'Neele and her Juicy Fruit and booze and gossip. Her off-kilter maternal warmth toward me and the comment that now sounded like a warning: *So much has gone wrong.* I needed Jackie, rejected by Adora, completely without filter, a woman who'd known my mother her entire life. Who very clearly wanted to say something.

Jackie's house was only a few minutes away, a modern mansion meant to look like an antebellum plantation home. A scrawny pale kid was hunched over a riding mower, smoking as he drove back and forth in tight lines. His back was spackled with bumpy, angry zits so big they looked like wounds. Another meth boy. Jackie should cut out the middle man and just give the twenty bucks straight to the dealer.

I knew the woman who answered the door. Geri Shilt, a Calhoon High girl just a year ahead of me. She wore a starchy nurse's dress, same as Gayla, and still had the round, pink mole on her cheek that I'd always pitied her for. Seeing Geri, such a pedestrian face from the past, almost made me turn around, get in my car, and ignore all my worries. Someone this ordinary in my world made me question what I was thinking. But I didn't leave.

"Hi Camille, what can I do for you?" She seemed utterly uninterested in why I was there, a distinct lack of curiosity that separated her from the other Wind Gap women. She probably didn't have any girlfriends to gossip to.

"Hey, Geri, I didn't know you worked for the O'Neeles."

"No reason you would," she said plainly.

Jackie's three sons, born in a row, would all be in their early twenties: twenty, twenty-one, twenty-two, maybe. I remembered they were beefy, thick-necked boys who always wore polyester coach shorts and big gold Calhoon High rings with flaming blue jewel centers. They had Jackie's abnormally round eyes and bright white overbites. Jimmy, Jared, and Johnny. I could hear at least two of them now, home from school for the summer, throwing the football in the backyard. From Geri's aggressively dull look, she must have decided the best way to deal with them was to stay out of their way.

"I'm back here . . ." I began.

"I know why you're here," she said, neither accusingly nor with any generosity. Just a statement. I was simply another obstacle in her day.

"My mom is friends with Jackie and I thought . . ."

"I know who Jackie's friends are, believe me," Geri said.

She didn't seem inclined to let me in. Instead she looked me up and down, then out to the car behind me.

"Jackie is friends with a lot of your friends' moms," Geri added.

"Mmmm. I don't really have many friends around here these days." It was a fact I was proud of, but I said the words in a deliberately disappointed manner. The less she resented me, the quicker I'd get in there, and I felt an urgent need to speak with Jackie before I talked myself out of it. "In fact, even when I lived here, I don't really think I had that many friends."

"Katie Lacey. Her mom hangs out with all them."

Good old Katie Lacey, who dragged me to the Pity Party and turned on me. I could picture her roaring around town in that SUV, her pretty little girls perched in back, perfectly dressed, ready to rule over the other kindergartners. They'd learn from Mom to be particularly cruel to the ugly girls, poor girls, girls who wanted to just be left alone. Too much to ask.

"Katie Lacey is a girl I'm ashamed of ever being friendly with."

"Yeah, well, you were okay," Geri said. Just then I remembered she'd had a horse named Butter. The joke was that of course even Geri's pet was fattening.

"Not really." I'd never participated in direct acts of cruelty, but I never stopped them, either. I always stood on the sidelines like a fretful shadow and pretended to laugh.

Geri continued to stand in the doorway, stretching at the cheap watch around her wrist, tight as a rubber band, clearly lost in her own memories. Bad ones.

So why, then, would she stay in Wind Gap? I'd run across so many of the same faces since I'd been back. Girls I grew up with, who never had the energy to leave. It was a town that bred complacency through cable TV and a convenience store. Those who remained here were still just as segregated as before. Petty, pretty girls like Katie Lacey who now lived, predictably, in a rehabbed Victorian a few blocks from us, played at the same Woodberry tennis club as Adora, made the same quarterly pilgrimage to St. Louis for shopping. And the ugly, victimized girls like Geri Shilt were still stuck cleaning up after the pretty ones, heads lowered glumly, waiting for more abuse. They were women not strong enough or smart enough to leave. Women without imagination. So they stayed in Wind Gap and played their teenage lives on an endless loop. And now I was stuck with them, unable to pull myself out.

"Let me tell Jackie you're here." Geri went the long way to the back stairs – around through the living room rather than the glass-paneled kitchen that would expose her to Jackie's boys.

The room I was ushered into was obscenely white with glaring splashes of color, like a mischievous child had been finger painting. Red throw pillows, yellow-and-blue curtains, a glowing green vase packed with ceramic red flowers. A ludicrous leering black-and-white photo of Jackie, hair overblown, talons curled coyly beneath her chin, hung over the mantelpiece. She was like an over-groomed lapdog. Even in my sickened state I laughed.

"Darling Camille!" Jackie crossed the room with arms outstretched. She was wearing a satin house robe and diamond earrings like blocks. "You've come to visit. You look horrible, sweetheart. Geri, get us some Bloody Marys, stat!" She howled, literally, at me, then at Geri. I guess it was a laugh. Geri lingered in the doorway until Jackie clapped at her.

"I'm serious, Geri. Remember to salt the rim this time." She turned back to me. "So hard to get good help these days," she muttered earnestly, unaware no one really says that who's not on TV. I'm sure Jackie watched TV nonstop, drink in one hand, remote control in the other, curtains pulled as morning talk shows yielded to soaps, glided into court TV, moved on to reruns, sitcoms, crime dramas, and late-night movies about women who were raped, stalked, betrayed, or killed.

Geri brought in the Bloodys on a tray, along with containers of celery, pickles, and olives, and, as instructed, closed the drapes and left. Jackie and I sat in the dim light, in the freezing air-conditioned white room, and stared at each other a few seconds. Then Jackie swooped down and pulled out the drawer of the coffee table. It held three bottles of nail polish, a ratty Bible, and more than half a dozen orange prescription bottles. I thought of Curry and his clipped rose thorns.

"Painkiller? I got some good ones."

"I should probably keep some of my wits about me," I said, not quite sure if she was serious. "Looks like you could almost start your own store there."

"Oh sure. I'm terribly lucky." I could smell her anger mixed with tomato juice. "OxyContin, Percocet, Percodan, whatever new pill my latest doctor has stock in. But I got to admit, they're fun." She poured a few round white tablets into her hand and shot them back, smiled at me.

"What do you have?" I asked, almost afraid of the answer.

"That's the best part, sweetie. No one fucking knows. Lupus says one, arthritis says another, some sort of autoimmune syndrome says a third, it's all in my head says the fourth and fifth."

"What do you think?"

"What do *I* think?" she asked, and rolled her eyes. "I think as long as they keep the meds coming, I probably don't care all that much." She laughed again. "They're really fun."

Whether she was putting on a brave face or was really addicted, I couldn't tell.

"I'm sort of surprised Adora hasn't gotten herself on the sick track," she leered. "Figured once I did, she'd have to up the stakes, right? She wouldn't have silly old lupus, though. She'd find a way to get . . . I don't know, brain cancer. Right?"

She took another sip of the Bloody Mary, got a slash of red and salt across her upper lip, which made her look swollen. That second swallow calmed her, and just as she had at Natalie's funeral, she stared at me like she was trying to memorize my face.

"Good God, it's so weird to see you grown up," she said, patting my knee. "Why are you here, sweetheart? Is everything okay at home? Probably not. Is it . . . is it your momma?"

"No, nothing like that." I hated being so obvious.

"Oh." She looked dismayed, a hand fluttering to her robe like something out of a black-and-white movie. I'd played her wrong, forgot that down here it was encouraged to openly crave gossip.

"I mean, I'm sorry, I wasn't being frank just now. I do want to talk about my mother."

Jackie immediately cheered. "Can't quite figure her out, huh? Angel or devil or both, right?" Jackie placed a green satin pillow under her tiny rump and aimed her feet onto my lap. "Sweepea, will you just rub a little? They're clean." From under the sofa she pulled a bag of mini–candy bars, the kind you give out at Halloween, and placed them on her belly. "Lord, I'm going to have to get rid of these later, but they'll taste good going down."

I took advantage of this happy moment. "Was my mother always . . . the way she is now?" I cringed at the awkwardness of the question, but Jackie cackled once, like a witch.

"What's that, Sweepea – Beautiful? Charming? Beloved? Evil?" She wiggled her toes as she unwrapped a chocolate. "Rub." I began kneading her cold feet, the soles rough like a turtle shell. "Adora. Well, damn. Adora was rich and beautiful and her crazy parents ran the town. They brought that damn hog farm to Wind Gap, gave us hundreds of jobs – there was a walnut plant then, too. They called the shots. Everyone bootlicked the Preakers."

"What was life for her like . . . at home?"

"Adora was . . . overly mothered. Never saw your grandma Joya smile at her or touch her in a loving way, but she couldn't keep her hands off her. Always fixing the hair, tugging at clothes, and . . . oh, she did this *thing*. Instead of licking her thumb and rubbing at a smudge, she'd lick Adora. Just grab her head and lick it. When Adora peeled from a sunburn – we all did back then, not as smart about SPF as your generation – Joya would sit next to your momma, strip off her shirt, and peel the skin off in long strips. Joya loved that."

"Jackie . . ."

"I am not lying. Having to watch your friend

stripped naked in front of you, and . . . groomed. Needless to say, your momma was sick all the time. She was always having tubes and needles and such stuck in her."

"What was she sick with?"

"Little bit of everything. Lot of it just the stress of living with Joya. Those long unpainted fingernails, like a man's. And long hair she let go silver, down her back."

"Where was my grandfather in all this?"

"Don't know. Don't even remember his name. Herbert? Herman? He was never around, and when he was, he was just quiet and . . . away. You know the type. Like Alan."

She popped another chocolate and wiggled her toes in my hands. "You know, having you should have ruined your mother." Her tone was reproachful, as if I'd failed a simple chore. "Any other girl, got knocked up before marriage, here in Wind Gap way back when, it'd be all over for her," Jackie continued. "But your mother always had a way of making people baby her. *People* – not just boys, but the girls, their mothers, the teachers."

"Why is that?"

"Sweet Camille, a beautiful girl can get away with anything if she plays nice. You certainly must know that. Think of all the things boys have done for you over the years they never would have done if you hadn't had that face. And if the boys are nice, the girls are nice. Adora played that pregnancy beautifully: proud but a little broken, and very secretive. Your daddy came for that fateful visit, and then they never saw each other again. Your momma never spoke about it. You were all hers from the beginning. That's what killed Joya. Her daughter finally had something in her that Joya couldn't get at."

"Did my mother stop being sick once Joya was gone?"

"She did okay for a while," Jackie said over her glass. "But wasn't that long before Marian came along, and she didn't really have time to be sick then."

"Was my mother . . ." I could feel a sob welling up in my throat, so I swallowed it with my watered-down vodka. "Was my mother . . . a nice person?"

Jackie cackled again. Popped a chocolate, the nougat sticking to her teeth. "That's what you're after? Whether she was nice?" she paused. "What do *you* think?" she added, mocking me.

Jackie dug into her drawer again, unscrewed three pill bottles, took a tablet from each, and arranged them from largest to smallest on the back of her left hand.

"I don't know. I've never been close with her."

"But you've been close *to* her. Don't play games with me, Camille. That exhausts me. If you thought your momma was a nice person, you wouldn't be over here with her best friend asking whether she's nice."

Jackie took each pill, largest to smallest, smashed it into a chocolate, and swallowed it. Wrappers littered her chest, the smear of red still covered her lip, and a thick fudgy coating clung to her teeth. Her feet had begun to sweat in my hands.

"I'm sorry. You're right," I said. "Just, do you think she's . . . sick?"

Jackie stopped her chewing, put her hand on mine, and took a sigh of a breath.

"Let me say it aloud, because I've been thinking it too long, and thoughts can be a little tricky for me – they zip away from you, you know. Like trying to catch fish with your hands." She leaned up and squeezed my arm. "Adora devours you, and if you don't let her, it'll be even worse for you. Lookit what's happening to Amma. Look at what happened to Marian."

Yes. Just below my left breast, *bundle* began tingling.

"So you think?" I prompted. *Say it.*

"I think she's sick, and I think what she has is contagious," Jackie whispered, her shaky hands making the ice in her glass chime. "And I think it's time for you to go, Sweepea."

"I'm sorry, I didn't mean to overstay my welcome."

"I mean leave Wind Gap. It's not safe for you here."

Less than a minute later I closed the door on Jackie as she stared at the photo of herself leering back from the mantelpiece.

Chapter Fourteen

I nearly tumbled down Jackie's steps, my legs were so wobbly. Behind my back I could hear her boys chanting the Calhoon football rally. I drove around the corner, parked under a copse of mulberry treees, and rested my head against the wheel.

Had my mother truly been sick? And Marian? Amma and me? Sometimes I think illness sits inside every woman, waiting for the right moment to bloom. I have known so many *sick* women all my life. Women with chronic pain, with ever-gestating diseases. Women with *conditions.* Men, sure, they have bone snaps, they have backaches, they have a surgery or two, yank out a tonsil, insert a shiny plastic hip. Women get *consumed.* Not surprising, considering the sheer amount of traffic a woman's body experiences. Tampons and speculums. Cocks, fingers, vibrators and more, between the legs, from behind, in the mouth. Men love to put things inside women, don't they? Cucumbers and bananas and bottles, a string of pearls, a Magic Marker, a fist. Once a guy wanted to wedge a Walkie-Talkie inside of me. I declined.

Sick and sicker and sickest. What was real and what was fake? Was Amma really sick and needing my mother's medicine, or was the medicine what was making Amma sick? Did her blue pill make me vomit, or did it keep me from getting more ill than I'd have been without it?

Would Marian be dead if she hadn't had Adora for a mother?

I knew I should call Richard but couldn't think of anything to tell him. I'm scared. I'm vindicated. I want to die. I drove back past my mother's house, then east out toward the hog farm, and pulled up to Heelah's, that comforting, windowless block of a bar where anyone who recognized the boss's daughter would wisely leave her to her thoughts.

The place stank of pig blood and urine; even the popcorn in bowls along the bar smelled of flesh. A couple of men in baseball caps and leather jackets, handlebar mustaches and scowls, looked up, then back down into their beers. The bartender poured me my bourbon without a word. A Carole King song droned from the speakers. On my second round, the bartender motioned behind me and asked, "You lookin' for him?"

John Keene sat slumped over a drink in the bar's only booth, picking at the splintered edge of the table. His white skin was mottled pink with liquor, and from his wet lips and the way he smacked his tongue, I guessed he'd vomited once already. I grabbed my drink and sat across from him, said nothing. He smiled at me, reached his hand to mine across the table.

"Hi Camille. How're you doing? You look so nice and clean." He looked around. "It's . . . it's so dirty here."

"I'm doing okay, I guess, John. You okay?"

"Oh sure, I'm great. My sister's murdered, I'm about to be arrested, and my girlfriend who's stuck to me like glue since I moved to this rotten town is starting to realize I'm not the prize anymore. Not that I care that much. She's nice but not . . ."

"Not surprising," I offered.

"Yeah. Yeah. I was about to break up with her before Natalie. Now I can't."

Such a move would be dissected by the whole town – Richard, too. *What does it mean? How does it prove his guilt?*

"I will not go back to my parents' house," he muttered. "I will go to the fucking woods and kill myself before I go back to all of Natalie's things staring at me."

"I don't blame you."

He picked up the salt shaker, began twirling it around the table.

"You're the only person who understands, I think," he said. "What it's like to lose a sister and be expected to just deal. Just move on. Have you *gotten over it*?" He said the words so bitterly I expected his tongue to turn yellow.

"You'll never get over it," I said. "It infects you. It ruined me." It felt good to say it out loud.

"Why does everyone think it's so strange that I should mourn Natalie?" John toppled the shaker and it clattered to the floor. The bartender sent over a disgruntled look. I picked it up, set it on my side of the table, threw a pinch of salt over my shoulder for both of us.

"I guess when you're young, people expect you to accept things more easily," I said. "And you're a guy. Guys don't have soft feelings."

He snorted. "My parents got me this book on dealing with death: *Male in Mourning.* It said that sometimes you need to drop out, to just deny. That denial can be good for men. So I tried to take an hour and pretend like I didn't care. And for a little bit, I really didn't. I sat in my room at Meredith's and I thought about . . . bullshit. I just stared out the window at this little square of blue sky and kept saying, *It's okay, it's okay, it's okay.* Like I was a kid again. And when I was done, I knew for sure nothing would ever be okay again. Even if they caught who did it, it wouldn't be okay. I don't know why everyone keeps saying we'll feel better once someone's arrested. Now it looks like the someone who's going to be arrested is me." He laughed in a grunt and shook his head. "It's just fucking insane." And then, abruptly: "You want another drink? Will you have another drink with me?"

He was smashed, swaying heavily, but I would never steer a fellow sufferer from the relief of a blackout. Sometimes that's the most logical route. I've always believed clear-eyed sobriety was for the harder hearted.

I had a shot at the bar to catch up, then came back with two bourbons. Mine a double.

"It's like they picked the two girls in Wind Gap who had minds of their own and killed them off," John said. He took a sip of bourbon. "Do you think your sister and my sister would have been friends?"

In that imaginary place where they were both alive, where Marian had never aged.

"No," I said, and laughed suddenly. He laughed, too.

"So your dead sister is too good for my dead sister?" he blurted. We both laughed again, and then quickly soured and turned back to our drinks. I was already feeling dazed.

"I didn't kill Natalie," he whispered.

"I know."

He picked up my hand, wrapped it around his.

"Her fingernails were painted. When they found her. Someone painted her fingernails," he mumbled.

"Maybe she did."

"Natalie hated that kind of thing. Barely even allowed a brush through her hair."

Silence for several minutes. Carole King had given way to Carly Simon. Feminine folksy voices in a bar for slaughterers.

"You're so beautiful," John said.

"So are you."

John fumbled with his keys in the parking lot, handed them to me easily when I told him he was too drunk to drive. Not that I was much better. I steered him blurrily back to Meredith's house, but he just shook his head when we got close, asked if I'd drive him to the motel outside town lines. Same one I'd stayed at on my way down here, a little refuge where one could prepare for Wind Gap and its weight.

We drove with the windows down, warm night air blowing in, pasting John's T-shirt to his chest, my long sleeves flapping in the wind. Aside from his thick head of hair, he was so utterly bare. Even his arms sprouted only a light down. He seemed almost naked, in need of cover.

I paid for the room, No. 9, because John had no credit cards, and opened the door for him, sat him on the bed, got him a glass of lukewarm water in a plastic cup. He just looked at his feet and refused to take it.

"John, you need to drink some water."

He drained the cup in a gulp and let it roll off the side of the bed. Grabbed my hand. I tried to pull away – more instinct than anything – but he squeezed harder.

"I saw this the other day, too," he said, his finger tracing part of the *d* in *wretched*, just tucked under my left shirtsleeve. He reached his other hand up and stroked my face. "Can I look?"

"No." I tried again to pull away.

"Let me see, Camille." He held on.

"No, John. No one sees."

"I do."

He rolled my sleeve up, squinted his eyes. Trying to understand the lines in my skin. I don't know why I let him. He had a searching, sweet look on his face. I was weak from the day. And I was so damned tired of hiding. More than a decade devoted to concealment, never an interaction – a friend, a source, the check-out girl at the supermarket – in which I wasn't distracted anticipating which scar was going to reveal itself. Let John look. Please let him look. I didn't need to hide from someone courting oblivion as ardently as I was.

He rolled up the other sleeve, and there sat my exposed arms, so naked they made me breathless.

"No one's seen this?"

I shook my head.

"How long have you done this, Camille?"

"A long time."

He stared at my arms, pushed the sleeves up farther. Kissed me in the middle of *weary*.

"This is how I feel," he said, running his fingers over the scars until I got a chill of goosebumps. "Let me see it all."

He pulled my shirt over my head as I sat like an obedient child. Eased off my shoes and socks, pulled down my slacks. In my bra and panties, I shivered in the frosty room, the air conditioner blasting a chill over me. John pulled back the covers, motioned for me to climb in, and I did, feeling feverish and frozen at once.

He held up my arms, my legs, turned me on my back. He read me. Said the words out loud, angry and nonsensical both: *oven, queasy, castle.* He took off his own clothes, as if he sensed an unevenness, threw them in a ball on the floor, and read more. *Bun, spiteful, tangle, brush.* He unhooked my bra in front with a quick flick of his fingers, peeled it off me. *Blossom, dosage, bottle, salt.* He was hard. He put his mouth on my nipples, the first time since I began cutting in earnest that I'd allowed a man to do that. Fourteen years.

His hands ran all over me, and I let them: my back, my breasts, my thighs, my shoulders. His tongue in my mouth, down my neck, over my nipples, between my legs, then back to my mouth. Tasting myself on him. The words stayed quiet. I felt exorcised.

I guided him into me and came fast and hard and then again. I could feel his tears on my shoulders while he shuddered inside me. We fell asleep twisted around each other (a leg jutting out here, an arm behind a head there) and a single word hummed once: *omen.* Good or bad I didn't know. At the time I chose to think good. Foolish girl.

In the early morning, dawn made the tree branches glow like hundreds of tiny hands outside the bedroom window. I walked naked to the sink to refill our cup of water, both of us hungover and thirsty, and the weak sunlight hit my scars and the words flickered to life again. Remission ended. My upper lip curled involuntarily in repulsion at the sight of my skin, and I wrapped a towel around me before I got back into bed.

John drank a sip of water, cradled my head and poured some into my mouth, then gulped the remainder. His fingers tugged at the towel. I held tight to it, hard as a dishrag on my breasts, and shook my head.

"What's this?" he whispered into my ear.

"This is the unforgiving light of morning," I whispered back. "Time to drop the illusion."

"What illusion?"

"That anything can be okay," I said, and kissed his cheek.

"Let's not do that yet," he said, and wrapped his arms around me. Those thin, hairless arms. A boy's arms. I told myself these things, but I felt safe and good. Pretty and clean. I put my face to his neck and smelled him: liquor and sharp shaving lotion, the kind that squirts out ice blue. When I opened my eyes again, I saw the red twirling circles of a police siren outside the window.

Bang bang bang. The door rattled as if it could have easily broken down.

"Camille Preaker. Chief Vickery. Open up if you're in there."

We grabbed our scattered clothes, John's eyes as startled as a bird's. The sounds of belt buckles and shirt rustles that would give us away outside. Frantic, guilty noises. I threw the sheets back on the bed, ran fingers through my hair, and as John placed himself in an awkwardly casual standing position behind me, fingers hooked through his belt loops, I opened the door.

Richard. Well-pressed white shirt, crisply striped tie, a smile that dropped as soon as he saw John. Vickery beside him, rubbing his mustache as if there were a rash beneath it, eyes flitting from me to John before he turned and stared at Richard head on.

Richard said nothing, just glared at me, crossed his

arms and inhaled deeply once. I'm sure the room smelled of sex.

"Well, looks like you're just fine," he said. Forced a smirk. I knew it was forced because the skin above his collar was as red as an angry cartoon character's. "How're you, John? You good?"

"I'm fine, thanks," John said, and came to stand at my side.

"Miss Preaker, your mother called us a few hours ago when you failed to come home," mumbled Vickery. "Said you'd been a bit sick, taken a tumble, something like 'at. She was real worried. Real worried. Plus with all this ugliness going on, you can't be too careful. I suppose she'll be glad to hear you're . . . here."

The last part asked as a question I had no intention of answering. Richard I owed an explanation. Vickery no.

"I can phone my mother myself, thanks. I appreciate you looking up on me."

Richard looked at his feet, bit his lip, the only time I've ever seen him abashed. My belly turned, oily and fearful. He exhaled once, a long hard gust, put his hands on his hips, stared at me, then at John. Kids caught misbehaving.

"C'mon John, we'll take you home," Richard said.

"Camille can take me, but thanks, Detective Willis."

"You of age, son?" Vickery asked.

"He's eighteen," Richard said.

"Well fine then, you two have a real nice day," Vickery said, hissed a laugh in Richard's direction, and muttered "already had a nice night," under his breath.

"I'll phone you later, Richard," I said.

He raised a hand, flicked it at me as he turned back to the car.

John and I were mostly silent on the ride to his parents', where he was going to try to sleep in the basement rec room for a bit. He hummed a snatch of some old '50s bebop and tapped his fingernails on the door handle.

"How bad do you think that was?" he finally asked.

"For you, maybe not bad. Shows you're a good American boy with healthy interest in women and casual sex."

"That wasn't casual. I don't feel casual about that at all. Do you?"

"No. That was the wrong word. That was just the opposite," I said. "But I'm more than a decade older than you, and I'm covering the crime that . . . it's a conflict of interest. Better reporters have been fired for such a thing." I was aware of the morning sunlight on my face, the wrinkles at the edges of my eyes, the age that hung on me. John's face, despite a night of drinking and very little sleep, was like a petal.

"Last night. You saved me. That saved me. If you hadn't stayed with me, I would have done something bad. I know it, Camille."

"You made me feel very safe, too," I said, and meant it, but the words came out in the disingenuous singsong of my mother.

———

I dropped John off a block from his parents' house, his kiss landing on my jaw as I jerked away at the last second. *No one can prove anything happened,* I thought at that moment.

Drove back to Main Street, parked in front of the police station. One streetlight still glowed. 5:47 a.m. No receptionist on call yet in the lobby, so I rang the nightbell. The room deodorizer near my head hissed a lemon scent right on my shoulder. I hit the bell again, and Richard appeared behind the slit of glass in the heavy door leading to the offices. He stood staring at me a second, and I was waiting for him to turn his back to me again, almost willing him to, but then he opened the door and entered the lobby.

"Where do you want to begin, Camille?" He sat on one of the overstuffed chairs and put his head in his hands, his tie drooping between his legs.

"It wasn't like it looked, Richard," I said. "I know it sounds cliché but it's true." *Deny deny deny.*

"Camille, just forty-eight hours after you and I had sex, I find you in a motel room with the chief subject in my child-murder investigation. Even if it's not what it looks like, it's bad."

"He did not do it, Richard. I absolutely know he didn't do it."

"Really? Is that what ya'll discussed when he had his dick in you?"

Good, anger, I thought. *This I can handle. Better than head-in-the-hands despair.*

"Nothing like that happened, Richard. I found him at Heelah's drunk, dead drunk, and I really thought he might harm himself. I took him to the motel because I wanted to stay with him and hear him out. I need him for my story. And you know what I learned? Your investigation has ruined this boy, Richard. And what's worse, I don't even think you really believe he did it."

Only the last sentence was entirely true, and I didn't realize it until the words came out of me. Richard was a smart guy, a great cop, extremely ambitious, on his first major case with an entire outraged community bellowing for an arrest, and he didn't have a break yet. If he had more on John than a wish, he'd have arrested him days ago.

"Camille, despite what you think, you don't know everything about this investigation."

"Richard, believe me, I've never thought that I did. I've never felt anything but the most useless outsider. You've managed to fuck me and still remain airtight. No leaks with you."

"Ah, so you're still pissed about that? I thought you were a big girl."

Silence. A hiss of lemon. I could vaguely hear the big silver watch on Richard's wrist ticking.

"Let me show you what a good sport I can be," I said. I was back on autopilot, just like the old days: desperate to submit to him, make him feel better, make him like me again. For a few minutes last night, I'd felt so comforted, and Richard's appearing outside that motel door had smashed what was left of the lingering calm. I wanted it back.

I lowered myself to my knees, and began unzipping his pants. For a second he put his hand on the back of my head. Then instead he grabbed me roughly by the shoulder.

"Camille, Christ, what are you doing?" He realized how hard his grip was and loosened it, pulled me to my feet.

"I just want to make things okay with us." I played with a button on his shirt and refused to meet his eyes.

"That won't do it, Camille," he said. He kissed me almost chastely on the lips. "You need to know that before we go any further. You just need to know that, period."

Then he asked me to leave.

I chased sleep for a few darting hours in the back of my car. The equivalent of reading a sign between the cars of a passing train. Woke up sticky and peevish. Bought a toothbrush kit at the FaStop, along with the strongest-smelling lotion and hairspray I could find. I brushed my teeth in a gas-station sink, then rubbed the lotion into my armpits and between my legs, sprayed my hair stiff. The resulting smell was sweat and sex under a billowing cloud of strawberry and aloe.

I couldn't face my mother at the house and crazily thought I'd do work instead. (As if I were still going to write that story. As if it weren't all about to go to hell.) With Geri Shilt's mention of Katie Lacey fresh in my mind, I decided to go back to her. She was a mother's aide at the grade school, for both Natalie and Ann's classes. My own mother had been a mother's aide, a coveted, elite position in the school that only women who didn't work could do: swoop into classrooms twice a week and help organize arts, crafts, music, and, for girls on Thursdays, sewing. At least in my day it'd been sewing. By now it was probably something more gender neutral and modern. Computer usage or beginners' microwaving.

Katie, like my mother, lived at the top of a big hill. The house's slender staircase cut into the grass and was bordered with sunflowers. A catalpa tree sat slim and elegant as a finger on the hilltop, the female match to the burly shade oak on its right. It was barely ten, but Katie, slim and brown, was already sunning herself on the widow's walk, a box fan breezing her. Sun without the heat. Now if she could only figure out a tan without the cancer. Or at least the wrinkles. She saw me coming up the stairs, an irritating flicker against the deep green of her lawn, and shaded her eyes to make me out from forty feet above.

"Who is that?" she called out. Her hair, a natural wheaty blonde in high school, was now a brassy platinum that sprung out of a ponytail atop her head.

"Hi, Katie. It's Camille."

"Ca-meeel! Oh my God, I'm coming down."

It was a more generous greeting than I'd expected from Katie, who I hadn't heard from again after the night of Angie's Pity Party. Her grudges always came and went like breezes.

She bounded to the door, those bright blue eyes glowing from her suntanned face. Her arms were brown and skinny as a child's, reminding me of the French cigarillos Alan had taken to smoking one winter. My mother had blocked him off into the basement, grandly called it his smoking room. Alan soon dropped the cigarillos and took up port.

Over her bikini Katie had thrown a neon pink tank, the kind girls picked up in South Padre in the late '80s, souvenirs from wet T-shirt contests over Spring Break. She wrapped her cocoa-buttered arms around me and led me inside. No A/C in this old house either, just like my momma's, she explained. Although they did have one room unit in the master bedroom. The kids, I guessed, could sweat it out. Not that they weren't catered to. The entire east wing seemed to be an indoor playground, complete with a yellow plastic house, a slide, a designer rocking horse. None of it looked remotely played with. Big colored letters lined one wall: Mackenzie. Emma. Photos of smiling blonde girls, pug nosed and glassy eyed, pretty mouth breathers. Never a close-up of a face, but always framed in order to capture what they were wearing. Pink overalls with daisies, red dresses with polka-dot bloomers, Easter bonnets and Mary Janes. Cute kids, *really* cute clothes. I'd just created a tagline for Wind Gaps' li'l shoppers.

Katie Lacey Brucker didn't seem to care why I was in her home this Friday morning. There was talk of a celebrity tell-all she was reading, and whether childrens' beauty pageants were forever stigmatized by JonBenet.

Mackenzie is just dying to model. Well she's as pretty as her mother, who can blame her? *Why, Camille, that's sweet of you to say – I never felt like you thought I was pretty.* Oh of course, don't be silly. *Would you like a drink?* Absolutely. *We don't keep liquor in the home.* Of course, not what I meant at all. *Sweet tea?* Sweet tea is lovely, impossible to get in Chicago, you really miss the little regional goodies, you should see how they do their ham up there. So great to be home.

Katie came back with a crystal pitcher of sweet tea. Curious, since from the living room I saw her pull a big gallon jug out of the icebox. A hit of smugness, followed by a self-reminder that I wasn't being particularly frank, either. In fact, I'd cloaked my own natural state with the thick scent of fake plant. Not just aloe and strawberry, but also the faint strain of lemon air freshener coming from my shoulder.

"This tea is wonderful, Katie. I swear I could drink sweet tea with every meal."

"How do they do their ham up there?" She tucked her feet under her legs and leaned in. It reminded me of high school, that serious stare, as if she were trying to memorize the combination to a safe.

I don't eat ham, hadn't since I was a kid and went to visit the family business. It wasn't even a slaughtering day, but the sight kept me up nights. Hundreds of those animals caged so tightly they couldn't even turn around, the sweet throaty scent of blood and shit. A flash of Amma, staring intently at those cages.

"Not enough brown sugar."

"Mmmhmm. Speaking of which, can I make you a sandwich or something? Got ham from your momma's place, beef from the Deacons', chicken from Coveys. And turkey from Lean Cuisine."

Katie was the type who'd bustle around all day, clean the kitchen tile with a toothbrush, pull the lint from the floorboards with a toothpick before she spoke much about anything uncomfortable. Sober at least. Still, I maneuvered her to talk of Ann and Natalie, guaranteed her anonymity, and started up my tape recorder. The girls were sweet and cute and darling, the obligatory cheery revisionism. Then:

"We did have an incident with Ann, on Sewing Day." Sewing Day, still around. Kind of comforting, I suppose. "She jabbed Natalie Keene in the cheek with her needle. I think she was aiming for the eye, you know, like Natalie did to that little girl back in Ohio." *Philadelphia.* "One minute the two were sitting nice and quiet next to each other – they weren't friends, they were in different grades, but Sewing's open. And Ann was humming something to herself and looking just like a little mother. And then it happened."

"How hurt was Natalie?"

"Mmm, not too bad. Me and Rae Whitescarver, she's the second-grade teacher now. Used to be Rae Little, few years below us . . . and *not little*. At least not then – she's dropped a few pounds. Anyway, me and Rae pulled Ann off and Natalie had this needle sticking right out of her cheek just an inch below her eye. Didn't cry or nothing. Just wheezed in and out like an angry horse."

An image of Ann with her crooked hair, weaving the
needle through cloth, remembering a story about Natalie
and her scissors, a violence that made her so different.
And before she thought it through, the needle into flesh,
easier than you'd think, hitting bone in one quick thrust.
Natalie with the metal spearing out of her, like a tiny silver harpoon.

"Ann did it for no clear reason?"

"One thing I learned about those two, they didn't
need a reason to strike out."

"Did other girls pick on them? Were they under
stress?"

"Ha Ha!" It was a genuinely surprised laugh, but it
came out in a perfect, unlikely "Ha Ha!" Like a cat looking at you and saying "Meow."

"Well, I wouldn't say school days were something
they looked forward to," Katie said. "But you should ask
your little sister about that."

"I know you say Amma bullied them . . ."

"God help us when she hits high school."

I waited in silence for Katie Lacey Brucker to gear
up and talk about my sister. Bad news, I guessed. No
wonder she was so happy to see me.

"Remember how we ran Calhoon? What we thought
was cool became cool, who we didn't like everyone
hated?" She sounded fairy-tale dreamy, as if she were
thinking of a land of ice cream and bunnies. I only nodded. I remember a particularly cruel gesture on my part:
An overearnest girl named LeeAnn, a leftover friend
from grade school, had displayed too much concern

about my mental state, suggested I might be depressed. I snubbed her pointedly one day when she came scurrying over to speak with me before school. I can still remember her: books bundled under her arms, that awkward printed skirt, her head kept a bit low whenever she addressed me. I turned my back on her, blocked her from the group of girls I was with, made some joke about her conservative church clothes. The girls ran with it. For the rest of the week, she was pointedly taunted. She spent the last two years of high school hanging out with teachers during lunch. I could have stopped it with one word, but I didn't. I needed her to stay away.

"Your sister is like us times three. And she has a major mean streak."

"Mean streak how?"

Katie pulled a soft pack of cigarettes from the end-table drawer, lit one with a long fireplace match. Still a secret smoker.

"Oh, she and those three girls, those little blonde things with the tits already, they rule the school, and Amma rules them. Seriously, it's bad. Sometimes funny, but mostly bad. They make this fat girl get them lunch every day, and before she leaves, they make her eat something without using her hands, just dig her face in there on the plate." She scrunched up her nose but didn't seem otherwise bothered. "Another little girl they cornered and made her lift up her shirt and show the boys. Because she was flat. They made her say dirty things while she was doing it. There's a rumor going around that they took one of their old friends, girl named Ronna Deel they'd fallen out with, took her to a party, got her drunk and . . . kind of gave her as a present to some of the older boys. Stood guard outside the room till they were done with her."

"They're barely *thirteen*," I said. I thought of what I'd done at that age. For the first time I realized how offensively young it was.

"These are precocious little girls. We did some pretty wild things ourselves at not much older." Katie's voice got huskier with her smoke. She blew it up and watched it hover blue above us.

"We never did anything that cruel."

"We came pretty damn close, Camille." *You did, I didn't.* We stared at each other, privately cataloguing our power plays.

"Anyway, Amma fucked with Ann and Natalie a lot," Katie said. "It was nice your mom took so much interest in them."

"My mom tutored Ann, I know."

"Oh, she'd work with them during mother's aide, have them over to your house, feed them after school. Sometimes she'd even come by during recess and you could see her outside the fence, watching them on the playground."

A flash of my mother, fingers wrapped between the fence wire, hungrily looking in. A flash of my mother in white, glowing white, holding Natalie with one arm, and a finger up to her mouth to hush James Capisi.

"Are we done?" Katie asked. "I'm sort of tired of talking about all this." She clicked the tape recorder off.

"So, I heard about you and the cute cop," Katie smiled. A wisp of hair came unhooked from her ponytail, and I could remember her, head bent over her feet, painting her toenails and asking about me and one of the basketball players she'd wanted for herself. I tried not to wince at the mention of Richard.

"Oh, rumors, rumors." I smiled. "Single guy, single girl . . . my life isn't nearly that interesting."

"John Keene might say different." She plucked another cigarette, lit it, inhaled and exhaled while fixing me with those china blue eyes. No smile this time. I knew this could go two ways. I could give her a few tidbits, make her happy. If the story had already reached Katie at ten, the rest of Wind Gap would hear by noon. Or I could deny, risk her anger, lose her cooperation. I already had the interview, and I certainly didn't care about staying in her good graces.

"Ah. More rumors. People need to get some better hobbies around here."

"Really? Sounded pretty typical to me. You were always open to a good time."

I stood up, more than ready to leave. Katie followed me out, chewing the inside of her cheek.

"Thanks for your time, Katie. It was good seeing you."

"You too, Camille. Enjoy the rest of your stay here." I was out the door and on the steps when she called back to me.

"Camille?" I turned around, saw Katie with her left leg bent inward like a little girl's, a gesture she had even in high school. "Friendly advice: Get home and wash yourself. You stink."

I did go home. My brain was stumbling from image to image of my mother, all ominous. *Omen.* The word beat again on my skin. Flash of thin, wild-haired Joya with the long nails, peeling skin from my mother. Flash of my mother and her pills and potions, sawing through my hair. Flash of Marian, now bones in a coffin, a white satin ribbon wrapped around dried blonde curls, like some bouquet gone stale. My mother tending to those violent little girls. Or trying to. Natalie and Ann weren't likely to suffer much of that. Adora hated little girls who didn't capitulate to her peculiar strain of mothering. Had she painted Natalie's fingernails before she strangled her? After?

You're crazy to think what you're thinking. You're crazy to not think it.

Chapter Fifteen

Three little pink bikes were lined up on the porch, bedecked with white wicker baskets, ribbons streaming off the handlebars. I peeked in one of the baskets and saw an oversized stick of lipgloss and a joint in a sandwich bag.

I slipped in a side door and padded up the steps. The girls were in Amma's room giggling loudly, shrieking with delight. I opened the door without knocking. Rude, but I couldn't bear the idea of that secret shuffle, that rush to pose innocently for the grown-up. The three blondes were standing in a circle around Amma, short shorts and miniskirts baring their shaved stick legs. Amma was on the floor fiddling with her dollhouse, a tube of super glue beside her, her hair piled on top of her head and tied with a big blue ribbon. They shrieked again when I said hello, flashing outraged, exhilarated smiles, like startled birds.

"Hey, Mille," blurted Amma, no longer bandaged, but looking tweaked and feverish. "We're just playing dolls. Don't I have the most beautiful dollhouse?" Her voice was syrupy, modeled after a child on a 1950s family show. Hard to reconcile this Amma with the one who gave me drugs just two nights before. My sister who supposedly pimped out her friends to older boys for laughs.

"Yeah, Camille, don't you love Amma's dollhouse?" echoed the brassy blonde in a husky voice. Jodes was the only one not looking at me. Instead she was staring into the dollhouse as if she could will herself inside.

"You feel better, Amma?"

"Oh, indeed I do, sister dear," she whinnied. "I hope you feel well also."

The girls giggled again, like a shudder. I shut the door, annoyed with a game I didn't understand. "Maybe you should take Jodes with you," one of them called from behind the closed door. Jodes wasn't long for the group.

I ran a warm bath despite the heat – even the porcelain of the tub was rosy – and sat in it, naked, chin on my knees as the water slowly snaked up around me. The room smelled of minty soap and the sweet, spittoon scent of female sex. I was raw and thoroughly used and it felt good. I closed my eyes, slumped down into the water and let it flow into my ears. *Alone.* I wished I'd carved that into my skin, suddenly surprised that the word didn't grace my body. The bare circle of scalp Adora had left me pricked with goosebumps, as if volunteering for the assignment. My face cooled, too, and I opened my eyes to see my mother hovering over the oval of the tub rim, her long blonde hair encircling her face.

I lurched up, covered my breasts, splashing some water on her pink gingham sundress.

"Sweetheart, where did you go? I was absolutely frantic. I'd have come looking for you myself but Amma had a bad night."

"What was wrong with Amma?"

"Where were you last night?"

"What was wrong with Amma, Mother?"

She reached for my face and I flinched. She frowned and reached again, patted my cheek, smoothed my wet hair back. When she removed her hand, she looked stunned at the wetness, as if she'd ruined her skin.

"I had to take care of her," she said simply. Goosebumps blossomed on my arms. "You cold, honey? Your nipples are hard."

She had a glass of bluish milk in her hand, which she gave to me silently. *Either the drink makes me sick and I know I'm not insane, or it doesn't, and I know I'm a hateful creature.* I drank the milk as my mother hummed and ran her tongue over her lower lip, a gesture so fervent it was nearly obscene.

"You were never such a good girl when you were little," she said. "You were always so willful. Maybe your spirit has gotten a bit more broken. In a good way. A necessary way."

She left and I waited in the bathtub for an hour for something to happen. Stomach rumblings, dizziness, a fever. I sat as still as I do on an airplane, when I worry one rash movement will send us into a tailspin. Nothing. Amma was in my bed when I opened the door.

"You are so gross," she said, arms lazily crossed over her. "I cannot believe you fucked a *babykiller*. You are just as nasty as she said."

"Don't listen to Momma, Amma. She's not a trustworthy person. And don't . . ." *What? Take anything from her? Say it if you think it, Camille.* "Don't turn on me, Amma. We hurt each other awfully quickly in this family."

"Tell me about his dick, Camille. Was it nice?" Her voice was the same cloying, put-on she'd used with me earlier, but she wasn't detached: She squirmed under my sheets, her eyes a bit wild, face flushed.

"Amma, I don't want to talk about this with you."

"You weren't too grown up a few nights ago, sister. Are we not friends anymore?"

"Amma, I've got to lie down now."

"Hard night, huh? Well, just wait – everything's going to get worse." She kissed me on the cheek and slid out of the bed, clattered down the hall in her big plastic sandals.

Twenty minutes later the vomiting began, wrenching, sweaty upheavals in which I pictured my stomach contracting and bursting like a heart attack. I sat on the floor next to the toilet between hacking, propped against the wall in only an ill-fitting T-shirt. Outside I could hear blue jays bickering. Inside, my mother called Gayla's name. An hour later and I was still vomiting, off-green nauseous bile that came out of me like syrup, slow and sinewy.

I pulled on some clothes and brushed my teeth gingerly – inserting too much of the toothbrush in my mouth made me start gagging again.

Alan was sitting on the front porch reading a large, leatherbound book entitled only *Horses*. A bowl made of bumpy orange carnival glass perched on the armrest of his rocking chair, a lump of green pudding at its center. He was in a blue seersucker suit, a Panama hat atop his head. He was serene as a pond.

"Your mother know you're leaving?"

"I'll be back soon."

"You've done much better with her lately, Camille, and for that I thank you. She seems quite improved. Even her dealings with . . . Amma are smoother." He always seemed to pause before his own daughter's name, as if it had a slightly dirty connotation.

"Good, Alan, good."

"I hope you're feeling better about yourself too, Camille. That's an important thing, liking oneself. A good attitude infects just as easily as a bad one."

"Enjoy the horses."

"I always do."

The drive to Woodberry was punctuated with lurching twists into the curb where I threw up more bile and a little blood. Three stops, one in which I vomited down the side of the car, unable to get the door open fast enough. I used my old warm cup of strawberry pop and vodka to wash it off.

St. Joseph's Hospital in Woodberry was a huge cube of golden brick, cross-sectioned with amber-shaded windows. Marian had called it the waffle. It was a mellow place for the most part: If you lived farther west, you went to Poplar Bluff for your health; farther north, to Cape Girardeau. You only went to Woodberry if you were trapped in the Missouri boot heel.

A big woman, her bust comically round, was sending off Do Not Disturb signals from behind the Information desk. I stood and waited. She pretended to be intently reading. I stood closer. She trailed an index finger along each line of her magazine and continued to read.

"Excuse me," I said, my tone a mix of petulance and patronizing that even I disliked.

She had a mustache and yellowed fingertips from smoking, matching the brown canines that peeked out from beneath her upper lip. *The face you give the world tells the world how to treat you,* my mother used to say whenever I resisted her grooming. This woman could not be treated well.

"I need to track down some medical records."

"Put a request in with your doctor."

"My sister's."

"Have your sister put in a request with her doctor." She flipped the page of her magazine.

"My sister is dead." There were gentler ways of putting this, but I wanted the woman to snap to. Even still, her attention was grudging.

"Ah. Sorry for your loss. She die here?" I nodded.

"Dead on Arrival. She had a lot of emergency treatment here and her doctor was based here."

"What was the date of death?"

"May 1, 1988."

"Jesus. That's a pace back. Hope you're a patient woman."

Four hours later, after two screaming matches with disinterested nurses, a desperate flirtation with a pale, fuzzy-faced administrator, and three trips to the bathroom to vomit, Marian's files were flopped on my lap.

There was one for each year of her life, progressively thicker. Half the doctors' scratches I couldn't understand. Many involved tests ordered and completed, never to any use. Brain scans and heart scans. A procedure involving a camera threaded down Marian's throat to examine her stomach as it was filled with radiant dye. Heart-apnea monitors. Possible diagnoses: diabetes, heart murmur, acid reflux, liver disease, pulmonary hypertension, depression, Crohn's disease, lupus. Then, a feminine, pink sheet of lined stationery. Stapled to a report documenting Marian's week-long hospital stay for the stomach tests. Proper, rounded cursive, but angry – the pen had indented each word deeply into the paper. It read:

> *I am a nurse who has attended Marian Crellin for her tests this week, as well as several previous inpatient stays. I am of the very strong* ["very strong" underlined twice] *opinion that this child is not sick at all. I believe were it not for her mother, she would be perfectly healthy. The child exhibits signs of illness after spending time alone with the mother, even on days when she has felt well up until maternal visits.*

*Mother shows no interest in Marian when she is well,
in fact, seems to punish her. Mother holds child only
when she is sick or crying. I and several other nurses,
who for political reasons choose not to sign their
names to my statement, believe strongly the child, as
well as her sister, should be removed from the home
for further observation.*

Beverly Van Lumm

Righteous indignation. We could have used more of
that. I pictured Beverly Van Lumm, busty and tight
lipped, hair gathered in a determined bun, scrawling out
the letter in the next room after she was forced to leave
limp Marian in my mother's arms, only a matter of time
until Adora cried out for nursing attention.

Within an hour I had tracked the nurse down in the
pediatric ward, which was actually just a big room holding four beds, only two of them in use. One little girl
was reading placidly, the little boy next to her was sleeping upright, his neck held in a metal brace that seemed
to screw right into his spine.

Beverly Van Lumm was not a bit like I pictured.
Maybe late fifties, she was tiny, her silver hair cropped
tight to her head. She wore flowered nursing pants and
a bright blue jacket, a pen propped behind her ear. When
I introduced myself, she seemed to immediately remember me, and appeared none too surprised I'd finally
shown up.

"It's so nice to meet you again after all these years,
although I hate the circumstances," she said in a warm,

deep voice. "Sometimes I daydream that Marian herself comes in here, all grown up, maybe with a baby or two. Daydreams can be dangerous."

"I came because I read your note."

She snorted, capped her pen.

"Bully lot of good that did. If I hadn't been so young and nervous and awestruck by the great *docteurs* around here, I would have done more than write a note. 'Course back in that time, accusing mothers of such a thing was almost unheard of. Nearly got me fired. You never really want to believe such a thing. Like something out of Brothers Grimm, MBP."

"MBP?"

"Munchausen by Proxy. The caregiver, usually the mother, *almost always* the mother, makes her child ill to get attention for herself. You got Munchausen, you make yourself sick to get attention. You got MBP, you make your child sick to show what a kind, doting mommy you are. Brothers Grimm, see what I mean? Like something a wicked fairy queen would do. I'm surprised you haven't heard of it."

"It sounds familiar," I said.

"It's becoming quite a well-known disease. Popular. People love new and creepy. I remember when anorexia hit in the eighties. The more TV movies on it, the more girls starved themselves. You always seemed okay, though. I'm glad."

"I'm okay, mostly. I have another sister, a girl born after Marian, I worry about."

"You should. Dealing with an MBP mom – it doesn't

pay to be the favorite. You were lucky your mother didn't take more of an interest in you."

A man in bright green scrubs zipped down the hall-way in a wheelchair, followed by two fat laughing guys, similarly outfitted.

"Med students," Beverly said, rolled her eyes.

"Did any doctors ever follow up on your report?"

"I called it a report, they saw it as some childless, jealous nurse's pettiness. Like I said, different time. Nurses get a *leetle* more respect now. Just a *leetle*. And to be fair, Camille, I didn't push it. I was just off a divorce, I needed to keep my job, and bottom line was, I wanted someone to tell me I was wrong. You need to believe you're wrong. When Marian died, I drank for three days. She was buried before I hinted around again, asked the head of pediatrics if he'd seen my note. I was told to take the week off. I was one of those hysterical women."

My eyes were suddenly stinging and wet, and she took my hand.

"I'm sorry, Camille."

"God, I'm so angry." Tears spilled down my cheeks and I rubbed them away with the back of my hand until Beverly gave me a tissue pack. "That it ever happened. That it took this long for me to figure it out."

"Well, sweetheart, she's your mother. I can't im-agine what it must be like for you to come to grips with it. At least it looks like justice will be served now. How long has the detective been on the case?"

"Detective?"

"Willis, right? Good-looking kid, sharp. He Xeroxed every single page in Marian's files, quizzed me until my fillings hurt. Didn't tell me there was another little girl involved. He told me you were okay, though. I think he has a crush on you – he got all squirmy and bashful when he mentioned you."

I stopped crying, wadded up the tissues, and tossed them in the trash next to the reading girl. She glanced into the basket curiously, as if the mail had just come in. I said my thanks to Beverly and made my way out, feeling wild and in need of blue sky.

Beverly caught up to me at the elevator, took both my hands in hers. "Get your sister out of that home, Camille. She's not safe."

Between Woodberry and Wind Gap was a biker bar off exit 5, a place that sold six-packs to go with no call for ID. I'd gone there a lot in high school. Next to the dartboard was a pay phone. I grabbed a handful of quarters and phoned Curry. Eileen picked up, as usual, that voice soft and steady as a hill. I started sobbing before I got more than my name out.

"Camille, sweetheart, what is it? Are you okay? Of course you're not okay. Oh, I'm so sorry. I told Frank to get you out of there after your last call. What is it?"

I kept sobbing, couldn't even think what to say. A dart hit the board with a solid thunk.

"You aren't . . . hurting yourself again? Camille? Sweetheart, you're scaring me."

"My mother . . ." I said, before collapsing again. I

was heaving with sobs, purging from deep in my belly, nearly bent over.

"Your mother? Is she all right?"

"Noooo." A long wail like a child. A hand over the phone and Eileen's urgent murmur of Frank's name, the words *something's happened . . . horrible,* a silence of two seconds and the crash of glass. Curry got up from the table too quickly, his tumbler of whiskey wobbling to the floor. Just a guess.

"Camille, talk to me, what's wrong." Curry's voice was gruff and startling like hands on both my arms giving me a shake.

"I know who did it, Curry," I hissed. "I know it."

"Well, that's no reason to cry, Cubby. The police made an arrest?"

"Not yet. I know who did it." *Thunk* on the dartboard.

"Who? Camille, talk to me."

I pressed the phone to my mouth and whispered, "My mother."

"Who? Camille, you have to speak up. Are you at a bar?"

"My mother did it," I yelped into the phone, the words coming out like a splatter.

Silence for too long. "Camille, you are under a lot of stress, and I was very wrong to send you down there so soon after . . . Now, I want you to go to the nearest airport and fly back here. Don't get your clothes, just leave your car and come home here. We'll deal with all that stuff later. Charge the ticket, I'll pay you back when you get home. But you need to come home now."

Home home home, like he was trying to hypnotize me.

"I'll never have a home," I whimpered, began sobbing again. "I have to go take care of this, Curry." I hung up as he was ordering me not to.

Richard I tracked down at Gritty's having a late supper. He was looking at clippings from a Philadelphia paper about Natalie's scissors attack. He nodded grudgingly at me as I sat down opposite him, looked down at his greasy cheese grits, then back up to study my swollen face.

"You okay?"

"I think my mother killed Marian, and I think she killed Ann and Natalie. And I know you think that, too. I just got back from Woodberry, you fuck."

The sorrow had turned to outrage somewhere between exits 5 and 2. "I can't believe that all the while you were making time with me, you were just trying to get information about my mother. What kind of sick fuck are you?" I was shaking, the words stuttering out of my mouth.

Richard took a ten out of his wallet, tucked it under the plate, walked to my side of the table, and took my arm. "Come with me outside, Camille. This isn't the place." He walked me through the doors, to the passenger side of the car, his arm still on mine, and put me inside.

He drove us in silence up the bluff, his hand shooting up whenever I tried to say something. I finally turned away from him, aimed my body at the window, and watched the woods flash by in a blue-green rush.

We parked in the same spot where we'd overlooked the river weeks before. It roiled down below us in the dark, the current catching the moonlight in patches. Like watching a beetle hustle through fall leaves.

"Now my turn for the cliché," Richard said, his profile to me. "Yes, I was first interested in you because I was interested in your mother. But I genuinely fell for you. As much as you can fall for a person as closed off as you are. Of course, I understand why. At first I thought I'd formally question you, but I didn't know how close you and Adora were, I didn't want you to tip her off. And I wasn't sure, Camille. I wanted time to study her a bit more. It was only a hunch. Purely a hunch. Gossip here and there, about you, about Marian, about Amma and your mother. But it's true that women don't fit the profile for this kind of thing. Not serial child murder. Then I started to look at it differently."

"How?" My voice dull as scrap metal.

"It was that kid, James Capisi. I kept coming back to him, that fairy-tale wicked witch of a woman." Echoes of Beverly, Brothers Grimm. "I still don't think he actually saw your mother, but I think he remembered something, a feeling or subconscious fear that turned into that person. I started thinking, what kind of woman would kill little girls and steal their teeth? A woman who wanted ultimate control. A woman whose nurturing instinct had gone awry. Both Ann and Natalie had been . . . tended to before they were killed.

Both sets of parents noted uncharacteristic details. Natalie's fingernails were painted a bright pink. Ann's legs had been shaved. They both had lipstick applied at some point."

"What about the teeth?"

"Isn't a smile a girl's best weapon?" Richard said. Finally turning to me. "And in the case of the two girls, literally a weapon. Your story about the biting really focused things for me. The killer was a woman who resented strength in females, who saw it as vulgar. She tried to mother the little girls, to dominate them, to turn them into her own vision. When they rejected that, struggled against that, the killer flew into an outrage. The girls had to die. Strangling is the very definition of dominance. Slow-motion murder. I closed my eyes one day in my office after writing down the profile, and I saw your mother's face. The sudden violence, her closeness with the dead girls – she has no alibi for either night. Beverly Van Lumm's hunch about Marian adds to it. Although we'll still have to disinter Marian to see if we can get more solid evidence. Traces of poisoning or something."

"Leave her be."

"I can't, Camille. You know it's the right thing. We'll be very respectful of her." He put his hand on my thigh. Not my hand or my shoulder, but my thigh.

"Was John ever really a suspect?" Hand removed.

"His name was always swirling around. Vickery was kind of obsessed. Figured Natalie was kind of violent, maybe John was, too. Plus he was from out of town, and you know how suspicious out-of-towners are."

"Do you have any real proof, Richard, about my mother? Or is this all supposition?"

"Tomorrow we're getting the order to search the place. She'll have kept the teeth. I'm telling you this as a courtesy. Because I respect and trust you."

"Right," I said. *Falling* lit up on my left knee. "I need to get Amma out of there."

"Nothing will happen tonight. You need to go home and have a regular evening. Act as naturally as possible. I can get your statement tomorrow, it'll be a good help to the case."

"She's been hurting me and Amma. Drugging us, poisoning us. Something." I felt nauseous again.

"Camille, why didn't you say something before? We could have had you tested. That'd be a great thing for the case. Goddammit."

"Thanks for the concern, Richard."

"Anyone ever tell you you're overly sensitive, Camille?"

"Not once."

Gayla was standing at the door, a watchful ghost at our house atop a hill. With a flicker she was gone, and as I pulled up to the carriage porch, the light in the dining room switched on.

Ham. I smelled it before I hit the door. Plus collard greens, corn. They all sat still as actors before curtain. Scene: Suppertime. My mother poised at the head of the table, Alan and Amma to each side, a place set for me at the opposite end. Gayla pulled the chair out for me, whispered back into the kitchen in her nurse's garb. I was sick of seeing nurses. Beneath the floorboards, the washing machine rumbled on, as ever.

"Hello, darling, nice day?" my mother called too loudly. "Sit down, we've been holding dinner for you. Thought we'd have dinner as a family since you'll be leaving soon."

"I will?"

"They're set to arrest your little friend, dear. Don't tell me I'm better informed than the reporter." She turned to Alan and Amma and smiled like a congenial hostess passing appetizers. She rang her little bell, and Gayla brought the ham in, gelatin-wobbly, on a silver serving tray. A pineapple slice slid stickily down its side.

"You cut, Adora," Alan said to my mother's raised eyebrows.

Wisps of blonde hair fluttered as she carved finger-thick slices, passed them around on our plates. I shook my head at Amma as she proffered me a serving, then sent it on to Alan.

"No ham," my mother muttered. "Still haven't grown out of that phase, Camille."

"The phase of not liking ham? No, I haven't."

"Do you think John will be executed?" Amma asked me. "Your John on death row?" My mother had outfitted her in a white sundress with pink ribbons, braided her hair tightly on both sides. Her anger came off her like a stench.

"Missouri has the death penalty, and certainly these

are the kind of murders that beg for the death penalty, if anything deserves that," I said.

"Do we still have an electric chair?" Amma asked.

"No," Alan said. "Now eat your meat."

"Lethal injection," my mother murmured. "Like putting a cat to sleep."

I pictured my mother strapped to a gurney, exchanging pleasantries with the doctor before the needle plunged in. Suitable, her dying from a poisoned needle.

"Camille, if you could be any fairy-tale person in the world, who would you be?" Amma asked.

"Sleeping Beauty." To spend a life in dreams, that sounded too lovely.

"I'd be Persephone."

"I don't know who that is," I said. Gayla slapped some collards on my plate, and fresh corn. I made myself eat, a kernel at a time, my gag reflex churning with each chew.

"She's the Queen of the Dead," Amma beamed. "She was so beautiful, Hades stole her and took her to the underworld to be his wife. But her mother was so fierce, she forced Hades to give Persephone back. But only for six months each year. So she spends half her life with the dead, and half with the living."

"Amma, why would such a creature appeal to you?" Alan said. "You can be so ghastly."

"I feel sorry for Persephone because even when she's back with the living, people are afraid of her because of where's she's been," Amma said. "And even when she's with her mother, she's not really happy, because she knows she'll have to go back underground." She grinned at Adora and jabbed a big bite of ham into her mouth, then crowed.

"Gayla, I need sugar!" Amma yelled at the door.

"Use the bell, Amma," my mother said. She wasn't eating either.

Gayla came in with a bowl of sugar, sprinkled a big spoonful over Amma's ham and sliced tomatoes.

"Let *me*," Amma whined.

"Let Gayla," my mother said. "You put too much on."

"Will you be sad when John's dead, Camille?" Amma said, sucking on a slice of ham. "Would you be more sad if John died or I did?"

"I don't want anyone to die," I said. "I think Wind Gap has had too much death as it is."

"Hear-hear," Alan said. Oddly festive.

"Certain people should die. John should die," Amma continued. "Even if he didn't kill them, he still should die. He's ruined now that his sister is dead."

"By that same logic, I should die, because my sister is dead and I'm ruined," I said. Chewed another kernel. Amma studied me.

"Maybe. But I like you so I hope not. What do you think?" she turned to Adora. It occurred to me she never addressed her directly, no Mother or Momma, or even Adora. As if Amma didn't know her name but was trying not to be obvious about it.

"Marian died a long, long time ago, and I think maybe we should have all ended with her," my mother said wearily. Then suddenly bright: "But we didn't, and we just keep moving on, don't we?" Ringing of bell, gathering of plates, Gayla circling the table like a decrepit wolf.

Bowls of blood-orange sorbet for dessert. My mother disappearing discreetly into the pantry and surfacing with two slender crystal vials and her wet pink eyes. My stomach lurched.

"Camille and I will have drinks in my bedroom," she said to the others, fixing her hair in the sideboard mirror. She was dressed for it, I realized, already in her nightgown. Just as I had as a child when I was summoned to her, I trailed her up the stairs.

And then I was inside her room, where I'd always wanted to be. That massive bed, pillows sprouting off it like barnacles. The full-length mirror embedded in the wall. And the famous ivory floor that made everything glow as if we were in a snowy, moonlit landscape. She tossed the pillows to the floor, pulled back the covers and motioned for me to sit in bed, then got in next to me. All those months after Marian died when she kept to her room and refused me, I wouldn't have dared to imagine myself curled up in bed with my mother. Now here I was, more than fifteen years too late.

She ran her fingers through my hair and handed me my drink. A sniff: smelled like brown apples. I held it stiffly but didn't sip.

"When I was a little girl, my mother took me into the North Woods and left me," Adora said. "She didn't seem angry or upset. Indifferent. Almost bored. She didn't explain why. She didn't say a word to me, in fact. Just told me to get in the car. I was barefoot. When we got there, she took me by the hand and very efficiently pulled me along the trail, then off the trail, then dropped my hand and told me not to follow her. I was eight, just a small thing. My feet were ripped into strips by the time I got home, and she just looked up at me from the evening paper, and went to her room. This room."

"Why are you telling me this?"

"When a child knows that young that her mother doesn't care for her, bad things happen."

"Believe me, I know what that feels like," I said. Her hands were still running through my hair, one finger toying with my bare circle of scalp.

"I wanted to love you, Camille. But you were so hard. Marian, she was so easy."

"Enough, Momma," I said.

"No. Not enough. Let me take care of you, Camille. Just once, need me."

Let it end. Let it all end.

"Let's do it then," I said. I swallowed the drink in a belt, peeled her hands from my head, and willed my voice to be steady.

"I needed you all along, Momma. In a real way. Not a need you created so you could turn it on and off. And I can't ever forgive you for Marian. She was a baby."

"She'll always be my baby," my mother said.

Chapter Sixteen

I fell asleep without the fan on, woke up with the sheets stuck to me. My own sweat and urine. Teeth chattering and my heartbeat thumping behind my eyeballs. I grabbed the trash can beside my bed and threw up. Hot liquid, with four kernels of corn bobbing on top.

My mother was in my room before I pulled myself back onto the bed. I pictured her sitting in the hall chair, next to the photo of Marian, darning socks while she waited for me to sicken.

"Come on, baby. Into the bathtub with you," she murmured. She pulled my shirt over my head, my pajama bottoms down. I could see her eyes on my neck, breasts, hips, legs for a sharp blue second.

I vomited again as I got into the tub, my mother holding my hand for balance. More hot liquid down my front and onto the porcelain. Adora snapped a towel from the rack, poured rubbing alcohol into it, wiped me down with the objectivity of a window cleaner. I sat in the bathtub as she poured glasses of cold water over my head to bring the fever down. Fed me two more pills and another glass of milk the color of weak sky. I took it all with the same bitter vengeance that fueled me on two-day benders. *I'm not down yet, what else you got?* I wanted it to be vicious. I owed Marian that much.

Vomiting into the tub, draining the tub, refilling, draining. Icepacks on my shoulders, between my legs. Heat packs on my forehead, my knees. Tweezers into the wound on my ankle, rubbing alcohol poured after. Water flushing pink. *Vanish, vanish, vanish,* pleading from my neck.

Adora's lashes were plucked clean, the left eye dribbling plump tears, her upper lip continually bathed with her tongue. As I was losing consciousness, a thought: *I am being cared for. My mother is in a sweat mothering me. Flattering. No one else would do this for me. Marian. I'm jealous of Marian.*

I was floating in a half-full bath of lukewarm water when I woke again to screams. Weak and steaming, I pulled myself out of the bath, wrapped a thin cotton robe around me – my mother's high screams jangling in my ears – and opened the door just as Richard busted in.

"Camille, are you okay?" My mother's wails, wild and ragged, cutting the air behind him.

Then, his mouth fell open. He tilted my head to one side, looked at the cuts on my neck. Pulled open my robe and flinched.

"Jesus Christ." A psychic wobbling: He teetered between laughter and fear.

"What's wrong with my mother?"

"What's wrong with you? You're a cutter?"

"I cut words," I muttered, as if it made a difference.

"Words, I can see that."

"Why is my mother screaming?" I felt woozy, sat down on the floor, hard.

"Camille, are you sick?"

I nodded. "Did you find something?"

Vickery and several officers tumbled past my room. My mother staggered by a few seconds later, her hands wrapped in her hair, screaming at them to get out, to have respect, to know they'll be very sorry.

"Not yet. How sick are you?" He felt my forehead, tied my robe shut, refused to look at my face anymore.

I shrugged like a sulking child.

"Everyone has to leave the house, Camille. Put on some clothes and I'll get you to the doctor's."

"Yes, you need your evidence. I hope I have enough poison left in me."

By evening, the following items were removed from my mother's panty drawer:

Eight vials of anti-malarial pills with overseas labels, big blue tablets that had been discontinued due to their tendency to induce fever and blurred vision. Traces of the drug were found in my toxicology tests.

Seventy-two tablets of industrial-grade laxative, used primarily for loosening the bowels of farm animals. Traces of which were found in my toxicology tests.

Three dozen anti-seizure tablets, the misuse of which can cause dizziness and nausea. Traces of which were found in my toxicology tests.

Three bottles of ipecac syrup, used to induce vomiting in case of poisoning. Traces of which were found in my toxicology tests.

One hundred and sixty-one horse tranquilizers. Traces of which were found in my toxicology tests.

A nurses' kit, containing dozens of loose pills, vials, and syringes, none of which Adora had any use for. Any good use for.

From my mother's hat box, a flowered diary, which would be entered as a court document, containing passages such as the following:

SEPTEMBER 14, 1982

I've decided today to stop caring for Camille and focus on Marian. Camille has never become a good patient – being sick only makes her angry and spiteful. She doesn't like me to touch her. I've never heard of such a thing. She has Joya's spite. I hate her. Marian is such a doll when she's ill, she dotes on me terribly and wants me with her all the time. I love wiping away her tears.

MARCH 23, 1985

Marian had to go to Woodberry again, "trouble breathing since the morning, and sick to her stomach." I wore my yellow St. John suit, but ultimately didn't feel good about it – I worry with my blonde hair I looked washed-out. Or like a walking pineapple! Dr. Jameson is very masterful and kind, interested in Marian, but *not a busybody.* He seems quite impressed with me. Said that I was an angel, and that every child should have a mother like me. We had a bit of a flirtation, despite the wedding rings. The nurses are somewhat troubling. Probably jealous. Will have to really dote next visit (surgery seems likely!). Might have Gayla make her mince meat. Nurses love little treats for their break area. Big green ribbon around the jar, maybe? I need to get my hair done before the next emergency... hope Dr. Jameson (Rick) is on call...

MAY 10, 1988

Marian is dead. I couldn't stop. I've lost 12 pounds and am skin and bones. Everyone's been incredibly kind. People can be so wonderful.

The most important piece of evidence was discovered under the cushion of the yellow brocade love seat in Adora's room: a stained pair of pliers, small and feminine. DNA tests matched trace blood on the tool to Ann Nash and Natalie Keene.

The teeth were not found in my mother's home. I had images for weeks after of where they might have gone: I saw a baby blue convertible driving, top up as always – a woman's hand jutting out the window – a spray of teeth into the roadside thicket near the path into the North Woods. A set of delicate slippers getting muddied at the edge of Falls Creek – teeth plopping like pebbles into the water. A pink nightgown floating through Adora's rose garden – hands digging – teeth buried like tiny bones.

The teeth were not found in any of these places. I had the police check.

Chapter Seventeen

On May 28, Adora Crellin was arrested for the murders of Ann Nash, Natalie Keene, and Marian Crellin. Alan immediately paid the punishing bail sum so she could await trial in the comfort of her home. Considering the situation, the court thought it best for me to take custody of my half sister. Two days later I drove north, back to Chicago, with Amma beside me.

She exhausted me. Amma was wildly needy and afire with anxiety – took to pacing like a caged wildcat as she fired angry questions at me (Why is everything so loud? How can we live in such a tiny place? Isn't it dangerous outside?) and demanded assurance of my love. She was burning off all that extra energy from not being bedridden several times a month.

By August she was obsessed with female killers. Lucretia Borgia, Lizzie Borden, a woman in Florida who drowned her three daughters after a nervous breakdown. "I think they're special," Amma said defiantly. Trying to find a way to forgive her mother, her child therapist said.

Amma saw the woman twice, then literally lay on the floor and screamed when I tried to take her for a third visit. Instead, she worked on her Adora dollhouse most hours of the day. Her way of dealing with the ugly things that happened there, her therapist said when I phoned. Seems like she should smash the thing then, I answered. Amma slapped me in the face when I brought home the wrong color of blue cloth for Adora's dollhouse bed. She spat on the floor when I refused to pay $60 for a toy sofa made of real walnut. I tried hug therapy, a ridiculous program that instructed I clutch Amma to me and repeat *I love you I love you I love you* as she tried to wriggle away. Four times she broke free and called me a bitch, slammed her door. Fifth time we both started laughing.

Alan loosened some cash to enroll Amma at the Bell School – $22,000 a year, not counting books and supplies – just nine blocks away. She made quick friends, a little circle of pretty girls who learned to yearn for all things Missouri. The one I really liked was a girl named Lily Burke. She was as bright as Amma, with a sunnier outlook. She had a spray of freckles, oversized front teeth, and hair the color of chocolate, which Amma pointed out was the exact shade of the rug in my old bedroom. I liked her anyway.

She became a fixture at the apartment, helping me cook dinner, asking me questions about homework, telling stories about boys. Amma got progressively quieter with each of Lily's visits. By October, she'd shut her door pointedly when Lily came by.

One night I woke to find Amma standing over my bed.

"You like Lily better than me," she whispered. She was feverish, her nightgown clinging to her sweaty body, her teeth chattering. I guided her into the bathroom, sat her down on the toilet, wet a washcloth under the cool, metallic water of the sink, wiped her brow. Then we stared at each other. Slate blue eyes just like Adora's. Blank. Like a winter pond.

I poured two aspirin into my palm, put them back in the bottle, poured them back onto my palm. One or two pills. So easy to give. Would I want to give another, and another? Would I like taking care of a sick little girl? A rustle of recognition when she looked up at me, shaky and sick: *Mother's here.*

I gave Amma two aspirin. The smell made my mouth water. I poured the rest down the drain.

"Now you have to put me in the bathtub and wash me," she whined.

I pulled her nightgown over her head. Her nakedness was stunning: sticky little girl's legs, a jagged round scar on her hip like half a bottle cap, the slightest down in a wilted thatch between her legs. Full, voluptuous breasts. Thirteen.

She got into the bathtub and pulled her legs to her chin.

"You need to rub alcohol on me," she whimpered.

"No Amma, just relax."

Amma's face turned pink and she began crying.

"That's how she does it," she whispered. The tears

turned into sobs, then a mournful howl.

"We're not going to do it like she does it anymore," I said.

On October 12, Lily Burke disappeared on her way home from school. Four hours later, her body was found, propped tidily next to a Dumpster three blocks from our apartment. Only six of her teeth had been pulled, the oversized front two and four on the bottom.

I phoned Wind Gap and waited on hold twelve minutes until police confirmed my mother was in her home.

I found it first. I let the police discover it, but I found it first. As Amma trailed me like an angry dog, I tore though the apartment, upending seat cushions, rummaging through drawers. *What have you done, Amma?* By the time I got to her room, she was calm. Smug. I sifted through her panties, dumped out her wish chest, turned over her mattress.

I went through her desk and uncovered only pencils, stickers, and a cup that stank of bleach.

I swept out the contents of the dollhouse room by room, smashing my little four-poster bed, Amma's day bed, the lemon yellow love seat. Once I'd flung out my mother's big brass canopy and destroyed her vanity table, either Amma or I screamed. Maybe both of us did. The floor of my mother's room. The beautiful ivory tiles. Made of human teeth. Fifty-six tiny teeth, cleaned and bleached and shining from the floor.

—

Others were implicated in the Wind Gap child murders. In exchange for lighter sentences in a psychiatric hospital, the three blondes admitted to helping Amma kill Ann and Natalie. They'd zipped out in Adora's golf cart and idled near Ann's home, talked her into coming for a ride. *My mother wants to say hi.*

The girls putted to the North Woods, pretended they'd have a tea party of sorts. They prettied Ann up, played with her a bit, then after a few hours, got bored. They started marching Ann to the creek. The little girl, sensing an ill wind, had tried to run away, but Amma chased her down and tackled her. Hit her with a rock. Got bitten. I saw the wound on her hip, but had failed to realize what that jagged half moon meant.

The three blondes held Ann down, while Amma strangled her with a clothesline she'd stolen from a neighbor's tool shed. It took an hour to calm Jodes down and another hour for Amma to pull the teeth, Jodes crying the whole time. Then the four girls carried the body to the water and dumped it, zipped back over to Kelsey's home, cleaned up in the back carriage house, and watched a movie. No one could agree what it was. They all remembered they ate cantaloupe and drank white wine from Sprite bottles, in case Kelsey's mom peeked in.

James Capisi wasn't lying about that ghostly woman. Amma had stolen one of our pristine white sheets and fashioned it into a Grecian dress, tied up her light-blonde hair, and powdered herself until she glowed. She was Artemis, the blood huntress. Natalie had been bewildered at first when Amma had whispered into her ear, *It's a game. Come with me, we'll play.* She spirited Natalie through the woods, back again to Kelsey's carriage house, where they held her a full forty-eight hours, tending to her, shaving her legs, dressing her up, and feeding her in shifts as they enjoyed the increasing outcry. Just after midnight on the 14th, the friends held her down while Amma strangled her. Again, she pulled the teeth herself. Children's teeth, it turns out, aren't too hard to remove, if you put real weight on the pliers. And if you don't care how they end up looking. (Flash of Amma's dollhouse floor, with its mosaic of jagged, broken teeth, some mere splinters.)

The girls putt-putted in Adora's golf cart to the back side of Main Street at four in the morning. The aperture between the hardware store and beauty parlor was just wide enough to allow Amma and Kelsey to carry Natalie by hands and feet, single file, to the other side, where they propped her up, waited for the discovery. Again Jodes cried. The girls later discussed killing her, worried she might crumble. The idea was almost in action when my mother was arrested.

Amma killed Lily all by herself, hit her on the back of the head with a stone, then strangled her with bare hands, plucked the six teeth, and cut her hair. All down an alley, behind that Dumpster where she'd left the body. She'd brought the rock, pliers, and scissors to school in the hot pink backpack I'd bought for her.

Lily Burke's chocolate-colored hair Amma braided into a rug for my room in her dollhouse.

Epilogue

Adora was found guilty of murder in the first degree for what she did to Marian. Her lawyer is already preparing the appeal, which is enthusiastically chronicled by the group that runs my mother's Web site, freeadora.org. Alan shut down the Wind Gap house and took an apartment near her prison in Vandelia, Missouri. He writes letters to her on days he can't visit.

Quickie paperbacks were released about our murderous family; I was showered with book offers. Curry pushed me to take one and quickly backed off. Good for him. John wrote me a kind, pain-filled letter. He thought it was Amma all along, had moved into Meredith's place in part to "keep watch." Which explained the conversation I'd overheard between him and Amma, who'd enjoyed toying with his grief. Hurt as a form of flirtation. Pain as intimacy, like my mother jabbing her tweezers into my wounds. As for my other Wind Gap romance, I never again heard from Richard. After the way he looked at my marked-up body, I knew I wouldn't.

Amma will remain locked up until her eighteenth

birthday, and likely longer. Visitors are allowed twice a month. I went once, sat with her in a cheerful playground area surrounded by barbed wire. Little girls in prison slacks and T-shirts hung on monkey bars and gym rings, under supervision of fat, angry female guards. Three girls slipped jerkily down a warped slide, climbed the ladder, went down again. Over and over, silently for the duration of my visit.

Amma had cut her hair close to the scalp. It may have been an effort to look tougher, but instead gave her an otherworldly, elven aura. When I took her hand, it was wet with sweat. She pulled it away.

I'd promised myself not to question her about the killings, to make the visit as light as possible. Instead it came out almost immediately, the questions. Why the teeth, why these girls, who were so bright and interesting. How could they have offended her? How could she do it? The last line came out chidingly, as if I was lecturing her on having a party when I wasn't home.

Amma stared bitterly at the three girls on the slide and said she hated everyone here, all the girls were crazy or stupid. She hated having to do laundry and touch people's stuff. Then she went silent for a minute and I thought she was simply going to ignore my question.

"I was friends with them for a while," she said finally, talking into her chest. "We had fun, running around in the woods. We were wild. We'd hurt things together. We killed a cat once. But then she" – as always Adora's name went unsaid – "got all interested in them. I could never have anything to myself. They weren't my secrets anymore. They were always coming by the house. They started asking me questions about being sick. They were going to ruin everything. She didn't even realize it." Amma rubbed her shorn hair harshly. "And why did Ann have to bite . . . her? I couldn't stop thinking about it. Why Ann could bite her, and I couldn't."

She refused to say more, answered only in sighs and coughs. As for the teeth, she took the teeth only because she needed them. The dollhouse had to be perfect, just like everything else Amma loved.

I think there is more. Ann and Natalie died because Adora paid attention to them. Amma could only view it as a raw deal. Amma, who had allowed my mother to sicken her for so long. *Sometimes when you let people do things to you, you're really doing it to them.* Amma controlled Adora by letting Adora sicken her. In return, she demanded uncontested love and loyalty. No other little girls allowed. For the same reasons she murdered Lily Burke. Because, Amma suspected, I liked her better.

You can come up with four thousand other guesses, of course, about why Amma did it. In the end, the fact remains: Amma enjoyed hurting. *I like violence,* she'd shrieked at me. I blame my mother. A child weaned on poison considers harm a comfort.

The day of Amma's arrest, the day it finally, completely unraveled, Curry and Eileen parked themselves on my couch, like concerned salt and pepper shakers. I slipped a knife up my sleeve, and in the bathroom, I stripped off my shirt and dug it deep into the perfect circle on my back. Ground it back and forth until the skin was shredded in scribbly cuts. Curry broke in just before I went for my face.

Curry and Eileen packed my things and took me to their home, where I have a bed and some space in what was once a basement rec room. All sharp objects have been locked up, but I haven't tried too hard to get at them.

I am learning to be cared for. I am learning to be parented. I've returned to my childhood, the scene of the crime. Eileen and Curry wake me in the mornings and put me to bed with kisses (or in Curry's case, a gentle chuck under the chin). I drink nothing stronger than the grape soda Curry favors. Eileen runs my bath and sometimes brushes my hair. It doesn't give me chills, and we consider this a good sign.

It is almost May 12, one year exactly from my return to Wind Gap. The date also happens to be Mother's Day this year. Clever. Sometimes I think about that night caring for Amma, and how good I was at soothing her and calming her. I have dreams of washing Amma and drying her brow. I wake with my stomach turning and a sweaty upper lip. Was I good at caring for Amma because of kindness? Or did I like caring for Amma because I have Adora's sickness? I waver between the two, especially at night, when my skin begins to pulse.

Lately, I've been leaning toward kindness.

Acknowledgments

Much Thanks to my agent, Stephanie Kip Rostan, who walked me gracefully through this whole first-book thing, and to my editor, Sally Kim, who asked incisive questions and supplied many, many answers while helping me whittle this story into shape. Smart and encouraging, they also happen to be charming dinner companions.

Gratitude also to D. P. Lyle, M.D., Dr. John R. Klein, and Lt. Emmet Helrich, who helped me sort out facts involving medicine, dentistry, and police work, and to my editors at *Entertainment Weekly*, particularly Henry Goldblatt and managing editor Rick Tetzeli (clever kicker TK, I swear).

More thanks to my great circle of friends, particularly those who offered repeated readings, advice, and good cheer while I was writing *Sharp Objects*: Dan Fierman, Krista Stroever, Matt Stearns, Katy Caldwell, Josh Wolk, Brian "Ives!" Raftery, and my four witty sister-cousins (Sarah, Tessa, Kam, and Jessie) all provided kind words at crucial points, like when I was about to burn the thing. Dan Snierson may be the most consistently optimistic and decent human being on the planet — thanks for your unwavering confidence, and tell Jurgis to be gentle in his review. Emily Stone gave guidance and humor from Vermont, Chicago, and Antarctica (I highly recommend her Crazytown shuttle service); thanks to Susan and Errol Stone for that lake-house refuge. Brett Nolan, world's best reader – a compliment not given lightly – steered me away from accidental *Simpsons* references and is the author of the most reassuring two-word e-mail ever. Scott Brown, Monster to my Mick, has read countless iterations of *Sharp Objects*, poor thing, and also joined me on many a needed retreat from reality – me, Scott, and a neurotic unicorn with a daddy complex. Thanks to all.

Finally, much love and appreciation to my massive Missouri family – who I'm happy to say were absolutely no inspiration for the characters in this book. My faithful parents have encouraged me in my writing since third grade, when I declared I wanted to be either an author or a farmer when I grew up. The farming thing never really took off, so I hope you like the book.

Reading Notes

In Brief

Camille Preaker is a reporter in Chicago. Sounds glamorous, but the *Daily Post*, the fourth largest paper in the city, is a far cry from the *New York Times*. Camille's editor, Frank Curry, believes that one 'right' story will get his paper noticed. When a child disappears in Wind Gap, a town where a girl had been murdered the previous year, Frank smells a serial killer, and who better to get the inside story than Camille, his very own ex-resident of Wind Gap. So Camille has to go home; a journey back to a tragic past, and secrets she *really* doesn't want to uncover.

In Detail

Wind Gap has a population of around 2,000, consisting of 'Old money and trash', Camille tells her editor. 'I'm trash. From old money,' she adds.

There aren't many ties to undo in Chicago, so she is soon

heading down to her home town. When she reaches Wind Gap, her paper's budget dictates that she'll stay with her mother; a prospect which serves to fill her only with bourbon.

She soon gets to work and talks to a reluctant police Chief Vickery. It turns out that Ann Nash had been strangled the previous August, and dumped in the creek. The search for the missing girl, Natalie Keene, is still ongoing, and Camille joins it in the North Woods. Talking to the townspeople as they search, she learns that the Nash girl had had all her teeth removed by her killer, meaning he must have been 'some crazy man' riding through town. Not a local . . . Surely . . .

Camille calls in to the Nash home after leaving the fruitless search and learns more odd things about the killing of Ann. Unusually for this type of crime she was unmolested. 'No bruises, no cuts, no sign of any kind of . . . torture. Just strangled her. Pried her teeth out.'

Camille has put off going to her childhood home for as long as she possibly can, but the evil moment can be postponed no longer, and she is soon looking at her mother's 'massive house . . . an elaborate Victorian replete with a widow's walk.' So she is home, with her hypochondriac mother, Adora; but then wouldn't you be extra careful if your daughter Marian had died in childhood? Is it any wonder that her care of Amma, Camille's thirteen-year-old half sister, is so smothering?

After a disturbed night, Camille decides to stake out the police station for a quote before the search recommences. As she drives down a near deserted Main Street she sees a small group of people. Why would a middle-aged woman be 'sitting in the middle of the sidewalk, legs splayed, staring at the side of a building'? As Camille approaches, the horror is revealed.

Camille continues her investigations, and becomes increasingly disturbed by Wind Gap: her sister's chameleon existence – is she a vamp, or a little girl? Her mother's seeming isolation from reality; and the inevitable pull back to her own damaged and damaging childhood. She finds a boy who saw a woman in a nightgown snatch Natalie, but no one believes him. As out-of-town detective Richard Willis joins the investigation of the bizarre crimes, Camille starts to put the whole thing together, a puzzle that just gets her skin zinging. An itch that just needs a sharp little scratch . . .

About the Author

Gillian Flynn was born in Kansas city, the daughter of Penn Valley reading instructor Judith Flynn. After completing her Masters, she worked at a trade magazine before moving to *Entertainment Weekly*, where she is now chief television critic. She lives in Chicago.

For Discussion

• 'Good editors don't see bark, they see leaves' What do you think the author means by this when she introduces us to Frank Curry, Camille's editor?

• 'The Victorians . . . needed a lot of room to stray away from each other . . . to avoid rapacious lust, to wall themselves away from sticky emotions. Extra space is always good.' How much does Adora's home add to the problem? Would a two-room apartment have helped?

• 'Natalie was buried in the family plot, next to a gravestone that already bore her parents' names. I know the wisdom, that no parents should see their child die, that such an event is like nature spun backward. But it's the only way to truly keep your child. Kids grow up, they forge more potent allegiances. They find a spouse or a lover. They will not be buried with you. The Keenes, however, will remain the purest form of family. Underground.' Macabre but true?

• 'Outside on the porch I saw a changeling.' How do you feel about Amma? Is she a changeling in the traditional sense of the word? Or a chameleon forced to adapt to her unnatural environment?

• 'When you die, you become perfect. I'd be like Princess Diana. Everyone loves her now.' Is Amma right? Does this apply in the world of Wind Gap? In our lives is this also true?

• Do you think there is any significance to the letter A in *Sharp Objects*? Think of Camille's family in particular.

• '*I'm here*. I don't usually feel that I am.' How has Camille's past shaped her? Do you agree with her shrinks that her 'weightlessness' is due to her ignorance of her history?

• '"Oh, now look what you've done. I'm bleeding." My

mother held up thorn-pricked hands, and trails of deep red began to roll down her wrists.' What does this image in Camille's mind tell us of her view of her mother?

• 'I jammed a floppy blue teddy bear under my head, then felt guilty and returned him to the foot of the bed. One should have allegiance to one's childhood things.' How else does Camille's allegiance manifest itself? Would she be better without it, or do you agree with her?

• How important do you think the outward appearance of the people in *Sharp Objects* is to their personalities. Ugliness and beauty are themes throughout the book, but are they the key themes? Or do the characters rise above the visual?

• 'A ring of perfect skin.' One on Camille's back, and another on her mother's wrist. What significance does this have do you think? How alike are they?

• 'Sometimes I think illness sits inside every woman, waiting for the right moment to bloom.' How far do you agree with this? Can you see how Camille has come to think this?

Suggested further reading

Dolores Claiborne by Stephen King
The Bitch Goddess Notebook by Martha O'Connor
The Stepford Wives by Ira Levin
A Child's Game by John Connor